THE RAINBIRD PATTERN

Victor Canning's first novel, *Mr Finchley Discovers his England*, was published in 1934, since when he has been a full-time author and has over thirty novels to his credit. He is also the author of many short stories and serials which have been published in the principal newspapers and magazines of England and America. Born in Plymouth in 1911, he was a features writer for the *Daily Mail* before World War II, during which he was commissioned in the Royal Artillery. He has worked as a scriptwriter in Hollywood and now lives in Andover. His recent novels include *The Python Project, Queen's Pawn, The Great Affair* and *The Runaways*. *The Rainbird Pattern* has recently won the Crime Writers Association's Silver Dagger Award.

Sutile = T.H.N.

By the same author in Pan Books

THE
RAINBIRD PATTERN

VICTOR CANNING

PAN BOOKS LTD
LONDON AND SYDNEY

First published 1972 by William Heinemann Ltd
This edition published 1974 by Pan Books Ltd,
Cavaye Place, London SW10 9PG
ISBN 0 330 24298 9
© Victor Canning 1972

Printed in Great Britain by
Richard Clay (The Chaucer Press) Ltd, Bungay, Suffolk

For Diana with love

CHAPTER ONE

ON THE LOW centre table in the hall was a wide, shallow bowl full of blue and pink hyacinths, stiff, heraldic, unnatural flowers. At the side of the bowl was a small washleather bag, a jeweller's optic and a pair of fine balances. In a little while now, Bush thought, somebody was going to walk in from the cold March night and check the contents of the bag. Whoever it was would come by car. It was now two o'clock at night. Outside the floodlights swamped the approach road to the Officers' Mess building of the Army Aviation Centre with a sallow primrose light. The helicopter, stripped of radio, was waiting a hundred yards away on the football field. The pilot would be sitting there, blowing on his cold hands, briefed to follow instructions absolutely; one deviation from his orders, one irresistible spurt of heroics and he would be axed.

Bush moved round the table to the fireplace and lit a cigarette. Above the mantel was a coloured portrait of the Queen. The fireplace was masked with a great fan of green decorative paper. He noticed that one of the lower folds had been singed by a carelessly thrown cigarette. Bush had been trained to notice things and then lodge them in his memory until they were needed. He was a plump man, firmly in his thirties, with thinning brown hair, hazel eyes and a rubicund complexion that never took tan. His usual expression was mild, even kindly, and far from matched his real nature. He was a likeable man when he wanted to be liked. But it was only one of his tricks. He could be all sorts of men according to the brief he had to follow.

He contemplated the bowl of hyacinths. The last time the bowl had been full of potted bronze chrysanthemums. The lower leaves of two of the plants had been infested with green-fly. The last time it had been a woman who had come in from the night, raincoated, her face silk-scarf swathed to the eyes. This time Bush felt that it would be a man. The first time, and now again, the code name 'Trader' had been used, and the press always referred to the 'Trader Kidnappings'. The thought of the publicity, deliberately instigated by 'Trader', angered Bush. The first kidnapping had been successful and the woman had gone free. Anyway, if they had grabbed her, broken the protocol laid down and taken the risk that the stated threat would not be carried out, he was sure that they would have got little from her. This time the man would come out of vanity, masculine pride or even an impresario's delight in knowing his own creation.

Grandison was across the hall, near the door. He was study-ing a framed map of the school and its training areas. Bush knew that every detail on the map was being effortlessly ab-sorbed, programmed into his chief's mind. Grandison turned and came over.

He was a great pirate of a man – a wooden leg and black eye patch all that were missing. In place of the patch he wore a monocle, its red silk cord looping down over the lapel of his thick tweed jacket. His bulk was enormous, but never clumsy. He was black-haired and black-bearded, and his broad face was time-creased and experience-scarred from fifty years of hard, violent and joyous living. He was friendly now. When he wanted he could make Privy Councillors sweat under the arm-pits. He had the ear of those who mattered. He had dined once a fortnight with each of the Prime Ministers under whom he had served.

Bush said, 'History about to repeat itself.'

Grandison nodded. 'It has to. Repetition is reproduction. Reproduction is survival. You know, of course, that this time it will be the man?'

'Yes.'

'What would be your bet for the third time?'

'The third?'

Grandison flicked a bushy eyebrow and the monocle fell across his chest. 'You should have got as far as that, Bush.' He

8

nodded towards the washleather bag. 'Last time and this – all preliminaries. "Trader" himself sending a letter to the press each time – playing for maximum publicity up to a point. And what for? Just a handful of diamonds each time? Twenty thousand pounds' worth? Too modest. Nobody plays this kind of game for that kind of money. Naturally, you've realized that there must be a third time.'

'Frankly, no.' Nobody in the department ever called Grandison 'sir'. It was his own edict.

'Then you bloody well ought to have done.' The voice was good-natured. 'When we've finished with this little lot, put a cushion under your arse and work me out the logical projection.' He grinned and reset his monocle. 'If it's not right I'll send you to the salt mines. Want a tip?'

'Well, I . . .'

'An idle word "Well". The human sigh. The grunt of delay. Just say "Yes" or "No".'

'Yes.'

'Publicity, the power of the press, public opinion.' He stared past Bush at the Queen's portrait. 'Fascinating. You just use other people's weapons and their piddling fears about their own status, and the world is at your feet.'

On the reception desk at the door the telephone rang. It was answered by Bush's immediate superior, the Deputy Head of the department, Sangwill, his horn-rimmed spectacles pushed back on his forehead, a cigarette lodged in the corner of his mouth.

'Yes?' He listened, pursing his lips, playing a soft tattoo on the desk with his free hand. 'All right. Hold the car there on the way out.'

Bush smiled. At the gate they all knew the car had to be held. Not that it would help. Sangwill liked to reinforce the obvious. That's why he sat mostly on a cushion. *Rond-de-cuir*. Bureaucrat. A nice, gentle man, Sangwill, the caretaker that every department had to have.

Sangwill turned to them. 'Coming up now. From what they said – prepare yourself for a giggle.' He sighed and flicked his glasses down.

Through the half-glass door of the hall Bush saw the car pull up. It was a hired car, the firm's advertising plaque a lighted crescent on its roof. The headlight glare dropped to low beam. Grandison tipped his head to the door and Bush went out.

March night. A strong westerly wind going, shaking the bare wistaria branches on the front of the building. No cloud. Stars like diamond chips. Moon in its first quarter.

The man who got out of the car touched the night with pantomime.

The car driver, one arm hooked over his door, watched, grinning to cover uneasiness, and called hoarsely, 'Want me to wait, guv?'

Bush answered for the visitor. 'No.'

They would hold the driver at the gate. They would squeeze everything they could out of him and it wouldn't help a bit. The visitor watched as the car drove away, then he turned and came up the steps.

Bush logged him, detail by detail – five feet ten or eleven, slim build, easy mover. Everything was clear under the fierce glare of the overhead door light; black shoes indifferently polished, a length of grey flannel trousering and above that a wind-flapped, single-fronted raincoat. He had a black towelling scarf (the kind golfers and fishermen wear against rain) tight about his throat. Above all, crowning everything, he wore the face of pantomime – a papier-mâché mask, a crude, red-painted, bulbous-nosed, fat-cheeked carnival face, grotesque with dark, drooping moustaches – a vulgar, moronic, leering front. Bush showed no surprise. He stepped aside, pushed the door open and the man went in. Inchwide elastic, caught at the sides of the mask, stretched across the back of the man's head. The hair that showed was blond and long. Could be a wig. Bush made a note to try to check the colour of the wrist hairs when the visitor took his hands from his pockets. He would be wearing gloves, of course, but they might be short enough to reveal something.

Coming in from the freshness of the night air, the sweet, bready smell of the hyacinths was strong in the hall. Grandison was on the far side of the low table, monocle screwed into his eye. Nothing on his face changed. Fantasy was no stranger in their lives. Sangwill stood below the Queen's portrait. There was a raised movement of his pale eyebrows behind the thick rims of his spectacles. A joke-weary father humouring another family prank. The visitor took his right hand from his pocket. The left stayed where it was, and with it, Bush knew, there would be an automatic.

Grandison said, 'You've missed All Hallow's Eve by a few months.' He wagged a long forefinger towards the washleather bag.

The visitor said nothing. His left hand came out of the pocket holding an automatic. He put it on the edge of the bowl of hyacinths, where it was nearer to hand than four inches lower on the table. He did it neatly, not a bloom or leaf disturbed. The flower growth almost hid the weapon so that Bush could not identify it. Maybe one of the hidden cameras would get it. For a moment he was tempted to look up to the decorative ceiling boss to check the line.

The man wore long black cotton gloves and they reached up under the raincoat sleeves. He picked up the washleather bag, pulled the toggled cords loose and tipped the diamonds on to the table. They were – as had been specified – uncut blue whites. They looked like nothing. Cutting and polishing would bring them to life. You could sell them, no questions asked, in hundreds of different markets. The visitor splayed the stones around with a gloved finger. He picked one up, rolled it casually in his hand, rocking it on the black palm, and then slid it back with the others. Slowly he put all the diamonds back in the bag.

Grandison said, 'Your trust in us is flattering.'

The man made no reply. They all knew that no word would come from him, any more than it had from the woman. No curt 'Yes' 'No' or 'Maybe' to be caught by the tapes, that might give a fractional vocal vibration of accent, national or regional, or the bare echo of social class. You could put a detail like that in Sangwill's computer with a yeasty collection of other facts and out would come a few hundred samples that

11

could be followed up and might lead to a rare identification. Not even in the helicopter would this man speak. He would do what the woman had done the first time, produce pencil and notepad and write the instructions in block letters, never letting the pilot handle the pad, and taking it with him when the trip was done. This man could fail only by his own mistakes. He was making none. His security lay in the power of death he held over another man ... a man waiting now, somewhere, for release. He would have no cause to use that power. The men above Grandison had decided that.

If the decision had been left solely to Grandison it would have been different. Other people's deaths were commonplace. The thought of his own held no great concern for him. Whenever it was ordained it would come. Bush knew his philosophy well. Meet threats with thrusts and send messages of condolence to the families of innocent casualties. There is no sanity in any community, no true safety, the moment you acknowledge the imperatives of any tyranny, large or small. The world had got to learn that it was better to die than to be dishonoured, that evil could not be expunged either by prayer or payment. Only a sacrifice of life or lives could make living safe – and whether you lived safe or were sacrificed was the luck of the draw. Unchristian, of course. But for Grandison, himself and Sangwill and all the others in the department, Christianity had long been relegated to a footnote in the first training manual. Man had outgrown it. It had served its purpose like the apposition of thumb and fingers. There was more to life now, whether you liked it or not, than the simple ability to pick bananas from a tree in the jungle. There was now a different kind of jungle slowly enfolding the whole world.

Bush watched the washleather bag go into the right-hand pocket. The automatic was picked up and went in the other pocket. Ignoring them the man walked to the door. He pushed it open with his shoulder and held it, waiting. Bush went out past him, as he had once gone out past the woman.

They went down a floodlit drive, turned into a pathway half dark with the black scribbles of leafless shrub shadows. Bush walked ahead, out on to the football field where the helicopter

12

waited. A few moments later the machine took off. Its rotors flattened the tall grasses of the outfield as it rocked gently and then rose and headed eastwards. The navigation lights winked until it hit a thousand feet and then they were switched off.

Bush went back to the hall. In his absence a tray of drinks had been brought in and rested on the table. Grandison had dropped into a black leather armchair beyond the fireplace. A large glass of neat whisky was perched close to him on a side table. He was slumped deep in the chair, reading a small leather-bound, gold-tooled book. Wherever he moved there was always a book in his pocket. He had removed himself from them now because for two, three or more hours there was nothing for him to do. Sangwill, a long, weak whisky and water at his side, was at the reception desk on the telephone to the gate, listening, grunting now and then and making notes with his free hand.

Bush helped himself to a whisky and soda. Sangwill would be getting the driver's details. The plaque on its roof-top had said – *Riverdale Motor Hire – Reading.* Their visitor, Bush guessed, had come out of the station or appeared on the corner of a street, flagged the car and got in... He didn't pursue conjecture any further. Sangwill would get it all, and none of it would help. He found himself a chair, slumped in it, took a long pull at his drink and then stared up at the ceiling and began to think about the third time. He was conscientious and ambitious and successful. With every year that passed he found himself raising his sights higher.

George Lumley stood at the low bedroom window of his cottage and stooped a little to look through to see what the morning was doing. It was, he thought, doing a typical basinful of March stuff. Stinking. Rain coming down like stair-rods. A mad west wind banging away at the old elms down the side of the field track. He watched a handful of rooks tossed and sucked up above the trees by the wind. A swirl of burnt paper scattering across the grey sky. Poetic. He felt good and alive. Early morning sex did that for him always. Not Blanche. She just flopped back. Three deep sighs and she was away for another hour's shut-eye.

He turned back to the bedroom and looked at her. He ought to get a bigger bed. She was a diagonal dozer. Pick one up at a sale, somewhere. A mahogany monster that you could lose yourself in. She could sleep diagonal, vertical or horizontal then. All the points of the compass. Trouble was they'd never get it up the stairs. Floppy woman, he thought. Everything about Blanche flopped beautifully. Except her mind. By God, he had to give her that. He leaned over and kissed her right nipple then gently tucked the smooth mass of her breast back into the shelter of the green silk nightdress. She gave a small noise, a puppy whimper, and smiled in her sleep.

He went down the steep awkward stairs. When he had money he would put in a funicular. Albert slept on the mat at the bottom. There was no movement as he stepped over the black and white, pint-sized, nondescript animal. Great watch-dog, Albert. A burglar would have to jump on him to find trouble. Cunning bastard, Albert, too. There'd be no move-ment from him until he heard the grating of the opener on the can of dog food. Lucky Albert, too. All you had to do was wag an occasional tail and lick a hand and you were housed, fed and coddled for the rest of your life. Like me with Blanche. Yes, but that was only temporary. Everything was only tem-porary. Always had been. That was the trouble.

He whistled to himself and went into the kitchen. His do-main. George Lumley, gastronome – overboil an egg and burn toast with the best of them. Another Escoffier, that was him. What sauce! He laughed aloud at his own poor joke and began his chores.

He was a big, clumsy man admitting to being near forty, and certain that he had the best years of his life to come. Success for George was always around the corner. The shape success should take changed constantly, tantalizing him like a mirage. The only way he would ever be able to pin it down would be when he had money. Real money. Not the piddling remittance through lawyers from a family that had written him off long ago, a process that had begun years back when he'd

14

been caught *in flagrante delicto* with the young matron at his third-rate public school and had been kicked out.

Sometimes, after a drink or two, George would try to remember her in detail, but he never could. Blonde, brunette? God alone knew. All he really vividly remembered was that it hadn't been much good. Willing, but maladroit like a raw stallion put to its first mare. Never mind. Good times were coming. He'd read it in his horoscope in the *Daily Mail* yesterday.

While he was waiting for the coffee to heat up, he plugged in his electric razor and shaved and hummed a little tune to himself. Like Pooh, he thought. Had there ever really been a time, he puzzled, when his mother had read that to him? She hadn't been as tough as the others, but tough enough. Anyway she had had no chance against the old man. Alive still, the old man. And still kicking. The shave finished, he examined his face in the slip of kitchen mirror.

Smooth as a baby's B, he thought. Only a few veins breaking here and there. A bland, warm, friendly face. One you would trust. He grinned and took the opportunity to examine his teeth. Even, regular, healthy. Hardly a row of pearls, though. He was overdue for some scaling but it would have to wait until he had paid the dentist's last bill. He turned and caught the coffee milk before it boiled over. Coffee, toast and marmalade. Not the kind of breakfast Blanche had at her own place. Two eggs, three rashers and a sausage on the side. But she knew what to expect here. She'd never marry him. She was too fly for that. Anyway, he didn't want marriage. He'd tried that once, thank you. Disastrous. Thank God another bloke had fancied it and taken it off his hands. Nice chap. Manager of a printing works in Wakefield. Must have been mad.

He looked out of the kitchen window to the untidy paddock at the back of the cottage. A long, wire-netting aviary ran down one side of it. There was no sign of the birds, budgerigars, ornamental pheasants, stray or injured birds, his feathered friends. They were all in the shelter of their hut. George, the bird man. He had been going to make a fortune breeding

15

and selling . . . two years ago that had been. What a flop! Still, it was nice to have a few birds about. What was life without colour?

He reached for the dog-food can and began to open it. Albert came in, walking stiffly.

George said, 'Hungry?'

Albert flicked a scut of tail.

'Not until you get the bloody paper. Paper. Savvy?'

Albert, following the hard-learnt routine, moved out of the kitchen and through the narrow hall. He came back with the *Daily Mail* from the doormat. It was damp and crumpled from the rain that had soaked through the delivery boy's bag. Albert laid it at George's feet.

'Oh, noble master, pray accept this tribute,' mocked George. As he bent for the paper, he ruffled the dog's ears. What would a man be without a dog, he thought? Man's greatest friend – but never good for a touch.

In between making three relays of toast, he leaned back against the kitchen sink and gutted the paper; the strip cartoons first, then the sports' page, and then the stock exchange to make sure that the few meagre holdings he had were in their usual debilitated state. He finished off with a quick sweep through the general news. Blanche read a newspaper meticulously from cover to cover and was sometimes a day behind. George could take all the meat off the bone in six minutes flat and burn three pieces of toast while he was doing it.

The only thing that really interested him this morning was the finish of the 'Trader' business – the Right Honourable James Archer, member of the Labour Party's Shadow Cabinet, had been kidnapped two weeks previously and had now been restored to anxious family and loving Opposition Party for a ransom of twenty thousand pounds, paid in uncut diamonds. There was a fancy piece of writing about it by a reporter who obviously hadn't been given many facts. Reading between the lines it was clear that the police were completely up a gum-tree about the whole thing. For the second time running the man had made fools of them – and the papers and the public weren't letting them forget it. George was inter-

16

ested only in the money aspect. To carry out dangerous stunts like that for such small beer seemed odd to him.

He loaded the breakfast on to a tray and climbed awkwardly up the stairs with it. Blanche was sitting up in bed, red hair brushed back, a short-sleeved bed jacket over her handsome broad shoulders and a happy sparkle in her green eyes. Looking at her George told himself, and not for the first time, that she was a gorgeous great woman, a Mother Ceres, a cornucopia of delights . . . thirty-five years and a hundred and eighty-odd pounds' worth of warm, milky womanhood. Wagnerian. He had known her two years and they had been good to and for one another.

George put the tray on the bed close to her and said, 'Stinking morning. March coming in still like a lion. George coming in like a waiter. Good morning, my love. Or have I said that before?'

'I seem to remember you did – one way or another.' Blanche's voice was as full and ripe as her figure and there was an earthiness in it of fairgrounds, bar parlours and the shouting crowds of race-courses. She went on, 'Keep that mangy dog out of here.'

'It's all right, love. He knows he's only allowed on the threshold.'

Albert sat at the top of the stairs and watched them. George buttered and marmaladed toast for Blanche and fixed her coffee the way she liked it. He did it from tenderness and devotion. He liked doing things for Blanche . . . most things, not all things, and he could see one of the 'not all things' coming up now. He could always tell by the way she stared past him suddenly – just as she did when she went into her professional touch – bright-eyed, rapt, in tune with the infinite. Not Blanche Tyler any longer, the good sport and the good romp, but Madame Blanche. The woman who was always there, every week in the classified advertisements of the *Psychic News*. MADAME BLANCHE TYLER. *Clairvoyance, postal readings, private appointments, groups, home circles visited, healing. 59 Maidan Road, Salisbury, Wilts.*

Without looking at him, a piece of toast half raised in her

hand like some holy symbol, she said, 'It came to me in a dream just now.'

'What did?'

'The name. It was coming from Henry. Not him in person. But his voice. And there was this wonderful blue cloud with a great shining star in the middle of it.'

'Come off it, Blanche.' George was, after all this time, always a little put out when she turned this kind of thing on. Not that he thought it was all fake. No, there were some things you couldn't put down to that. Like the healing, among others. She had a pair of hands that could wipe away a headache or a touch of the old fibrositis like magic. And he'd seen and heard a few other things that he had no answers for.

Blanche raised the toast a little higher, saluting the heavens, and said in a vibrant, ecstatic voice, 'It is to be called The Temple of Astrodel!'

Having made the announcement, she came back to earth immediately. She bit into the toast and smiled warmly at him as she began to chew.

'You're three streets ahead of me,' said George. 'What's all this about a temple?'

'My temple, stupid. George, you are dumb at times! I told you all about it last week.'

'Not me you didn't.'

Blanche considered this, and then said, 'No, of course not. It was that Mrs Cookson. Lord, if I had a fraction of her money I could set it up right away. She's very tight, though. I'm not surprised. She's got a very poor aura.'

George poured himself coffee, lit a cigarette and sat beside her on the bed.

'You're going to build a temple? Like Solomon?'

'You can joke, but I am. A temple, a church of spiritualism. The Temple of Astrodel.'

'Bit of an odd name, isn't it, old girl?'

'It came out of the blue cloud.'

George chuckled. 'Pity it wasn't something a bit more substantial. Like, say, the loot to build it with. I've got a chum who's a builder. He'd give me a rake-off if I got the contract for him.'

'The money will come,' said Blanche firmly. 'Henry has promised it.' She leaned forward and took his hand. 'You know, George – you're a very good man. Not just good for me when I have to relax from the strain of the etheric, but a good man. You've got a wonderful aura.'

'So you've said before. What's its cash value?'

Blanche ignored him. 'It's a willing, kindly aura, soothing and refined. It comes to me like a warm amber glow just faintly tinged with a smooth ripple of red flame round the edges. Most rare.'

'Sounds bloody uncomfortable to walk about with.'

'Dear George.' She kissed his hand.

'Don't fool me. You want something.'

She nodded and reached for a second piece of toast. 'I want the money for my project, my temple, and one day soon ... yes, soon, I'm going to have it, love. In the meantime will you do one of your jobs for me?'

'Oh, Blanche – not again.'

'Just this one.'

'That's what you always say.'

'Please.'

George shrugged his shoulders. The trouble with Blanche was that, as far as he was concerned, she was the hardest wo-man in the world to refuse. Sometimes he wondered if it would be worth falling in love with her in the hope that that might alter it. If she were his wife he really could say no sometimes.

'That's a good George. I'll pay you twenty this time.'

George held out his hand, palm up. 'Ten quid down and it's a deal – plus expenses.'

Blanche leaned over and pulled her handbag from under a pile of clothes on the bedside chair. She took out a fat roll of five-pound notes and counted off two which she put in his hand.

His eyes on the roll, George said, 'You're always loaded.'

'I work hard for it, bringing healing and comfort. My true

19

concern, George, is my work. That is always before me like a shining star. The money is incidental. Your trouble is the opposite.'

George smiled. 'You're an old faker.'

'Only in part, and you know it though you won't admit it. And, lovey, let me tell you that if you had the patience to sit quietly for half an hour, not fiddling to have the television on, or to go out for a beer or to take me to bed, I'd explain it to you.'

'Anything you say. I came under your spell two years ago in the saloon bar of the Red Lion.' He gave her a mock salaam. 'You rubbed the lamp, madame? I am your willing servant. Who or what is it this time?'

'She's a Miss Grace Rainbird. Reed Court, Chilbolton. She's around seventy and God knows how rich. Chilbolton's not far, George. Could you do it today?'

'But we were going to have today together.'

'You can do the preliminary stuff and be back here by six. That'll give us all the evening and through to bed. While you're gone I'll clean up this mess of a cottage of yours. But you take Albert. I don't want him pissing around.'

'What about his aura? Must be bad, eh?'

But Blanche had gone. She stared past him, a beatific glow over her large, handsome face. Raising her arms, so that the bed jacket slipped from her shoulders and her breasts swelled majestically above the lowcut nightdress, she intoned, 'The Temple of Astrodel . . . The Temple of Astrodel . . .'

George sighed and stood up. There was nothing for it but to get dressed and take off. Pity, because sometimes after breakfast he would go back to bed and they would entertain one another with a wide range of pleasures until it was time to think about drinks before lunch.

George's cottage, stone-built, thatched and inconvenient, though boasting electricity and septic-tank drainage, was about five miles south of Salisbury. It stood at the end of a rough track, flanked on one side by a row of tall elms, and quite close to the Hampshire Avon. George had bought it during a rare

20

period of prosperity ten years before. The thatch was soon going to need renewing. Sometimes he looked forward to that point and wondered cheerfully how the hell he was going to be able to afford something like a thousand pounds for the job. He thought about it now as he drove through the wild March gale that was blowing. The heavy rain would be dripping through the ceiling in the small spare bedroom and he had forgotten to warn Blanche to stand a bucket under the drip.

With Albert curled up on the seat alongside him, George thought about Blanche. She was a clever girl. Clever, and sometimes disturbing. He wasn't over-keen about all this spiritualism and medium stuff, but since knowing Blanche he'd picked up a fair amount of knowledge and quite a few of the tricks of the trade. His own personal view was that if there was a life after death he hoped that it was going to include a few of the greater pleasures of this one. As for human survival, he could only imagine that there was a softening of the brain conditional on it. Most of the messages that came through to Blanche either directly or through her control 'Henry' were pretty piffling. You'd have thought that someone like Sir Oliver Lodge or Sir Arthur Conan Doyle or Benvenuto Cellini would have come over with a pretty authoritative statement about living and working conditions and all the other relevant stuff. Mostly it was a load of old guff. 'Henry' once had relayed a message through Blanche to Mrs Cookson from George Washington. Mrs Cookson was marginally related to the Washington family. Washington had just kept on about Mrs Cookson not worrying about something that was the biggest problem in her life at the moment – problem not stated. But both George and Blanche knew that for years the rich widow had been trying to make up her mind about remarrying and had half a dozen suitors she could pick from. The whole thing, said George Washington, would be resolved happily by the end of the year. Peanut stuff from such a big man. Anyway it pleased Mrs Cookson. It had to be true, didn't it, seeing the man it came from?

George smiled to himself, dropped a free hand on Albert's head and scratched it for him. Clever girl, Blanche. Buttering up Mrs Cookson, who would be good for a hefty contribution to the establishment of her temple. Astrodel? What kind of name was that? And now Miss Grace Rainbird ... wealthy spinster. She was a new one. Had to be, or he wouldn't be slogging through the rain along the Salisbury Stockbridge road, heading for Chilbolton. Blanche, if she got the chance, always liked to have a few preliminary facts when she took on a new client. She justified it by saying it put her more in rapport with the person if she had an idea of some of their circumstances. With anyone coming in cold off the street there was a certain shyness on the part of the spirit world to give freely ... He chuckled to himself. It would be the same old routine. A shufti round the village. Good old George doing his stuff. Loosening a few tongues in the pub. Chat up the garage proprietor. Spread a little ground bait in the Post Office and village store. And check the church and graveyard. Wonderful what you could get there if a family had lived in the same place for any length of time. Oh, he knew all the tricks. And people took to him – which was fair enough after all because he was a friendly, gregarious soul and all the drinks he stood came out of expenses. He began to whistle. Life was good. That was the only way to look at it. Some day his ship would come limping into port.

Chilbolton was a few miles north of Stockbridge in the valley of the river Test. It was a longish, straggly village with pink and white thatched cottages, and some more substantial houses. Everything spick and span and one look told you that there was money around. George went into his routine.

First he found Reed Court. It was well outside the village. He couldn't see it from the road because it stood in its own grounds and was hidden by a tall bank of trees. George drove up the gravelled driveway to the front of the house, turned slowly round without stopping and drove out again. It only took a few seconds, but he was a quick observer and knew what he was looking for. From Reed Court he went back into the village and parked outside the Abbot's Mitre. Four drinks later his dossier on Miss Grace Rainbird was building up nicely. From the pub he went to the garage to get petrol,

22

bought some cigarettes in the village store, gave the Post Office a miss because he was doing very nicely and then went on to the church, which was at the far end of the village.

The church didn't impress him as much as Reed Court. It was a rather gloomy flint-built affair with an insignificant looking wooden spire perched on one corner. The weather vane on top bore the date 1897. Not the finest flowering period of English architecture. He walked round the graveyard with Albert dogging slowly after him. Well kept. Some nice chestnuts, biggish old yew, and at the back a pleasant run of meadows across to the river. George had an eye for beauty. Although the church didn't impress him, clearly Chilbolton was the kind of place where you could retire, provided you had the cash, and live a life of calm and contemplation. He found the sexton tidying up a path with a rake. The sexton took against Albert's being in the churchyard. George tucked Albert under his arm. He sweetened up the old man, and they had a pleasant chat, George running on affably in his good voice, a big, pleasant man, well dressed, clearly a gentleman to the inexpert eye, George well-content with four glasses of Guinness under his belt and in love with the world. The more he learnt about the Rainbird family – the more he envied what they'd had and still had. Without bitterness, he thought that if it hadn't been for that sexy matron at school and a considerable number of other things afterwards he might have been in the running for something like a Rainbird life. Far more modest, of course, but still a little paradise of place and possessions to wrap about himself like a soft, silky cocoon.

He got back to the cottage just as it was getting dark. Blanche was not there. She'd left a note saying she'd gone to Salisbury to do some shopping for him. George never re-provisioned until he went for something in the cupboard and found it wasn't there.

He sat with a whisky and soda and began to jot down his findings for Blanche. There was quite a nice little bundle of them. He hoped that he would not have to go rooting around for more. You never knew with Blanche. So far it was an easy twenty pounds. But if she wanted more he would have to get more and the price was not always renegotiable. Not that he minded. He almost loved Blanche. She was good to him, and she had remembered to put a bucket under the ceiling leak.

As George sat with his whisky in his cottage, Bush, too, sat with a similar drink reading through the two reports he had prepared for Grandison. He was working at home, which was a small flat near Chelsea Bridge with a restricted view of the Thames and a small corner of the Tate Gallery. His wife was in Norfolk, staying with her parents. She often stayed with her parents. Her father was a retired Major-General. One day, Bush knew, she would come to him and ask for a divorce. If he had wanted to he could easily have found out who it was, other than her parents, that drew her so often to Norfolk. His marriage had been a mistake, ambitiously entered, which now lingered like some autumn-buffeted weed waiting for the first sharp winter frost to cut it down. What love there had been had declined rapidly. Bush was not sorry for his wife. She had revealed physical and social needs which meant nothing to him. He had only one love, a twin-celled entity which was himself and his work. About his real work his wife knew nothing. To her he was something in the Foreign Office. Although he was listed on the staff of the *Arms Control and Disarmament Research Unit*, he did no work there and had only been inside the place about half a dozen times. Something the same applied to Sangwill. He was listed as a Senior Executive Officer at the Home Office in the *Establishment and Organisation Department*. Grandison was listed nowhere, but his offices were in Birdcage Walk, not far from Wellington Barracks, and with a pleasant view over St James's Park and its lake. Under him here worked Sangwill and Bush and half a dozen others, men and women, all dedicated, quiet, inconspicuous people who had been hand-picked by Grandison.

Bush read his first report through. It was a factual analysis of the two Trader kidnappings which had taken place in the last eighteen months. A comparison of the two kidnappings, both of prominent political figures, revealed very little of real information or of any progress on the department's part. There was a great mass of uncoordinated police facts. The police didn't like the department because it sat on top of them, using a power that came straight from the Prime Minister. Officially they had no knowledge of it. But in practical terms they knew it and resented it. There was rivalry between them which occasionally caused volcanic upheavals at near-Cabinet level. But there was no denying the logic behind the department's secret formation. It was anonymous, unidentifiable, and could use methods and take actions at home and abroad which no police department could risk – though it might be sorely tempted at times. The justification for its existence lay in the highly organized development of much modern crime which called for an uninhibited counter force unhampered by conventional police ethics. Over the last eight years it had achieved many quiet, ruthless successes that had never had any publicity.

Bush's second report was the projection which Grandison had asked for.

There have been two Trader abductions. Organized by one person with not more than two, possibly three people involved. Moderate ransoms have been demanded. Victims prominent political – male – personalities. Maximum publicity has been ensured by Trader messages to the press. Publicity has embarrassed police and Government, leading to heavy criticism of police and other establishments, and also of prominent individuals in the political, security and police fields. The pattern of these two abductions leads to the following projections:

(a) The next abduction is the main operation. The other two have been carried out to establish the right climate for it.

(b) The next victim will be someone much more highly placed than either of the last two.

(c) No publicity will be given. Trader will insist on complete secrecy, except, say, for a press handout that the victim is ill, confined to bed, to cover any embarrassment publicly.

(d) *Authority will accept this condition to protect the victim and, more pertinently, the reputations of individuals in Government and in the police echelons. These reputations are already at risk because of the public's growing anger at the way Trader has made a laughing stock of authority already.*

(e) *The ransom asked will be high. Half or a quarter of a million pounds?*

(f) *If it is not paid the victim will be killed. The character reading on Trader and the pattern of the last two make this clear. Trader is not playing a game.*

(g) *His victim will be of such eminence that Government and police will, in my opinion, agree to all terms and pay up, and the whole affair will never reach the domain of public knowledge.*

(h) *Trader will carry out his final kidnapping within the next six months. The closer it occurs to this last one the more anxious will be authority's wish for a complete news media blackout.*

(i) *Trader when successful will retire from the kidnapping scene.*

(j) *At the moment we have no information whatsoever which shows any promise of giving a lead to Trader.*

Who wouldn't retire, thought Bush, if he had half a million to live on? He wondered what line Grandison would take at his conference tomorrow. Grandison was unpredictable. He might say they were to sit and let the third kidnapping happen, or that they had to go all out to get Trader before he could act again. Already he had made the projection for himself, and he might have discussed it with those above him and already have had his instructions. Personally Bush hoped that they would be told to go for Trader now. Somewhere among the mass of information they already had there surely had to be something, no matter how small, which would give them a lead. He stood now at the window with his drink, watching the tree-and-building-framed section of river. The tide was flowing in, a brown, lusty flood with great squalls of March rain

26

sweeping across its surface. If he could find something, if he could get Trader, then Grandison would give him the credit and make it known where it counted. He was a generous man like that . . . Get Trader and he could climb high. Not with this hybrid department necessarily. There were other spheres. Golden ones . . . He saw the woman coming up the steps with her scarf-wrapped face. He saw the man climbing them, grotesquely masked, and he fervently hoped that Grandison would not be instructed to close the case for them. He wanted to go on.

CHAPTER TWO

IT WAS A still, mild morning. The gales of the last two days had gone. From the tip of the great Wellingtonia across the driveway a blackbird finished a brief recital. Through the window of her sitting-room Miss Rainbird watched the cloud shadows move slowly across the green lawns studded with long sweeps of early daffodils. Spring was coming again. Spring would keep on coming, and humans would keep on going – and she with them after a handful more of years. It was a detached thought and had no personal significance for her. At seventy-three she had long ceased to be concerned with death. Most of her faculties were still strong. Moping and worrying was for the weak. She couldn't imagine either that this Madame Blanche, sitting across from her, was given to moping or worrying. The woman seemed to radiate cheerfulness and life. She was what Sholto – who had been vulgar at times – would have called 'a big, busty number'. Thirty-fivish, glowing almost with vitality, anything less like a medium or one concerned with the spiritual world she couldn't imagine. Sholto would have eyed her admiringly and patted his thin hands together gently, as though in applause, at the splendid sight. She hadn't been fond of Sholto, but at least there had been nothing hypocritical about him. He just openly said and did what he had to say and do. That was the trouble, too. There had been no turning him away from what he had to do.

Miss Rainbird, who wasn't always aware of her own frankness, said primly, 'I must make some things very, very clear to you, Madame ... Blanche.'

Blanche said, 'It's better right now if you just call me Miss Tyler. The other's professional.' She smiled, knowing she had to take things easy here. This old girl was as sharp as a needle.

'We haven't reached that stage yet. In fact I think you've half decided already that you have made a mistake. That Mrs Cookson perhaps over-persuaded you?'

Miss Rainbird considered this. Big and busty she might be, but this woman had a brain ... understanding, too. Briefly she was impressed.

'It might be so, yes. However, I would, as I said, like to make some things clear. I have an instinctive distrust of the ... the philosophy you represent. Although I'm a practising Christian it really is only a conventional performance. At heart I'm an agnostic. And, yes, I am beginning to regret asking you to come.'

Blanche nodded. 'It doesn't surprise me, Miss Rainbird. A lot of people begin that way. If you would like me to I'll go now. But before I do – and I'm sure you'll appreciate this – I'd like to say that ... well, it cuts both ways. I very soon know whether I can be of help to people. If I know I can't ... then I go. I'm not a performer, asking a fee. My vocation is to help people. Some, after a very short time, I know I can't help. You could be one of those, Miss Rainbird. I don't know yet.' She laid it down in her good voice, the voice for houses and people like this. The voice and acceptable speech forms had come years ago from elocution lessons, a good ear and an instinctive regard for the use of words. But they weren't natural. Blanche had been born in a fairground caravan at Nottingham. Alone with George or close friends she liked to relax.

Watching the faint expression of surprise on Miss Rainbird's face she knew that she was not going to be allowed to go. They were all the same. They wanted something – and she genuinely could and wanted to give them something, but they always put up the barriers first. Perhaps to hide their own embarrassment until they had got used to the idea.

Suddenly Miss Rainbird found herself liking this woman. There was no apparent cant about her. She spoke her mind and was unintimidated. Although she had meant to be far less direct, she found herself saying, 'You really believe deeply and sincerely in your ... your vocation?'

'Of course. My calling is full of ... well, doubtful types. Performers only interested in money. Read any authoritative work on psychic research and you'll find plenty of evidence for trickery and faking. If I had wanted to be a performer, Miss Rainbird, I would have found some other profession. But it just so happens that I have a gift, a precious one. Not for making spirits appear or silver trumpets float about a darkened room – I don't do that. I just happen to have been born with some extra little faculty for communication and, far more important, for understanding the human personality and its eternal nature.' It was a set speech, but she really did believe it. George could pull her leg and, okay, she did give herself a little help now and then to get things going but beyond that ... well, like it or not, it was just there and she had to do it.

'But this help you give, Miss Tyler. It is concerned with the spirit world, is it not?'

'Mostly, yes. But the spirit world covers all spheres of life. We, in a sense, are spirits – earthbound spirits. Sometimes people come to me, not because they want to know about their loved ones who have passed over, but because they have their own immediate problems. I'm not sure at the moment, Miss Rainbird, what you fancy you need from me in the way of help. But I would be a stupid person not to know you hope for something. My presence in this house at your request makes that clear. Let me say, Miss Rainbird, that if you want any crystal-ball gazing you won't get it from me.'

The slight hint of a reprimand or warning sharpened a natural tendency to quick temper in Miss Rainbird. She was an autocrat, used to being obeyed and, if conditions had to be imposed, she did it. So now she said, 'But surely that is what you did for Mrs Cookson? I know she's a rather impressionable person. In many ways a complete fool. But she tells me that you got in touch with George Washington for her. Now, surely that is ridiculous – even if she is distantly related to the family?'

Blanche smiled. She had the old girl going. Miss Rainbird had expected a 'Yes, ma'am – No, ma'am' type. Miss Rainbird, given a chance, could be a bully. Well, so what? Let 'em all come. All you had to do was to keep your nice voice on, smile, and never let them score an advantage.

'Mrs Cookson, Miss Rainbird, as you would be the first to admit, no doubt, is a very different person from you. She is a simple soul basically. But her need for comfort is as strong as anyone else's. I must explain that those who have passed over don't lose their human characteristics. My control – a really quite remarkable man called Henry – is a person with a sense of humour and also one who respects men and women of great achievements. Naturally he wouldn't bother a man like George Washington with some small problem like Mrs Cookson's. All she wants to know is which of three or four men she shall marry – if any. But she needs that help and she got it through Henry, who did what so many of the good ones who have passed over do. He merely put the problem back in Mrs Cookson's lap only in a different form. She will have to make the decision by herself. The spirits don't communicate with us to make life a bed of roses here, Miss Rainbird. We must all deal with our own human problems. Mrs Cookson will make a decision for herself before the end of the year. She will think George Washington helped her. Well, there is no harm in that. He did – through Henry. George Washington has more important things to do in his new life.' Blanche chuckled, a rich, earthy sound.

Miss Rainbird found herself chuckling, too.

'But, Miss Tyler, if one admits their existence – what kind of advice or help do they give?'

'They exist all right, Miss Rainbird. Chiefly they give the ones they have left behind the comfort of knowing there is survival after death and the comfort of communicating with them. And sometimes they help with earthly problems where the persons concerned are in no position to help themselves.'

'I see. And can you call for their help at will?'

'No, I can't. I can try always. Sometimes it happens and sometimes it doesn't. To them we are children. In this world, Miss Rainbird, much as parents love their children they do not always drop everything they are doing to answer their call. Unless it is one of alarm.'

'Could you try here and now? I mean, do you have to have special effects or conditions. A dark room, people holding hands and so on?'

Blanche laughed. 'No, I don't need special effects. They help sometimes when we do group work. But, anyway, I can't try here and now. That's right out of the question.'

'But why?'

'Because, Miss Rainbird – you have to want me to try and help you. How can I when for the moment you are a long way from deciding whether to treat me seriously? You are a highly intelligent, practical woman. You live in a world which is socially and economically far above mine. Madame Blanche Tyler – the medium. You mustn't be offended if I say that I know you must have had many a private little giggle to yourself about the very idea of such nonsense as you imagine I deal in. You can't imagine what possessed you to let Mrs Cookson persuade you to make an appointment with me.' Blanche stood up. This was the moment and she had known a hundred similar ones. 'I think it is best if you think it over for a few days and then let me know what your decision is. You're sceptical about all this. That I don't mind. You don't know whether you want to give it a try. I can't help you until you sincerely do hope that I can help you and are prepared to accept disappointment if I can't.'

'You really are a most unusual person, Miss Tyler.' Although Miss Rainbird's voice was tart there was an undertone of admiration in it. Blanche caught it and scored it up in her favour. She would be coming back here, she knew.

She said, 'Perhaps you'll be kind enough to let me know in a few days what you decide, Miss Rainbird? In the meantime, if it will comfort you, I can tell you that you won't be having any of your disturbing dreams, not, at least, for a few nights.'

Controlling herself, no sign of her surprise showing, Miss Rainbird said, 'What an extraordinary thing to say.'

'I didn't say it, Miss Rainbird. I merely passed it on. Henry's etheric presence has been in this room for the last few minutes and he's been saying it to me. Which means, of course, that someone has asked him to pass the message through.'

When Blanche had gone, Miss Rainbird poured herself a glass of dry sherry and sat with it in her favourite chair by the window. She was a small, neat woman. She had been pretty once, but now her cheeks were lean, the flesh of her face wrinkled and stretched without curve or softness over the bone structure. Her hair was grey and her eyes large and brown. There was about her an elfish quality, an ageing elf, a time-worn sprite, a little old lady who was used to having her own way and had very seldom been thwarted. And at this moment she completely puzzled by Blanche. It was true that Ida Cookson, a fool if ever there was one, had persuaded her to see Madame Blanche. But that had arisen originally because she was always teasing Ida about her belief in spiritualism. Only when the dreams had started did she ever begin to think about it and even then not seriously. In fact, looking back, she found it hard to decide when or why she had made the decision. Dreams were commonplace enough and there was a perfectly logical explanation for hers. The particular ones about Harriet upset and disturbed her. They would pass or she could live with them. She really couldn't understand why in the end she had made the appointment with Madame Blanche. The wo-man talked well with only the faintest hint of her real class echoing in her speech. She was amusing, and she didn't crucify the Queen's English. But what she was and where she came from were only too evident. Ida had told her something about Madame Blanche's early life. All that she must in fairness discount. But she wasn't going to be taken in. Madame Blanche, she was sure, had treated her to a routine approach for people of her nature. The woman was sharp-witted, intel-ligent and quick to adapt herself. But *how* could she have known about her dreams? Nobody but herself knew. The wo-man certainly couldn't have gleaned the information from any-one else.

Miss Rainbird sat with her thoughts and her very dry sherry, her eyes absently on the gardener who was forking through a rose bed. Harriet was a fool, of course. Always had

33

been. She and Sholto were both gone. If there were any truth in being able to communicate with the other world, then Sholto was the one to answer – and that was the last thing he was likely to do. Sholto had never gone back on anything he had said or done. A stubborn brute. Still, she smiled to herself, perhaps she ought to give it a try. Harriet might know more now that she had 'passed over'. It would be ironical if Harriet could do it, with Sholto standing by unable to stop her … No, the whole thing was a nonsense. How on earth had Madame Blanche guessed she was having bad dreams? Harriet whining every night, wringing her hands and talking about 'the right thing to do for the family'. Harriet who had caused all the trouble in the first place by being such a spineless creature! Although she had loved Harriet, really deeply loved her, she had to say it – Harriet had been really quite a useless person. No guts, no backbone … those big blue eyes always filling with tears. Why was that fool of a gardener forking the bed over before he'd done his pruning? She reached out and rang the bell for Syton, the butler.

Driving back to Stockbridge to pick up George, Blanche was placidly pleased with herself. Miss Rainbird would call for her. The thing which would get the old duck most was the challenge. She'd as good as told her that she wasn't up to facing something new. A starchy old biddy like Miss Rainbird wouldn't take that lying down. George had done a good job. To begin with, anyway. Most of it had come from the church and the sexton. There were half a dozen Rainbird headstones in the churchyard. The two latest were for Harriet Rainbird and Sholto Harold Rainbird. Sholto had been the only brother, unmarried, and had died at the age of seventy-six two years previously. Harriet Rainbird had died at the age of sixty-five two years before her brother. Both their parents were buried in the churchyard. Three children, all born with silver spoons in their mouths. Reed Court, a large Georgian country mansion, had been in the family for donkey's years. Once the Rainbirds had been big landowners. Now they held only about ten acres around Reed Court, but clearly no money had been lost in the process. Everything in and around Reed Court pointed to wealth; the gardens well kept, the house in good repair, a butler, two maids, a gardener and boy, a chauffeur, and a Rolls-Royce and a small station wagon in the garage. What a number George was for ferreting things out. Clever bastard ... too clever sometimes for his own good. Idle, too, unless he was prodded hard. But nice. Nice old George. If she could have made him over a bit she would have married him. But as he was – no thank you. She had other things in her sights ... and they might be on their way because of this Rainbird woman. All the money in the world, the middle child, probably sat on by this Sholto (they'd said a thing or two about him in the pub), and then inheriting everything when the bachelor tyrant died. Miss Rainbird had real freedom now, Blanche guessed. She would be generous if you really did something for her ... something big, something that meant everything in the world to her.

And that's what Henry had told her, lying there in bed after George had gone off to Chilbolton. He'd been filling the room and she'd just opened up her mind and spirit to him and it had all come through. Just like he'd been in the room at Reed Court a little while back. That bit about the dreams. She was no fool. Henry didn't always make things easy. Sometimes he came as clear as a bell, speaking right through her. The old girl had little dark bags from bad sleeping under her eyes. She looked otherwise as fit as a flea. Nothing wrong with her health, nothing wrong with her circumstances – bit mean, though, she could have offered a sherry seeing that it was half-past eleven on a sunny morning – so she probably had been sleeping badly because of dreams. And right then, Henry had said clearly, 'Dead right, me old dear. Bad dreams. Tell her I'll fix it for a few nights.' Sometimes Henry sounded just like George. Great joker Henry. Did it on purpose to tease her. But Henry, before he had passed over, had been a qualified railway engineer in the nineteenth century. He'd worked with someone called Brunel. She'd looked him up in a book she had, and there he was; and what's more there were a couple of lines about the work of his assistant – Henry Rees Morton. Her Henry.

The old girl had covered her surprise when she had told her about the dreams. She'd seen too many people put on a poker face when she said something that shook them. Specially this kind. The-don't-think-you-can-fool-me-Madame Blanche-type, all-done-by-mirrors-and-snooping-around-for-gossip. Well, why not? Henry wasn't going to help her to find things that were right under her nose. Henry and the others only came in when you really needed them. Bad dreams? What kind of bad dreams would Miss Rainbird have? She was a spinster and so had been Harriet. Probably thought that every man was after their money. And the old boy, Sholto. Bachelor, too. But with an eye for the girls. Probably decided that he could have all he wanted without the trouble of marriage. What *had* she been dreaming about? Henry would know. But he wouldn't break a confidence. He would have to know that Miss Rainbird wanted it revealed before he would come over. Perfect gentleman. He must have been like that down here and the fineness of character had naturally passed over with him.

Anyway, there was no doubt about one thing. Henry had made it clear that through wealthy Miss Rainbird she was going to have the Temple of Astrodel ... a splendid, real church. My God, not like some of the crummy places she sometimes went to, wedged between the pub and the public lavatories and as tatty inside as a third-rate whore's parlour. No wonder they got bad results or had to fake 'em a bit. What would anyone who had passed over to the shining glory of the other shore want to come back to joints like that for? The Temple of Astrodel, a blaze of purple and white and gleaming gold and well endowed. No counting the collection with a gloomy heart after the service.

George was waiting in the saloon bar of the Grosvenor Hotel at Stockbridge, sitting at a table with a glass of beer. He greeted her with his big grin, put an arm around her and gave her a hug. Nice, big, warm George.

He brought her a glass of stout and she took off her hat and gave her red hair a shake. She'd dressed soberly for Miss

Rainbird. None of the bright colours she liked. But the plain brown dress and brown coat barely dimmed the splendour and glowing fruitfulness of her ample body. Rubens would have stripped her in haste, his eyes filling with tears of joy.

George said, 'Well, how did it go?'

'We made some progress.'

George winked. 'Got her on the hook?'

'I don't like that kind of talk.'

'Upstage, eh? Professional etiquette. You don't fool me, love. You're in – or at least you will be soon. Good for you. Well, you must say I did a good job for you.'

Blanche finished her stout in a long, relishing swallow that made her creamy throat pulsate. She put the glass down and said, 'The job's not finished, Georgie-love. Get me another of those and I'll tell you what I want you to do.'

George groaned. 'Christ, no.'

'Christ, yes. And don't blaspheme.'

There were three of them in the room. The curtains drawn against the night. Outside a strong north-west wind was blowing with an occasional grenade-like burst of rain in it. Now and then a squall made the windows rattle. The storm swept down across Hyde Park and Green Park, ragging at the leafless trees, swirled across St James's Park, ruffling and disturbing the roosting wildfowl, and broke with a noisy turbulence against the solid block of the Houses of Parliament at the riverside. Grandison could hear it, wind and rain, and he liked the sound. He paused now and then in his talking, not to gather words for fresh speech, but just to catch the sound of the wind. The wind was power, undiluted power. It could lay a liner over on its beam-ends. He liked power. Unashamedly. But he made no display of it unless forced. He was an arrogant man, too. But he displayed that never. He moved a little about the bare, almost monastic room as he talked and the dress medals and decorations on his evening clothes made a small metallic sound now and then. After he left here he was going to a banquet sponsored by the Foreign Office for an Oxford-educated African Head of State whose father for tribal and often personal reasons had conducted many a human sacrifice. Many of the activities which were coordinated in this room had the same purpose. *Plus ça change* ...

Sangwill and Bush watched and listened.

'The projection we've made—' That was being generous to Bush, '—has been examined, considered, disputed and all the other official jargon. Tossed about and kicked about – and accepted. From there on everyone had to have their little say and then it was all wrapped up and said for them again by the Big Man himself. The third kidnapping must not happen – because if it did they would have to accept all the terms for the sake of ... well, I don't have to spell that out. Quite simply – and this if for you, Bush, because I'm dropping it in your lap – Trader has got to be scotched. Find him and those with him and we'll deal with them.' He smiled, scratched at his beard, and added, 'Very quietly, very unofficially, and permanently. And by the way, I think your projection is slightly wrong on one point. I don't feel that you will have six months to do it in. More like three at the most. Trader has no need to spin it out. He wants time only to set it up. The closer the third strike comes to the others the better from his point of view. It will reinforce his demand for complete secrecy. All right?'

'Yes.' Bush's mind was already racing ahead. This was what he wanted.

'Sangwill will give you everything you want. There are two things you should pay particular attention to. Evidence which seems to have no significance when it is first collected may turn out to be more than pertinent six months later. The other thing is that an ordeal recollected in calmness often throws up small facts, or uncovers minor lapses of memory, which don't come to the surface in the interrogation immediately after the ordeal. The human mind is unreliable in its recollection of facts and often rejects or even conceals small details because of the priority which it feels must be given to larger and, so it would seem, more cogent facts. I am sure you are aware of that already, but I get a pedantic pleasure out of stressing it.'

Bush smiled at this. The last sentence had been a characteristic form of apology in case he had been making two unnecessary points.

Later in his room Bush acknowledged that the first point he had been well aware of. The second had not occurred to him, though it might have done later. He picked up the telephone and called Sangwill and asked that appointments be made for him to see again the next day the two men who had been kidnapped. He had already seen them once individually. This time he wanted to see them together.

He looked at his watch. It was seven o'clock. He called the main office and asked for coffee and sandwiches to be sent up and then turned to the bundle of six orange-backed files which contained a complete record of all the inquiries which had been made by the police and his department on the kidnapping cases.

By midnight he had gone through the files meticulously and had made a list of points which warranted further investigation. He dictated a tape outlining the points and requesting that Scotland Yard be asked to deal with three of them. The others would be his concern.

The three points for Scotland Yard were –

1. A check over the last three years of the membership lists of Crowborough Beacon Golf Club and Tiverton Golf Club to be made and the names noted of any man or woman who was or had been a member of each club.

2. A similar check through the visitors' books of the clubs and a note made of all names appearing in each.

3. The photograph of the carnival mask worn by Trader to be circulated to all novelty manufacturers in the country for possible identification. If identified, a list of all retail and foreign outlets.

The points for himself were –

1. The rushing sound and the small bell ringing?

2. Travel limit radius by train or car. From Newbury and Reading after phone call. Two hours first, one hour second.

3. Water?

39

He walked home through the late-night streets to his flat, had a bath and went to bed. The next morning there was a letter in the post for him from his wife. She wrote to tell him that she was not coming back to him. She was willing – whichever way he chose, since it might have some effect on his professional status and future prospects – to give him the evidence for a divorce or let him give it. He put it in his pocket quite unmoved by it. Sometime or other soon he would think about it and let her know. There were other things on his mind at the moment.

Miss Rainbird woke for the second morning in succession without having dreamt. It was a refreshing feeling and she told herself sensibly that she must have been very stupid to let herself get into any kind of state because of them. Everyone had strange dreams at times. The thing to do was to ignore them. She couldn't understand how she'd ever let Ida Cookson persuade her to see that blowsy Madame Blanche.

When the maid brought her morning tea and drew the curtains on a sparkling morning, she told her to tell the chauffeur to have the Rolls ready at half-past nine. She was going to London. She would treat herself to a couple of hours' shopping in Harrods. It was still a keen pleasure to be able to come back at the end of the day and not be subject to a bad-tempered inquisition from Sholto as to where she had been and exactly how much money she had spent and on what. Sholto had really become impossible in his later years. It was a blessing when, very drunk, he had fallen down the main stairway and killed himself.

That morning George drove off for Chilbolton sorry that the weather was so fine. If you stood on the doorstep with the rain belting down or a cold wind running up the inside of your trousers you met more than one who would ask you inside for a cup of tea that always led to gossip. It always amazed him how people liked to talk. Loneliness it was. Anyone to natter to for half an hour. You rolled up with your important looking note-book. Doing a survey for a big London firm of Publicity and

Advertising Consultants. Half of them didn't know what you were talking about. What daily paper do you take? And magazines? Oh, yes. You're only the second one I've had this morning, madame, who takes that. Very high-class publication. Now what about the children, the rest of the family? To begin with, how many would you be in family? Out it would come. What does your husband do? was a gusher opener sometimes. You got what he did or didn't do and what he ought to do, and his ailments and the whole family picture.

'And Albert,' he said, reaching over and scratching the dog's head, 'somewhere along the line you hit some old trout who's worked at Reed Court. Some old dirt hoarder, or some old coughing, beer-drinking ancient who could and will give you the whole Doomsday book of scandal and gossip about everyone in the village. And Albert, just because I'm good at it, don't think I enjoy it. Really nasty some are. They do love to hand on a bit of dirt. Got to be careful, too, with some of the women, Albert. Fine-looking fellow like me. No funny stuff. Remember the matron at school. What the hell was her name? Had to be me that was caught and fourth in the queue by all accounts. Heigh-ho, the wind and the rain. Wish there bloody well was some.'

He began to whistle. He hadn't got a care in the world which he could do anything about.

That evening the two men who had been kidnapped came to see Bush in the department's guest room. Although they were both Members of Parliament they had no conception of the real function of the department. For them it was simply a discreet branch of the Home Office which specialized in liaison work with the police forces of the country and, unless invited, no one was encouraged to ask questions about it. Everything they said in the room was recorded on tape openly.

Richard Pakefield was a right-wing member of the Labour Party. He was an old Etonian, in his late thirties. He was an eager, excitable, restless man, brimming largely with impractical ideas, a tall, wide-eyed man who, despite the pipe nearly always in his mouth, gave the impression of an overgrown, precocious schoolboy.

On the night of his kidnapping he had decided to walk back to his hotel from a political meeting he had addressed in Southampton. He was crossing the dark forecourt of his hotel when someone had called his name from a group of parked cars. He had gone over to find a woman sitting at the driving wheel of the car, the window open. All he remembered of her was that she wore a dark coat with a large collar that was pulled up around her face. Her hair – she wore no hat – was short and seemed to be blonde or light brown. As he had bent to ask her what she wanted, someone – he presumed a man – had come up behind him. He had felt a sharp pain in the top of his left arm and had passed out before he could straighten up. The car, a stolen Rover 2000 saloon, was found abandoned the next morning in a layby on the Southampton Winchester road about three miles north of Southampton. The car belonged to a commercial traveller staying at the hotel who was sleeping soundly when the kidnappers appropriated it so that its loss was not reported until the following morning. When Pakefield had come to he was in the quarters where he was to spend the rest of his time until the night of his release.

The second victim, the Right Honourable James Archer, had had much the same thing happen to him. Archer was one of the doyens of the Labour Party. He was a man in his mid-sixties, a shrewd, earthy, frankly-spoken Trade Unionist who had begun life in a Yorkshire mine. He was observant and intelligent and had previously been a Cabinet Minister. He had been taken one week-end while staying with friends in the country near High Wycombe. He often stayed with them and it was his habit nearly always before going to bed to take a five-minute stroll down the lane for a breath of fresh air. As he had come abreast of a car parked off the road under the shadow of a tree, the car window had come down and the woman driver had beckoned to him. Wiser than Pakefield, he had remained where he was and called to ask what the driver wanted. Before she could reply he heard a soft scuffling sound behind him and began to turn. He was gripped from behind, had a glimpse of a masked face, and then felt the prick in his shoulder and had rapidly passed out. He was convinced that his assailant had been a man. Although not big he was a strong man, but he had been gripped and held one-armed with a strength he was sure no woman could have possessed. As for the woman in the car, she was bare-headed and, he swore, certainly not blonde or fair. Her hair was either dark brown or black. The car, a Volvo saloon, had been found abandoned the next afternoon on a little-used road through a wood near Maidenhead. It had been stolen from the staff car park of a High Wycombe Hospital and belonged to a young doctor who was doing all-night casualty service so that its loss was not reported until the next morning. Fingerprinting of the two cars had produced no helpful results. Clearly the man and woman concerned wore gloves and they had operated in the stolen cars safe in the knowledge that there would be no police call out for them. Equally clearly they had each time driven to their own car and made a transfer of their victim.

The two men had regained consciousness in the same place. Their descriptions of this and of their routine tallied. There were two windowless rooms. The outer room was a living-room with a wooden table and two chairs, one an upright cheap table chair for eating and the other a rexine or leather-covered lounging-chair. The inner room, smaller, contained a safari camp bed with the appropriate bedclothes. Behind a curtain was a low-suite lavatory and a wall washbasin which gave hot and cold water. There was a small mirror over it with an electric razor point. A razor – a Philips – was provided. The lighting in both rooms was from ceiling strips which they were at liberty to operate. There were ventilation ducts near the ceiling in both rooms and, if the men needed warmth, there was a Dimplex heater in each room which they could switch on and off. In the living-room, set in the wall, was a loud-speaker system which they could control. Most of the day and early part of the evening light classical and popular music was relayed through this. Above this system was another loud-speaker which they could not control. Over this they received their instructions. When a meal was about to be brought to

43

them they had to retire to the bedroom and close the door. There was no apparent lock on the door but they had both found that once inside it could not be opened on these occasions. Pakefield, examining it when it was opened, had seen that at three places down the length of the door jamb on the handle edge of the door there were three studs that moved across – obviously from an electric control outside their quarters – which married into three cylindrical cavities in the edge of the door itself. Someone had gone to a lot of trouble, Bush had long known, to ensure security, and that someone never took a random step. The voice giving them their instructions over the speaker was male, but it was always backed by some kind of electronic disturbance, sometimes to the point of making it difficult to know what was being said.

The door from the living-room to the outer world was of some stout wood, handleless on the inside. In the top half was inset a two-foot square of mirror. Both of the men had soon guessed that this was a one-way window through which they could be observed from the outside. Pakefield had tried to smash this mirror with the table chair but had only succeeded in breaking the chair, which was replaced without any comment. They were fed well and had a selection of magazines to read though these were never renewed.

They were provided with no newspapers whatever and at no time were they given any information relating to their abduction, though both of them realized that they must be being held for some kind of ransom. They were happily ignorant of the fact that a death sentence hung over them unless the ransom was paid within a certain time limit.

On the evening of their release the procedure had been the same for the two men. Over the speaker they had both been informed that they were being released, but if in any way they refused to carry out the instructions now to be given them then the release would be cancelled. The slightest attempt at heroics would merely prolong their stay. Naturally both of them had done as they were bid. They were told to take a dark blanket from their bed and wrap it securely around their heads and then to stand in the middle of the living-room. Both men had done this and – so far as they could tell – only one person had come into the room. Their right arms were taken and there followed the jab of a hypodermic needle and they passed out. Both men when picked up by the helicopter were in a highly sedated state. (A blood test on Archer – missed as far as Pakefield was concerned – had shown that the drug used was a highly sophisticated development of sodium theopentone and chlorpromezathine which was not generally available to the public.) The helicopter picking up Pakefield had landed near the first fairway of the Tiverton Golf Club in Devon. An open roadway ran near it. Archer had been picked up on the twelfth fairway of the Crowborough Beacon Golf Club in Sussex, and a roadway, screened by trees, ran alongside it. The drugged men, with their hands tied, were waiting on the ground fifteen yards from the landing spot of the helicopter. Both the girl, the first time, and the man the second time, had pointed out the man to the pilot and then, covering him with their automatic, had backed away into the night, leaving the pilot to get his load aboard unaided. The whole process so far as the kid-nappers were concerned was over in a few seconds. The pilot – briefed after his experience the first time – had waited some minutes in the hope of hearing a car move off. He would then have picked up his load and followed it to try and establish its identity. But there had been no sound. The man had just dis-appeared into the night. (This had been no surprise to Bush or Grandison. The kidnapper would have known the helicopter risk once he had moved away from it and had made provision for it.)

Listening to the tapes of the previous interrogations being played now, Bush was professionally full of admiration for the skill and intelligence behind the two abductions. Not only had the victims been studied in detail and arrangements made for their captivity which would leave them with little to tell when they were free, but the planning had for all that involved risk, the kind of risk, he was sure, in which the man behind it all would take a delight. Risk, the unforeseen trip of circum-stances to bring disaster, there always had to be. But more than that, and this was what he wanted, somewhere or other there had to be something on which the mind, his mind, could seize and from the faintest echo of sound or the turn of a tiny detail give him the lead he wanted, and which he was determined to have because he meant for purely professional and ambitious reasons to get to Trader.

When the interrogation tapes were finished, Bush said, 'Well, there it is, gentlemen. I'm sorry to put you through it all again, but as you've been told in confidence we're pretty sure this Trader might operate again. No man sets up this kind of operation just for forty thousand pounds.'

'It's a lot of money, lad,' said Archer. 'You ask my Union. They stumped up my twenty thousand. We could have used it for other things.' He began to roll himself a cigarette.

'It's the principle, not the money,' said Pakefield. 'So far as my family were concerned it didn't mean much. But that's not the integral point. When prominent men are put at risk, and by the very nature of their duties they are, then—'

Bush, sighing inwardly, interrupted. 'Yes, well, sir, that isn't quite the point at the moment. You've heard the tapes. What my department has been thinking is that now, studied and recollected in a calmer atmosphere, there is just the chance that there could be something, no matter how small, that has possibly been missed and which might help us. What I would like to do is to put a few questions to you which might lead us somewhere. If in doing so it stirs anything extra in your memory I'd be grateful if you would let me have it. No matter how small, no matter how vaguely remembered. Not facts necessarily, an idea, an impression.'

'Carry on, lad,' said Archer.

Pakefield, relighting his pipe, nodded.

Bush said, 'Thank you. First then. Would you say the water you used for washing was hard or soft or what?'

'Soft,' said Pakefield. 'Very definitely. Now that's interesting, isn't it? If you establish the soft-water areas of the country and then—'

'Dickey, lad,' said Archer, 'Mr Bush here knows that. Just let's stick to the answers and leave the deductions to him, lad. You may want to play detectives, but I want to get this over and be back at the House. The water was soft, lad.' He nodded at Bush.

'Do you remember the make of soap you were provided with?'

'It was yellowy, been used before so there was no name on it,' said Pakefield. 'I didn't like the smell.'

'It was Wright's Coal Tar soap,' said Archer. 'I'd know it anywhere from a boy. My mother used to scrub me with it.'

Bush said, 'These quarters. They were obviously adapted for the purpose. Would you say the installations were a professional job or a do-it-yourself effort?'

'Do-it-yourself,' said Pakefield. 'The wiring of lights and speakers just ran openly along the walls and ceiling. The partition that made the bedroom had been knocked up quite roughly. Everything worked, all quite functional—' Bush sighed inwardly again. Say what you mean once and leave it at that, he thought. '—but no attempt at refinement.'

'You both say that at times you were given white wine with meals. Any idea what it was?'

'Just white wine,' said Archer. 'Pretty dry stuff.'

Pakefield leaned back in his chair, took his pipe out of his mouth and stared at the ceiling. 'Can't see how knowing the wine would help. But, anyway, there was little doubt about it. I should say it was a Pouilly Fuissé 1966. The food was indifferent as I've said already. I would say that your man from a culinary point of—'

'Oh, I don't know,' interrupted Archer. 'I had some very good plaice and chips. And a Yorkshire pudding once that was passable.'

'I've just thought of something,' said Pakefield. 'That main door with the mirror. I believe there was something outside that. Like another door. From the bedroom when you were waiting for the food to come in, you'd hear a sort of rumbling sound before the sound of the main door being opened. And sometimes sitting in the main room there would be this rumble and, I don't think it's my imagination, there would be a change in the quality of the light behind or coming through the mirror. I would say, as a conjecture, that we were down in

47

some cellar system and that the entrance to our place was camouflaged in some way. A false wall that went across in the case of some unexpected visitor or inspection. This man, we know, had left nothing to chance. Somewhere he must be leading an outwardly ordinary life and—'

'What were the walls of your quarters made of, sir?' asked Bush.

'Stone slabs,' said Pakefield.

'Any idea what kind of stone?'

'No, I—'

'Limestone, lad,' said Archer. 'I should know that. And it had been there a long time. If it was a cellar then it doesn't belong to any modern house. And that makes me think of something else. That lavatory and washbasin. There was no drainage problem. Water went away fast enough. If we was in a cellar then there was a pretty good fallaway. House could have been on a slope.'

Pakefield said, 'I've just thought of something. After all, you have asked us for a kind of total recall. Any small, even apparently insignificant detail. Well, this comes into that category. I haven't mentioned it before because it has only just come back to me. It may surprise you to know, I'm really a bit of a sentimentalist. I like mementoes. Go on holiday and I like to bring something back ... well, I thought the same about this place. *If* I get out, I told myself, I'd like to have something, something I could frame for my study or put on a mantelpiece. So I stole one of the spoons. The cutlery and china as you know were all just plain, cheap stuff.'

To stop the long-windedness, Bush said, 'They took it from you, sir?'

'Yes, I had it in my pocket when they drugged me to come out. It wasn't there when I got back home.'

Archer chuckled. 'That happened to my feather. I found it on the floor of the main room one day after they brought the food. Stuck it in my pocket as a memento. Like Dickey, here, when I got back it was gone.'

'What kind of feather was it, sir?'

'It was a hackle feather. That's a small feather from the

neck of a bird. Kept pigeons when I were a lad. I wouldn't like to say what bird this came from though. It was sort of browny grey. Anyway it was gone.'

'They clearly searched us after we were drugged,' said Pakefield. 'Pity about that spoon, you know – kind of thing one's children would in time like to have.'

'Tell me, sir,' said Bush to Pakefield. 'You said previously that you thought you heard something over the intercom system. Could we go into that a little more?'

'Well, yes. It was a dual system clearly. Through the bottom speaker came this taped music. I should say home-made, Muzak stuff. During the day and early evening, if you switched on, it was usually going. The top speaker was dead until they switched on. You'd hear the click of the switch and then sometimes it would be a few seconds before the man – always the man – spoke. One day this happened. The man began to speak, the usual stuff about food coming in and I must go to the bedroom, and then there was an interruption. Only for a few seconds, though. I heard him make an angry ... no, rather exasperated noise. Like you might use when flapping away a wasp. And there was this little tinkle of sound and with it a sort of rushing of air. Then it stopped and he went on speaking.'

'If you had to put an explanation to it, sir, what would you say?'

'Well ... I'd have thought that he'd knocked something over, like a big pile of papers and some small glass object. Something on his desk or table.'

'Originally you said it was bell-like.'

'Well, it was in a way.'

Bush said, 'Did either of you ever hear any other noises? Not over the speaker. Say the sound of traffic or planes?'

Both men shook their heads. Then Archer said, 'The plates were always good and hot when we had a cooked meal. The stuff came on an open tray so the kitchen couldn't have been far away.'

'You've no recollection of being driven either to or from this place?'

Neither of them could remember anything of their journeys. There were no markings or makers' labels on any of their bed clothes. At meals they were served with plain white paper napkins.

When they were gone he ran the tape of their conversation. He hadn't been expecting anything very pertinent from them, and he hadn't got it. There was no disappointment in him. In his job you kept emotions at an even level. No joy, no pain, just hard grafting. The house – if it were a house – could be in limestone country with the kidnap quarters in the cellar. Fairly big cellar or cellar system. That meant a fairish-sized house. Near traffic noises or aircraft noises would have come through faintly maybe at night. Unless the cellar quarters were sound-proofed it could mean that the location was in the country somewhere ... almost certainly was because Trader wouldn't want the close presence of neighbours. The house could stand on a slope or hill. The rushing noise. Wind, falling papers? The tinkling sound? An ornament falling, a glass vibrating, some small bell?

He stood up and walked slowly about the room. This was going to be one of those hard, hard jobs of attrition. Almost certainly a closed van of some kind would have been used. The stolen cars were only safe enough for a few miles. Beyond that the risk was too great. He would have to get down to his maps and his timings. Trader had gone north from Southampton and south-east from High Wycombe. That wasn't significant. Trader would never use any direct route – but even he could not be independent of place, time and distance. Tiverton was in Devon and Crowborough in Sussex – a good two hundred miles apart. He poured himself a drink and considered the feather. Blown in by a draught when the door was opened for the meal to be brought? Or caught up on the sole of a muddy boot or shoe and brought in. From the kitchen? Few people plucked fowls in the kitchen these days. Or they might if it were a farm. Naturally Trader had searched the men before they left. Finding and taking the spoon was obvious. But the feather. Why take that? On principle? Then men were to go as they had come in. The spoon, yes. It could conceivably have given a lead. But why a feather, a small browny hackle feather little more than an inch long? If it had meant nothing Trader might not have bothered with it. The fact that he had, meant that he did not want it to go out. The assumptions had to be that either he was just sticking to a principle, or that he felt the feather might at a pinch have some significance ... say in the hands of a qualified ornithologist. And where on earth did he get the sodium theopentone-chlorpromezathine stuff? If it had been – his mind came swinging back to it suddenly – a hen, duck or turkey feather it would have helped no one. But take the extreme case – if it had been a feather from an un-usual bird and could be identified by an ornithologist then it might help. Trader was either just careful on principle – or he might own or have contact with a bird or birds which would not be classed as ordinary.

CHAPTER THREE

FOR THREE NIGHTS Miss Rainbird's sleep was clear of any disturbing dreams. On the fourth night Harriet returned. On the following day as Miss Rainbird was feeding the ornamental wildfowl on the small lake in the grounds of Reed Court she decided to send for Madame Blanche. Although she was inwardly still sceptical that Madame Blanche would be able to help her, she was forcing herself to be open-minded enough to give the experiment a trial. But one thing she was determined not to be was hoodwinked and so become a source of easy money for some charlatan.

Madame Blanche arrived at six o'clock that same evening and was shown in by Syton to the drawing-room. The curtains were drawn for the night and on a small table were set out a sherry decanter and cocktail biscuits. Madame Blanche, Miss Rainbird noted, was less soberly dressed than on her first visit. She wore a plum-coloured dress with matching shoes and there was a long string of large artificial pearls around her neck and looping down over her ample bosom. Over the telephone Miss Rainbird had already told Blanche that her dreams had returned. She had gone into no details of the dreams. To begin with she was quite determined not to help this woman in any way. She wanted first of all some positive demonstration that Madame Blanche did indeed possess some, at least, of the powers Mrs Cookson had claimed for her.

While she was offering Blanche a glass of sherry, which was accepted, she said quite frankly, 'This dream is one that recurs very often. I'm not prepared to say more at the moment than that it concerns someone who is dead and was very close to me. If I went into some of the circumstances of our relationship it might lead you – and forgive me for saying this – into conjectures and the possible formation of hypotheses which might influence you quite wrongly. You don't mind that I adopt this attitude, do you?'

Blanche sipped her sherry and smiled. The woman would have made a good headmistress of a girls' school. She talked like one often. But that didn't worry her. Gypsies, fairground people, crystal-ball gazers and, in the old days, actors were not house-trained and not to be trusted. The Miss Rainbirds of this world put up barriers which could be knocked for six when the moment was right. She said, 'All I want to know, Miss Rainbird, is that you really do in your heart hope I can help in some way. I don't ask that you believe in me. I just ask that you shall be fair and judge me by results. Quite frankly I may not be able to help you get across.'

'Get across?'

'To this person.'

'I see.'

'However, we can try, can't we?'

'Here and now?'

'That's why you asked me to come, Miss Rainbird.'

'Yes, of course.' For a moment Miss Rainbird felt a loss of confidence, and with it a slight feeling that she was being unfair to this woman, who met her outspoken scepticism, hostility almost, with a bland good-nature and understanding.

'All I ask,' Blanche said, 'is that you don't get upset at the beginning. Making contact is a strain. If I groan or seem, well, to be suffering – please don't let it worry you and, whatever you do, don't touch me. I'm sure Mrs Cookson must have explained something of what goes on.'

'Yes, she has.'

'Then let's have a crack at it, shall we?'

Seeing the expression on Miss Rainbird's face, Blanche laughed. 'Don't look surprised. I'm not being flippant. This is for me a gift like all the others I have. Seeing is a miracle, so is hearing. All part of life. And this psychic gift is part of life, this life and the greater life beyond. They are all one. I just see a little more and hear a little more than most people. Now, what I'd like you to do is to sit in your chair and relax your body and then forget me and think about this person. Think pleasantly and warmly about them. By the way, I should tell you that sometimes when I come round, I have no memory of what has happened or been said. And if you don't want to tell me, you don't have to. Naturally, if it is something you can tell without embarrassment, I would like to know because it does help at any later sittings. All right? Are we all set?'

Slowly Miss Rainbird smiled and gave a little laugh. When she laughed, thought Blanche, you saw something more of the pretty girl she had once been. Underneath she was sure that she wasn't such a bad old trout. For all her money and position, life hadn't been all good to her on the fun and frolic side. She should have married and had children, been regularly tupped by her man, and had the great kick of kids growing up about her. Only dedicated people like herself could seriously deny themselves most of that.

Blanche said, 'That's better. Now just sit back and let yourself go.'

Miss Rainbird sat back in her chair and shut her eyes for a moment, composing her thoughts, and trying to bring them around to Harriet. Perversely she found her mind suddenly full of the memory of Sholto. The whole thing had stemmed from him, from his sense of family and its good name. Harriet had been putty in his hands. She felt a little stir of anger at the thought that she hadn't known a thing about it until two years afterwards when Harriet had told her. Her eyes still shut, she heard Madame Blanche's voice.

'There is anger in you. Put it from you. It confuses and holds me back.'

Eyes opening, Miss Rainbird saw that Madame Blanche was sitting almost primly, stiffly even, upright in her chair. Her hands had gone to the long hanging loop of the pearls and she was holding it with lightly clenched fists. Her head was slightly raised and her eyes were shut.

'I'm sorry,' said Miss Rainbird.

Madame Blanche smiled. 'Anger is a tall black wall without a gateway. Love is the gateway. From us to them and from them to us.'

Miss Rainbird unaccountably had a quick mental picture of the wide, elaborately worked wrought-iron gates that led from the closed garden of Reed Court down a long stretch of greensward to the fringe of the ornamental lake where she had been that morning. She saw Harriet moving down to the lake, a blue poplin dress sweeping the sunbathed grass, straw hat swinging from its ribbon in her hand; Harriet at nineteen, the light summer breeze lifting the stray tendrils of her blonde hair. The memory pleased her. Almost as though Madame Blanche were sharing the pleasant memory with her, she saw her smile.

Madame Blanche breathed in and out deeply as though she were filling her nostrils with the perfume of some secret garden. Then slowly she dropped the pearls and raised her hands to her temples, her fingers smoothing at her brow, and she sighed deeply. Her hands came down from her forehead and held the ends of the arm-rests of the chair. The movement of the hands held Miss Rainbird's attention and she slowly realized that they were not resting easily on the ends but gripping hard at them, so hard that she could see the whitening of the knuckles. Madame Blanche began then to breathe quickly, her body tensing as though she were possessed by some inner struggle. For a moment or two Miss Rainbird was frightened. Not for Madame Blanche, but for herself, for being in this position, for letting herself consider even for a moment that there was any need for this ludicrous experiment. Harriet was dead. Only a memory to her now. And Sholto was dead and a far less pleasant memory. Only she lived and there was no one to command her to this charade ... Not even Harriet in her dreams.

Madame Blanche in an unexpectedly loud voice said, 'Somebody is here. Not closely, not willingly. No, not one ...' She broke off and a long, strange, almost animal groan broke slowly from her. Almost curtly, she cried, 'No, there are two. But very distant ... away, away at the end of a great vista, but I can see them. An old man and an elderly woman.' She paused and then said briskly, 'Henry? Are you there, too? Yes, you are. I get you now.' She laughed happily. 'Welcome, love.

55

What's all the trouble? Why do they stay so far away?'

Miss Rainbird, fascinated by the sudden change in Madame Blanche's manner and tone when she greeted and talked to Henry, watched her closely. Her hands were relaxed now and her body had slumped easily against the upholstered chair back. She was a big, slack, vulgarly handsome woman.

Madame Blanche gave a low laugh and said, her voice coarsening a little, 'Come on, Henry – don't you be difficult too. Not one of your bad days, is it, love? Tell me what's bothering them. Why won't they come closer?'

She was silent for a while and then with an accompanying quick jerk of her body Madame Blanche began to speak again, but now her voice had changed. It was a man's voice, not deep, but a firm, unemotional, deliberate voice just touched with some accent. Miss Rainbird felt the skin at the back of her neck begin to creep as she listened.

The voice said, 'There is forgiveness always here. There has to be that. The woodside that is cut down leaves a scar on the hill. But the trees grow again and the hill is what it was.'

Madame Blanche chuckled. 'I've someone here, Henry, who wants help. Can't you save the poetry for another time? Why do they stay so far away?'

Henry said, 'She knows why they stay far away. They won't come – even though there is now peace and forgiveness between them – unless they know she really wants them. She must not be offended, but there is a selfishness in her which keeps them away.'

Madame Blanche's head moved sharply towards Miss Rainbird.

'Is that true, Miss Rainbird?'

Stung, Miss Rainbird said pertly, 'All human beings are selfish. It's typical of the kind of excuse Sholto—' She cut herself off quickly. Madame Blanche had impressed her against her will, but she had no intention of giving any information away. Certainly not at this stage.

Madame Blanche smiled and said, 'We've got to be patient, Henry, ducks. Miss Rainbird isn't a believer. We can't expect that yet.'

Henry in an even, almost offhand voice said, 'With some it can only be blind faith. With others the growth of belief is the struggle of a wayward flower to bloom out of season. The gentlewoman with you must warm her scepticism with love. Belief will bloom.'

A little impatiently, Madame Blanche said, 'You've been runnin' around with too many poets up there, Henry. You're an engineer, remember? So make it plain.'

A man's laugh came from Madame Blanche and then Henry's voice. 'You're a bully, Blanche. Ask her if she knows who they are.'

Madame Blanche turned to Miss Rainbird. 'Do you know them?'

Miss Rainbird, becoming more at ease in these strange circumstances, said, 'I know who they might be. But I clearly can't know who they are.'

Madame Blanche said, 'There's your answer, Henry.'

Henry said, 'It is what I expected. But tell her that human selfishness is weaker than a love of justice. She knows this. That is why she came to you. Tell her they both now want to see justice done, but they can't help until she is ready. Tell her the family of Man is the only true family.'

Madame Blanche turned to Miss Rainbird. 'Do you understand what Henry means?'

'Yes, I do, of course. I'm familiar with all the platitudes—'

Henry, through Madame Blanche, laughed, and the quick switch in tones, from female to male, broke through Miss Rainbird's temporary ease and chilled her. She was suddenly anxious for this pantomime to stop.

Madame Blanche, disappointment in her voice, said, 'Why are they going, Henry? They're turning away.'

Henry said solemnly, 'They have been turned away, Blanche. We have love and understanding. We have powers which enable us to reach back to the old life. But we have no power to change the human heart. As an engineer I could pipe water a thousand miles and make a desert bloom. But neither I nor anyone else here can bring faith to you below as though it came from the strike of a match at the turning of a gas tap.'

Madame Blanche chuckled. 'You're behind the times, Henry. We have electricity now.'

Henry said, 'Old habits of thought die hard. So do long-held prejudices.'

Miss Rainbird saw Madame Blanche's shoulders slowly shiver as though coldness had swept like an icy wind over her.

Madame Blanche said, 'The man's gone, Henry. Why does the woman linger?'

'Love makes her drag her steps, Blanche. Two loves. A love she gave and a love she killed.'

Madame Blanche said to Miss Rainbird, 'Do you understand that?'

In a low voice, Miss Rainbird answered, 'I think I might.' Then suddenly dropping her head, she went on in a half-choked voice, 'Ask him to tell her ... to tell her ... Oh, no ...! Oh, no ...!' She was fighting now to stop herself from crying, fighting hard, one part of her wanting to abandon herself to it, and another strongly, angrily almost, upbraiding herself for being so stupid.

Henry said quietly, 'From tears the desert of the heart will bloom. Goodbye, Blanche ... Goodbye ...'

'Bye, Henry.' Madame Blanche's voice echoed after Henry's.

Miss Rainbird sat and slowly recovered her composure. When she looked up Madame Blanche was leaning comfortably back in her chair, eyes shut. Her hands came up slowly and held her pearls. She sat like this, her eyes closed, for a long time until Miss Rainbird, her own emotions now quietened, thought she had gone to sleep.

She said, 'Are you all right, Madame Blanche?'

Blanche opened her eyes slowly and smiled. She let out a long breath and said, 'My goodness! What was all that about? I feel as though I've been properly done over. Oh, dear ... Do you mind if I—' Her eyes went to the little table with its sherry decanter on a silver tray.

'Of course.' Miss Rainbird got up and poured sherry for them both. For a moment or two they sat and sipped at their drink and then Miss Rainbird said, 'Do you remember what happened?'

Blanche shook her head. 'No, I don't. I only know that Henry must have come. He always leaves me like this when he's been really moved about something.' She laughed. 'Honestly, sometimes I look to see whether I've actually been bruised. He's a frank, hard-speaking man, though sometimes he gets a little fancy in his talk.'

'You don't remember any of the conversation at all?'

'No, Miss Rainbird, I don't. Sometimes, in fact very often, I do. But there are times when Henry cuts me out. He's very discreet. Did it help you at all?'

Miss Rainbird finished her glass of sherry and looked at Blanche. She had been impressed, but she was not a gullible old woman. She was quite prepared to admit that there could be phenomena in the world which she knew nothing about. More things in heaven and on earth, Horatio ... But before she accepted anything new it had to be demonstrated beyond doubt. There was doubt here. Madame Blanche could have gone off into a mediumistic trance state and quite honestly didn't remember anything. But the mind and the memory still functioned in such a state, as it did in sleep, though on a different plane. And she was not unaware of the possibility of mental telepathy. There was an impressive body of research to support it. Some people had the uncanny knack of sensing others' thoughts or emotional moods. And some people who had such gifts, she knew, were not above furnishing them out with trickery.

Very deliberately, she said, 'There must have been some things about me and my family, Madame Blanche, that you have learned from Mrs Cookson.'

'Well, of course.' Blanche smiled. 'Sometimes it's not possible to stop Mrs Cookson telling things. She told me who you were and that you had an elder brother and a younger sister who are both dead. She told me too that you were very fond of your sister and ... well ... not quite so fond of your brother. That's all, Miss Rainbird.'

Miss Rainbird considered this. Ida Cookson was an habitual gossip. But, all things considered, there was little to gossip about. Sholto's reputation had been well known. The business about Harriet was a very closely guarded family secret. Ida Cookson could know nothing about that. And certainly no one but herself could have known about Harriet's dream appearances. Two people who stood a long way off ... at the end of a heavenly vista, no doubt. And they wouldn't come any closer, wouldn't communicate with her unless she had already made up her mind that it was her duty, no matter what it might cost in embarrassment and discomfort to her, to dedicate herself to Harriet's tearful, histrionic wishes. If Harriet had asserted her rights as a human being years and years ago there would never have been any of this foolery, no plump, over-ripe Madame Blanche sitting in the chair opposite with a warming smile on her face. Didn't remember a thing. What nonsense. She had just put on a ... well, yes, a very, very good performance based on the merest scraps of knowledge and – she would give the woman this – a sound knowledge of human psychology. And her Henry – a prosy fool if she had ever heard one.

Miss Rainbird stood up, making it clear that their session was finished and said, 'Well, thank you for coming, Madame Blanche. As you know by now I am not a woman who is afraid to say Yes or No. I must frankly say that at the moment I don't know what I feel.' She began to walk towards the room door as Blanche rose. 'I need time to think a little. It is not, I want you to understand this, a question of my faith or otherwise in you and your powers. I have a personal decision to make about going on which is nothing to do with you. I will let you know, and if this should turn out to be our last meeting, Madame Blanche, I will, of course, see that you are properly remunerated.' She pressed the bell push three times, a signal to Syton that a visitor was going.

Affably, Blanche said, 'That's all right, Miss Rainbird. If this is the last time I don't need any money. You know ... sort of seven days' free trial and no obligation. I can guess how you feel. It's all upsetting and strange and your mind is full of doubts about yourself and me. If I don't hear from you I shall quite understand and I won't in any way be put out. My problem is to find enough time to help those who do really need me.'

As Miss Rainbird opened the room door, Syton appeared. Blanche moved out and the butler helped her on with her coat. Then with a smile for Miss Rainbird she began to follow him across the hall, past the foot of the long, oak-balustraded stairway that ran down to the ground floor. At the foot of the stairs Madame Blanche suddenly came to a halt. It was almost as though some invisible hand had come out and planted itself firmly against her bosom, blocking further movement. She stood motionless for a moment, then slowly turned back and looked at Miss Rainbird, and said, 'Something happened here.' She looked up the curving run of steps. 'Something terrible happened here. I can feel it.' Her shoulders shook with a quick shivering spasm and she moved on, following Syton. When Syton turned back from seeing her out, Miss Rainbird had retired to the sitting-room.

She went straight to the decanter and poured herself another glass of sherry. She was full of disturbance. Normally she would not have dreamt of taking so much sherry on her own. Sholto's excesses had firmly reinforced her natural habit of moderation.

What an extraordinary woman! How could she have felt anything? Only she and Dr Harvey had known that Sholto had fallen drunkenly down the stairs. Although Sholto was dead, he had miraculously not broken any bones or been more than mildly bruised, but the shock of falling had been too much for his heart. Dr Harvey – their doctor for forty years – had for the sake of the family name and to save village gossip simply certified death from heart failure. Even in death Sholto kept upsetting her when she thought of him. And now that fool Harriet was aiding and abetting him. How dare they say there was a selfishness in her which kept them away? She wasn't selfish. At least, not unduly so. She just wanted to be left alone to enjoy her few remaining years of life in a tranquillity which had come only too late to her. She certainly didn't want another man about the place ... and all the talk it would mean in the village, the chatter and the knowing nods and their eyes on her ... on them. And most daunting of all, what kind of man would he be with Harriet as a mother? And the father a heedless, good-for-nothing who'd been killed commanding a tank in the Egyptian desert during the war? No, they could stay at the end of their long heavenly vista, all of them. They were dead and she was alive, and she wanted this house to herself.

George woke in the night and at once knew she was there. He lay without stirring and grinned to himself. What a girl! Once he was asleep an army could walk through the room and he wouldn't hear. Faithful Albert, too. Man's best and sleepiest friend. She was awake, he knew. But she wouldn't have dreamt of waking him until he came surfacing naturally. He could picture what had happened. Coming back late to her Salisbury house she had suddenly wanted company. His company. Impulsive Blanche wanting a change from the spirit world. Henry was no substitute for flesh and blood. Henry might know the mystery of life, tune in to the music of the spheres, but Henry wasn't George. He, George, was the world, the warm, muddled up, never-know-where-you-will-be-to-morrow world. Personally if the next one wasn't more or less a replica of this with a few improvements he wanted nothing of it. Just to wake up now, as he had often done in the past, and find that warm, bed-cosied cornucopia of delights beside him was worth a thousand years of sitting on a drifting cloud listening to hymns and the constipated music of harps.

He reached out and touched her. Her hand closed in his and he heard her sigh. After a moment she released his hand and he let it roam over the familiar contours, and the rich delights of the hills and valleys which were his estate. One day he *must* get a bigger bed. He and Blanche were made for the wide rolling spaces. Big people, titanic lovers. Lovely, tell your Mum. The only thing to make it absolutely perfect would be ten thousand a year tax-free. As he slowly slipped up her nightdress, Blanche sighed again and her lips found his as he came to her.

Swinging over the unkempt garden, quartering it for winter mice and voles, the silent white spectre of a barn owl banked gently close to the curtained window and heard the squeak of bed springs. Much later, coming back from a foray over the water meadow, the owl planed by the window and there was silence.

Out of euphoria George said, 'All right?'

Lazily Blanche said, 'You should patent it, love. Make you a fortune. Sometimes it's all music, sometimes all colour – like tonight. A great fan-shaped flame, purple with pearly lights through it.'

'Things didn't go too well with Miss Rainbird?'

'Why?'

'Because you're here. Come to George for comfort. Always on offer, and special for you. Not even old Henry can match it.'

'You leave Henry out of this.'

'Gladly. Three'd be a crowd. What about her?'

'She went through phase two almost copybook. She'll phone me the day after tomorrow when she's settled down and had another dream. Why didn't you tell me about the way the brother went?'

'What, old bottom-pincher?'

'Yes.'

'I did.' He moved a leg and rested it diagonally and comfortably across the broad acres of her thighs.

'No. You said he died of heart failure.'

'So he did.'

'So he might, but he got it from falling down the hallway stairs. I could feel it like a great scream as I went by. Didn't you know about that?'

'Of course I did – and I told you. One of the gabby old girls said something about it. It was only a rumour. I must have told you.'

'It doesn't matter, but you didn't. You should tell me everything, George. No matter how small. You didn't tell me.'

'Well, maybe I didn't. Sometimes something slips.'

'The family doctor must have hushed it up. The old boy was probably tight and took a tumble. No scandal like that allowed. That's one of her big things, though she never mentions it. The Rainbird family. Pride and good name. She's all right.'

Through his body contact with her he felt her suddenly shiver.

'What's the matter, love?'

'It was one of those sessions. I don't know why Henry does it to me. He knows I don't care for it much. I don't like it when I don't remember anything after.'

George chuckled. 'Well, Henry may not give you anything to remember after. But you can't say that of me.' He slid his hand over and caressed her left breast. She lay placidly for a long time, taking the slow caress and then, as she felt him stir and move closer to her, she said, 'You aren't beginning again?'

George nuzzled the side of her cheek and said, 'Why not, love? This time it'll be a pearly flame streaked with purple, and I hope Henry bites his fingernails in frustration.'

Although Bush was an ambitious man, he was far from being an optimistic one. The hope of turning up by accident something which would help him in his work on the Trader business never occurred to him. Anything he was going to get would come from research into the following up of known facts. But if he were not optimistic he could easily feel frustration. And frustration lived with him now. He had worked on his maps and his timings and he had to admit the deduction he had made was far from a firm one. In fact if it had been presented to him by a subordinate he would have ridiculed it scathingly.

He sat now at his desk watching the lunchtime strollers in the park and the movement of the water fowl on the lake. He wanted no lunch himself. Frustration had killed his appetite, which was never very robust at the best of times.

On the map of England before him was drawn in a rectangle. Its top left-hand corner lay at a point west of Cardiff in Wales and its top right-hand corner was at Woolwich, east of London. Perpendiculars dropping from these points passed on the west through Tiverton, on the east through Crowborough, and framed between them, on a base line running just south of the Isle of Wight, practically the whole of the South of England – with London included! He looked at it and wrinkled his face in disgust. Somewhere in the area probably, though he had little faith in the assumption, the two kidnapped Members of Parliament had been held. Somewhere in that area could be a country house on some sort of slope or hill, a house possibly built of limestone (which narrowed it without much comfort to areas like the Mendip and Cotswold hills and others – possibly. Limestone had been frequently used for building well outside limestone areas). Somewhere in the area was a house where the water was soft – but it need not be soft naturally. It could be in a hardwater area in a house equipped with a water softener. Somewhere in that area there was a house in which a feather had floated or been shoe-scuffed into a cellar. Knowing something of the fastidious nature of Trader the feather might belong either to some common bird like the domestic fowl or to a much more unusual bird. Or, for all he knew, it might have come out of a feather duster or mattress. Somewhere in the enormous haystack of the area he had outlined was a needle, and in an hour's time he was due at a top-level conference at Scotland Yard where nobody from the department got a warm welcome – though strict cooperation would be given – to explain the position and to ask that right down to local constabulary level information should be requested ... demanded ... for any house which might fit the bill. His heart sank as he thought of the looks, the mouth-corner smiles, the little lift of eyes to heaven as he laid it all out. Somebody would say something about old ladies with parrots, pensioners with canaries and Royal Dukes with acres of lake stocked with ornamental wild-fowl, ancestral homes in wild-life parks and pigeon fanciers in back streets. He'd look a fool. There was no escaping that. Anger turned in him at the thought. He was no fool but he was going to look one. He was up against a blank wall. He was tempted to pick up the telephone and call Grandison, who was in Paris at an Interpol conference, and put it to him that the meeting with Scotland Yard should be cancelled. But he knew what Grandison would say, divining the real reason for his request. 'If it's all you've got, then it's all you can give them to work on. If it makes you look a fool, then it does. Only a real fool would do nothing.' And then in that easy voice, some sweetener, sensing all his frustration, like, 'Great oaks from little acorns grow.'

Through the window he watched two office girls walk by, mini-skirted, Amazon-legged in the biting March air, and behind them a youth in jeans and a fringed leather jacket, long hair hanging lank over his shoulders, and at the sight his anger rose unaccountably. A brazen, bloody useless lot . . . shameless and grotesque. And then into his mind came the macabre picture of the mask Trader had worn. Scotland Yard would fall over themselves about that. It was a popular selling line – and bloody Mr Trader must have known that – which could be purchased at dozens of shops in London and dozens more all over the South of England.

He got up and walked to the cabinet on the far side of the room and helped himself to a drink. He poured his usual measure and then, almost without knowing he had done so, doubled it.

CHAPTER FOUR

GEORGE ON HIS recent visit to Chilbolton canvassing for information about the native reading habits had turned up a little gold mine in human form. She was a Mrs Gradidge who looked like Methuselah but was actually sixty-nine by her own account. She was a grey-haired, Punch-nosed, garrulous, shrewd number who took the *Daily Mirror* on weekdays, the *News of the World* on Sundays, and a weekly called *Saturday Titbits*. And titbits were the stuff of Mrs Gradidge's old age. Not a curtain was drawn closed in daytime, not a village girl a month overdue, not a tremor of scandal or gossip, or a breath of a feud or the whisper of someone behind with television or car instalments was ever missed by her, although she seldom stirred from her thatched cottage where she spent most of the day sitting in her patchwork-covered armchair behind a big bowl of artificial roses in her window. She was a dirty-minded, disgusting old woman and thrived cheerfully and vicariously on the lives of others. She took to George, snickering and working her loose mouth over badly fitting dentures, and told him that she had been a great one for the lads in her time, and opportunity was a fine thing and she could name a few in the village who now wouldn't give her the time of day but had forgotten that there was a time when they couldn't get her alone in a barn quick enough. George held down his nausea and played Prince Charming and duly claimed his reward.

Her husband, long dead – and happily so, George imagined – had been a river-cum-gamekeeper at Reed Court with the Rainbirds. Mrs Gradidge had worked there on and off as a kitchen maid and then as an occasional help. What she didn't know, her husband did. In the war of the classes it was as natural for her to listen at a door, or to take a look at a letter lying on a desk, as it was for her husband to edge within earshot of his gentlemen at a shooting party al fresco lunch, or to stand in shabby coat-and-breeches camouflage in some spinney or woodland ride and watch human nature parallel the courting and love-making tactics and patterns of the animals, fish and birds he knew so well.

From her George learned of Sholto's ways with the maids, visitors and county matrons. Sholto hadn't insisted on the *droits de seigneur*, but he was given them often. And he had drunk with a dedicated steadiness from half-past ten in the morning until he fell asleep at night. (George, burning toast in his kitchen as he thought back about Mrs Gradidge, was damned certain that he had told Blanche about the old boy falling drunk downstairs. Hadn't he? Well, he had certainly meant to. Could have slipped it in the mass of stuff he had told her, anyway. God, what a stinking old witch Mrs Gradidge was. He only hoped Blanche wouldn't want him to do any more research that would send him back to her.)

The richest vein to be mined had concerned Miss Rainbird's younger sister, Harriet. From Mrs Gradidge's talk it hadn't been difficult for George to piece the story together, filling in the gaps from his own fertile imagination.

Both the sisters were good-looking, pretty even, but whereas Grace Rainbird had been petite and birdlike her sister had been a tall, rather ungainly woman who – contrasted with Grace's poise – suffered from an almost pathological shyness and lack of self-confidence. By the time Harriet was in her early thirties (Mrs Gradidge was fantastic with dates – she could remember days, dates and occasions for years back) it was generally assumed that neither sister would ever marry. Grace, who had a sharp, critical manner, put most men off and the ones she quite liked she guessed or convinced herself were after her money. Harriet's shyness and lack of self-confidence were insurmountable barriers to any romance. On the few occasions that there was any sign of some determined man – money- or love-prompted – taking any notice of her, then Sholto, knowing and valuing the worth of two capable women to keep the house in order and willing to provide him with ample scope for his drinking and amours, promptly exerted his influence in a cold blast of disapproval to kill any relationship. Sholto was a selfish bully with a rough surface bonhomie.

But three years before the Second World War Sholto was packed off to hospital with a kidney complaint which kept him there for three weeks. And during those weeks Mother Nature saw her opportunity and played one of her beldam tricks. Grace and Harriet went to a charity dance at a near-by army garrison free of the usual Sholto chaperonage. Grace had a mildly pleasant evening. Harriet was taken in to supper by a slightly tight young Irish tank officer, urged to drink more wine than was her custom, slowly found herself uninhibited and enjoying life, and was seduced in the back of the officer's car while Grace was dancing a Paul Jones. Harriet kept her secret from Grace, riding high on the heady drug of a new and rare pleasure, and in the next three weeks met her *beau* in the woods by the river unknown to Grace, but not to old Gradidge who had a sixth sense for anything coupling within two hundred yards of him. The day before Sholto returned the officer was posted with his squadron to the Middle East. Harriet never heard from or saw him again. She said nothing to Grace, but when it was personally clear what was going to happen to her she told Sholto in private who, undoubtedly making sure that Grace was clear of the house, raised hell and promptly packed her off for a long visit to the home of a reliable crony of his in Northumberland. Here, in due course, she had a child and mothered it for twenty-four fours and then it was taken from her, never to be seen by her again, nor was she to know where it had gone or with whom.

It was to be many years before she told Grace her secret. By then the Irish officer had been fatally wounded in a tank engagement outside Tobruk.

This was the story Mrs Gradidge told – and which George had dutifully passed on to Blanche. Mrs Gradidge took a great glee in pointing out that, while quite a few in the village knew perfectly well what had happened up at Reed Court and in Northumberland, neither Sholto nor Miss Grace Rainbird had any inkling that the skeleton in their family cupboard had long been walking abroad.

And, Mrs Gradidge hinted, there were other things that could be told if one had a mind to. Not that she would because she didn't hold with gossip and scandalizing. Sometimes, for instance, the two lovers had used the old fishing hut where Gradidge kept reeds for thatching – and they hadn't been the first by a long street. George, who had had enough, escaped to the Abbot's Mitre where he had three quick whiskies to take the bad taste from his mouth.

Now, eating his burnt toast and marmalade and sipping at his coffee and thinking about Harriet and his dirt-digging for Blanche, he felt a strong distaste for the whole business. Something had gone wrong with his stars. Surely this kind of work and existence had been meant for someone else? Someone who could chuckle and snigger with the Mrs Gradidges of the world and enjoy it. Some damn fool up above had got the card index all mixed up and he'd been mistakenly assigned to this portion here below. If he had had to have an odd sort of life he'd have liked something more romantic and manly ... He wouldn't have minded the Irish tank officer's part, all except the being killed bit, or being a secret agent, suave, and with a cultivated taste for Continental beauties and collecting old porcelain and netsukes, whatever they were. He saw himself rescuing heroines in distress to be suitably rewarded later; succouring the poor and the weak, fighting tyranny, and confounding villainy.

He looked down to where Albert lay on the kitchen mat and said sharply, 'What the hell are you doing?'

Albert was chewing up the morning *Daily Mail* which he had brought in.

George rescued it and as he shook it limply and damply into shape, he made a decision. He'd got to reorganize his life. He had talent, looks, and intelligence, and integrity of a kind. To hell with all this pussyfooting around. People like Mrs Gradidge made him sick. And in a small way people like Blanche made him uneasy. He didn't know whether she was all fake or half fake or just completely and quietly off her nut about this

70

psychic bit. Anyway, he didn't – not at this moment certainly – go for fooling old ladies and shaking them down for a cheque towards any arse-ended idea like building a Temple of Astrodel. Who did Blanche think she was, the daughter of Solomon? And that stinking Henry. Where had she dreamt up that one? Probably read about him in the *Child's Book of British Railways* or something. No – he'd done enough for her. Friends, yes, they could remain, good friends, but he wasn't having any more of this kind of lark. He'd drive into Salisbury, have a quiet shufti round the Cathedral and think about a new life. What better place? Then lunch at the Red Lion and afterwards he'd go and see Blanche and tell her. Maybe he could persuade her to go for the new life bit . . . maybe.

He looked down at Albert and said, 'Things are going to be bloody different around here from now on.' Albert raised a grizzled eye-brow and wagged his tail.

While George was having his breakfast and planning a reorganization of his life, Miss Rainbird was having her breakfast, facing it with a listless appetite and feeling stiff and unrefreshed from a very disturbed night. Harriet had come to her again in her dreams and had been very persistent. It was curious – sometimes she came as a young woman, sometimes as an old woman. Between the two Miss Rainbird became very confused in her sleep. But there was no confusing what Harriet wanted. 'Find my boy. Find my boy and take him into the family. He's a Rainbird!' Often when she said, 'He's a Rainbird!' she got a weird echoing quality in her voice.

It had been a very bad night with Harriet whining and echoing around like a bad actress in a cheap drama. Find my boy, indeed! Bring him back to Reed Court, for it all to be his when she died . . . Ten to one if she could find him he'd turn out to be something quite unacceptable. And to bring him back would mean that the whole history would be made public in the village and district. Not that she was fool enough to think that there weren't some people around who had an idea of what had happened. What a fool Harriet had been. Not for falling in love, if that's what it was, rather than a physical

71

passion. But for acting like some stupid village girl. Using the fishing hut, did anyone ever hear of such indiscretion? And why hadn't she made sure that ... well, any half decent man would have taken precautions. What would the son of this man be like? A bad hat without doubt. Now, now ... that wasn't fair. And at least, if he could be found, one didn't have to declare oneself. He could be discreetly looked over and if he were entirely out of the question then one could quietly forget the whole affair. One could make some anonymous gift perhaps, do something that would keep Harriet quiet and satisfied.

With a little start, she suddenly realized that she was thinking of Harriet as though she were alive and a force that must be appeased. It was really quite odd, that.

She lit the first of the four cigarettes she allowed herself each day, refilled her coffee cup, and was slowly possessed with the thought that she was a lonely woman. She had no true friend in the world. Acquaintances, yes. Silly women like Ida Cookson, and sensible men like her doctor, solicitor and stockbroker. No friend. No one to talk to frankly. She held the thought for a while deliberately, considering it and considering herself in relation to it and then made a decision.

She rang for Syton and when he came she said, 'Syton, I want the car in half an hour. I'm going to Salisbury.'

Bush had breakfast in his flat; a glass of unsweetened grapefruit juice, corn flakes and milk without sugar and then an apple, imported, which he only half finished because it was like eating cheaply scented cottonwool. He was in a bad temper and, removed from the public eye, he was prepared to indulge it. Quite deliberately he picked up the half apple and threw it across the kitchen to smash into limp pulp against the door of the refrigerator.

The action gave him no relief. The memory of yesterday's conference at Scotland Yard smarted still. They had roasted him, politely and with nicely contained delight; the Assistant Commissioner, two Deputy Assistant Commissioners and two Commanders. Grandison's boy from the department – the wizard Bush with all the other bastards who secretly sat above them – asking them, someone had actually in an oversweet voice used the phrase, 'to find out from which bed mattress in the South of England had come a feather nobody had'! There had been worse and with more validity. For the first time since he had worked for Grandison he had been made to look a fool. They had all known that he was up against it and they had loved it – with the same passion as they hated the department. When he had said that, although the lines of inquiry were admittedly highly tenuous – in view of the seriousness of the matter – there could be no question of washing their hands of the whole tedious business, some wit had asked, 'With hard or soft water?'

The thought of that particular moment made him stir again now with anger. It didn't matter that they were going to do all they could. Had to do it. They were all privately convinced that nothing would come of it. They were all delighted. He had lit up a lousy, wintry March afternoon for them.

He went through to the sitting-room and sat at his desk. Frustration writhed in him like a snake trying to slough its skin. He wrote a letter to his wife in cold, barren tones telling her that he had no intention of providing her with evidence for a divorce and even less intention of proceeding against her on any evidence she might supply. If she were not prepared to come back to him, she could sit out a waiting period of five years' separation until she could obtain a divorce and remarry. Let her sweat it out, he thought. He didn't want her back, but there was the chance that without marriage ties her boy friend would cool off and she could go on living in limbo until she found a replacement.

The letter done and sealed in its envelope, he sat staring at it. Somewhere Trader was preparing his third assault, quietly, efficiently and with as near certainty as any man could hope for that it would be a success. And he, Bush, was completely blocked. When he got to the office this morning the golf club reports would be coming in, waiting to be sifted and analysed. His expectation of any help from them was minimal.

Miss Rainbird had telephoned Blanche to make sure that she would be free before she left for Salisbury. Blanche's house was in a quiet, prosperous residential area to the north-west of the town on high ground. It had a corner site and from its top windows Blanche could look across playing fields to the green mound of Old Sarum and the distant valley of the river Avon. Away to the left the slim pencil of the Cathedral spire rose above the huddle of town buildings. At night a red light shone from the tip of the spire as a warning to aircraft.

Miss Rainbird sat in the front sitting-room. She had expected a room with touches of the colourful flamboyance which marked Madame Blanche's clothes. She was wearing now, at eleven in the morning, a long purple gown, deeply V-cut at the neck. Tied around her waist was a length of red silk scarf. Her pearls today were wound in a close chain about her throat, and her red hair hung loose to her shoulders (beautiful hair, thought Miss Rainbird, well-brushed and obviously well cared for) giving her an oddly girlish look. The room itself, however, was well and quietly furnished. The two pictures were very good water colours of parts of old Salisbury.

Blanche sat listening to Miss Rainbird. The old girl's manner had changed quite completely. This was no surprise to her. She had seen similar changes in women many times before. Quite frankly, Miss Rainbird had given a description of her dreams about Harriet and had then gone on to explain the history of Harriet's love affair and the steps Sholto had taken to deal with it. Even though Harriet was dead, Blanche was sorry for her. She could see how it all had been. Bottled up for years and then some sprig of an officer turning it all on. Sholto sounded a bastard.

Miss Rainbird said, 'I realize now that my dreams were the result of a clash of conscience in me. Harriet's child – if he still lives – will be a man well in his thirties by now. What is more, he's a Rainbird. And what is even more important, my closest relative. Everything I own should go to him. Frankly, Madame Blanche, it was not an idea I took kindly to. Not the idea of leaving everything to him, but of finding him and to some substantial degree perhaps having to take him into the

74

life of Reed Court, which would mean explanations having to be made in the district and the history of Harriet's misadventure becoming known.'

Blanche nodded understandingly. 'You didn't want your nicely ordered life upset. Quite natural. But now, you've decided you must face that – because of your conscience?'

'Yes, indeed. That's why I'm here.'

'Have you thought about that? You might not need my help. All you have to do is to hire some private detective to trace him.'

'Naturally I've given that thought. But there are one or two things which make it impossible. No matter how discreet he was, he would have to make inquiries. Some in the village. I'm not fool enough to imagine that some people there hadn't an inkling of what happened. People don't have to know for certain. They put two and two together and then guess. The thought of my friends and the village people getting to know that I'm looking for him isn't a pleasant one. And anyway, even if I could overcome my reluctance about that there is a much more difficult problem. When Sholto died I went through all his private papers hoping that I could find some trace of what he had arranged for the child.'

'And you found nothing?'

'Quite. If there had been any papers he had destroyed them. My brother was an awkward, odd man but he had an almost exaggerated regard for the family name. His one object was to cut the child right out of Harriet's life and restore the *status quo* at Reed Court. He never forgave Harriet, of course.'

Blanche smiled. 'He has now I'm sure. Did you ever talk to him about all this?'

'No, not really. I tried once but it was quickly made clear that he would say nothing.'

'What about these friends in Northumberland? Do they know anything?'

'Only one of them is alive now. I visited her some little while ago and brought the matter up. But she knew nothing. Harriet went into a local nursing home – as a married woman. After the child's birth Sholto and a nurse collected it within two days and took it away. It was a monstrously cruel thing to do to Harriet, but Sholto did it. There was no question of her opposing him. Harriet wasn't like that. How could any private detective hope to do anything when there is no point from which he could start . . . at least . . .'

Blanche said, 'You mean at least down here in a physical, material way? That's why you've come here and told me all this, isn't it, Miss Rainbird?'

'Frankly, yes.'

'But you still don't believe it can be done?'

Miss Rainbird hesitated, and then said, 'How can I know? Frankly, it's hard to break the prejudices of a lifetime. But if it can be done discreetly then I'm willing to try. I want to try.' She smiled suddenly. 'I'm not enjoying Harriet coming whining to me in dreams, Madame Blanche. I like to sleep soundly at night. If the child – man now – can be found I am ready to accept him and to do my duty by him. Unless, of course, he proves entirely unacceptable.'

'Well,' Blanche stood up, 'we'd better get started, hadn't we? Let's see what Henry has to say about all this.'

Seeing the look of surprise on Miss Rainbird's face, Blanche touched her gently on the shoulder. 'You must get used to my attitude about these things, Miss Rainbird. For me it is just part of my life. The gift I have may seem wonderful to you, strange, even frightening. But there is nothing unusual about it. Everyone in this world has it, the ability to go beyond the body into another life. Only a few of us develop it – because to do that you have to have belief and faith. Henry is as real to me as you are sitting there. We talk to each other like human beings, laugh, have a giggle, argue and so on. What we'll do now is have a little chat with him and see what he has to say. He's been here quite a while.'

Repressing an impulse to look around the room, Miss Rainbird said, 'How *can* you know that?'

Blanche smiled and moved a wing of her long hair back from her shoulder. 'Because I can smell him, Miss Rainbird.' She chuckled. 'Now, don't give me that surprised look again. If you were sitting there blindfolded and with your ears plugged and a woman came into this room wearing a strong perfume, you would know that someone had come into the room. Sometimes with Henry it's just his ethereal vibrations, sometimes it's his aura quite clearly in my psychic sight, and sometimes it is an aroma. When it's the last, it's a kind of heathery, tangy wood-smoke smell. Masculine and out of doors.'

Blanche went to the window and pulled over an inner pair of translucent curtains, saying, 'I like to do this because the house is overlooked from across the road. We don't need darkness, but we do need privacy. One day ... when I have the money, I shall build a proper place of ministry and guidance. I like to think of it as a temple ... a temple of communications where love and comfort and advice can pass from the worlds beyond us to this one.'

Following an impulse, Miss Rainbird said, 'Madame Blanche, you really are a quite extraordinary woman.'

In the half light of the room Blanche shook her head. 'No. You are the extraordinary woman, Miss Rainbird. I am an ordinary woman, using all the gifts God gave me. You have the same gifts, all humans have, but for some strange reason they leave them unnoticed in the bottom of their Christmas stockings in their delight and greediness over what seem bigger and more splendid presents. Now, let's do exactly as we did before. You just sit there and relax and we'll see what old Henry has to say. I just do hope he won't be too poetical today.'

Miss Rainbird sat relaxed in her chair. She was, she told herself, really relaxed this time. She had taken a new step, made a decision. She wasn't fully committed. She wasn't going to throw her common-sense overboard, but she knew that there was some power and understanding that came from Madame Blanche which she had never met in anyone else before. In a way, it was soothing to abdicate partly one's self-dependence and firm authority ... to abandon oneself to another person.

She watched Madame Blanche lean back in her chair, her eyes closed. For a moment her fingers lightly touched the pearls at her neck and then dropped to her red silk sash. She took the loose ends of the bow and held them gently. For a while she breathed deeply, shoulders and bosom rising with the intake of air. Then the breathing quietened, seemed almost to cease altogether so that she sat there like a wax figure, the muscles of her face relaxed so that her mouth hung a little open and Miss Rainbird could see the wetness of saliva on her lower inner lip.

Abruptly, Madame Blanche said loudly, 'Henry?'

There was a long silence, and then she said almost crossly, 'Henry – don't do this to me! There is someone here who needs help. You know who it is.'

There was another silence and then she began to talk, carrying on a conversation with someone whose words were not heard.

'Yes, yes, I see ... Pictures? But words would be so much better ... Yes, I understand. They must prepare themselves ... They have difficulties to overcome ... Yes, I see it plainly. A young woman and a man by a river bank. The woman is blonde and carries a hat ... a straw hat. And the man is in uniform.' She was silent for a while and then said quickly, 'Yes, I see the boy ... My goodness, Henry, he's all messed up.' She laughed. 'Like any boy. But what's that on his wrist, Henry? ... Yes there is, there's something on his hand. I can't see clearly what it is ... Oh, Henry, this is like going through a family album and explaining nothing. And the pictures ... I can hardly make some of them out. Oh, that's nice. I like that. The baby in the woman's arms. She looks happy and the baby is smiling. Is that Harriet? It doesn't look like her ... No, I didn't think it was. She was blonde ... Oh!' Her exasperation was clear. 'Why are you like this today, Henry? Please, she wants to know what happened to the child. Where is he now? You've only got to bring them here ... Ask them ... Why not? ... Well, if you can't you can't and I'm not going to bully you. But if they won't come at the moment, you must know something ... Then tell me, is he happy at the moment? ... He is. Well, that's something. Is he married?' She suddenly sighed. 'Well, yes I understand that. It's not the first time

78

either that it's happened with other people. But you might have told me earlier instead of just flipping through all those pictures ... Yes, of course she'll understand ... Yes, yes ... yeess ... yeess ...' Madame Blanche's voice slowly faded away on a drowsy singing note.

Miss Rainbird watched her. She lay back in her chair, breathing evenly as though she were asleep. After a while her eyes opened slowly and then with a brisk stir of her body she was awake.

Blanche beamed at Miss Rainbird. 'Well,' she said cheerfully, 'that's what happens sometimes. I caught Henry on one of his bad days.' She got up and went to a sofa table, saying, 'I don't know about you, Miss Rainbird, but I need a little something. Yes?'

Miss Rainbird nodded and watched while Blanche poured sherry for them. She said, 'I don't understand?'

Blanche handed her a glass of sherry. 'It's simple. It's like getting a bad line on the telephone. Henry's always very polite about it. He says it's his fault, but it isn't, it's mine.'

'You remember what happened this time?'

'Yes. Yes, I do.'

'Perhaps you would explain?'

'I'll try, but sometimes to someone new it doesn't seem very credible. The chief thing is ... How shall I put it? You see the people over there aren't in any final state. There's nothing static about their lives. They're developing all the time. It's a long time before a complete understanding of the Great Mystery comes to them. They have powers but not absolute all-embracing powers. At least, not to begin with. That's why scientifically inclined or narrowly sceptical people say why don't the messages that come through really answer for us all the questions about life after death. The answer is that the majority of those who have crossed over haven't yet attained full knowledge. Most people here on earth couldn't explain technically how television or radar works. The same applies there. And over there our loved ones are very susceptible to mood and atmosphere, too. That's why the communication was bad today. Your brother and sister associate you closely with Reed Court. Seeing you here they retire. I think perhaps in future I should come to your house.'

'If you think that will help.'

'I do. All Henry could get today was a sort of glimpse of a family album. Harriet's child, now a man, is alive and happy.'

'Then why doesn't stupid Harriet just say where he is?' asked Miss Rainbird tartly.

Blanche laughed. 'Now, now, that's not fair. I've told you they don't have absolute powers. Some things they know and some things they have to find out. And sometimes even if they do, Henry won't pass it through.'

'Why ever not?'

'I'm surprised you ask that. Do you give a child its reward before it's done its little task? I don't want to say this to hurt you in any way, but frankly I sensed that Henry isn't sure of you. Maybe he catches sceptical vibrations from you. Maybe he is not convinced of your sincerity. Maybe Harriet and Sholto now feel the same. Harriet through Henry can't help you – much as she wants you to help her – if there is a barrier of disbelief between you.'

'It all seems very complicated and illogical.'

'It's another world, Miss Rainbird.'

Miss Rainbird had to admit the force of this argument, though she could not help feeling that she was being given a very capable sales talk by Madame Blanche. She would have been more convinced of this were it not for one thing.

She said, 'When you saw the picture of the boy, you remember?'

'Oh, yes. He was all mussed up and untidy. Like any boy out for a day's fun.'

'You said he had something on his hand or on his wrist. Couldn't you see what it was?'

'No, I couldn't. It was a very muzzy picture.'

'Was it large or small?'

'Largish. I thought at first it might be a table tennis bat.'

Miss Rainbird agreed to telephone Blanche in a few days, to let her know if she would like another meeting at Reed Court. But as she was driven home, a small figure lost in the back of the Rolls-Royce, she had no doubt that she would want Madame Blanche to continue to help her. Although she had decided to say nothing today about it, Madame Blanche had impressed her with the description of the boy. When she had described Harriet and the officer walking by the river she had had a vivid picture of the scene. With it had come back a small scrap of detail that Harriet had once given her when she had talked of her love affair. The Irish officer was passionately interested in falcony and – so Harriet had said – on one of his visits he had brought over with him a kestrel he had trained. They had walked along the river with the bird to hunt starlings. The son could have inherited the same love. She was sure that the thing on his wrist had been a hawk of some kind. As Madame Blanche had described the boy she had seen it vividly in her imagination. An untidy schoolboy, carrying a hawk. How very extraordinary.

CHAPTER FIVE

THE AFTERNOON LIGHT was going. The sun was already low, hidden behind the high-banked clouds in the west. Northwards, ten miles away, clear in the frost-bound air, Martin Shoebridge could see the grey glint of the sea with the high plug of Steep Holm rising rocky and green-capped from the water. Farther out was the lower, squat shape of Flat Holm. In another hour the light out there would come on marking the mouth of the Severn River. In another two hours he would be on his way back to school, the week-end exeat over. Although he liked most being at home, the thought of school gave him no concern. He handled things as they came, liking some, stoically accepting others.

He went steadily up the long limestone scarp of the hills, the red setter bitch at his heels, the hooded goshawk on his gloved fist, the crisp feel of frosted, sheep-bitten grass under his feet and his old canvas satchel thumping gently against his side. His eyes watched and assessed every movement and change of light, his ears marked all sound above the low sough of the north-easterly breeze. This was what he liked, to be alone with the hawk and the dog. Liked most because also it was what his father liked. They understood it all without having to talk about it. Being alone, being yourself.

At the crest the wind strengthened in his face and ruffled the slaty-blue feathers of the goshawk's wing coverts. In the valley below him he marked roads, villages and farmhouses, and the dull shine of the Blagdon and Chew Valley lakes. He'd fished there often with his father for the stew-pond-bred trout. He liked it, but loved more the fishing in small, wild Welsh mountain streams. Halfway down the hillslope was a hangar of tall beech trees. He had time to work through the top half before he would have to turn for home. Fifty yards from the edge of the trees he stopped. He loosened the braces at the back of the hawk's hood with his free hand and his teeth and let her slip. He manned and used his birds to his own rules. His father was the purist, not he. He watched her rake away low and then rise, long-tailed and short-winged, to the first high branch of an outlying tree. She settled, and the dog behind him whined. He stopped it with a touch of his hand on its wet nose. He didn't like other people's rules. You had to find your own way of doing things. If he lost birds flying them in a high gale of wind, then he lost them, but they never carried swivel-link jesses to trap them on post or wire. They flew to freedom.

He went into the trees without a glance at the hawk. She would follow from tree to tree and he would hear the small, sharp sound of her bell. He sent the dog ahead to work the bushes and underscrub and the tall patches of winter-brown grass and dead nettles that hid the fallen beech mast.

Within fifteen yards the dog put up a rabbit and the boy called, 'Hoo-haaa!'; not to set the waiting hawk on but because he liked to call. The hawk was already past him, swooping low between the trees, wings fast beating, twisting and turning and then plunging in a short stoop to the rabbit, binding to it as it moved, so that fur and feather rolled together for a few yards.

He brought the dog to heel and went forward. The rabbit was already near dead, the claws of the long-legged hawk strangling it. He took the hawk to his fist, rewarded it with a small piece of meat from his satchel, and then picked up the rabbit by its hind legs and smacked its head against the smooth grey bole of a tree to finish it off. He stuffed it into the game pocket at the back of his satchel and put the hawk on the wing again. She went up ahead of him to a tree and he moved forward again with the dog.

They worked caterways down the slope and through the trees. They took another rabbit, winter-thin, lost a wood-pigeon that came up fast from foraging in the beech mast, and raised a magpie from a holly bush to be killed in a short fast stoop that sent a scattering of black feathers idling into the wind. He had no feeling about killing, made no excuses to himself that the rabbits would feed the other birds in the mews, or that the magpie was a nest-robber. He and the hawk and the dog were hunting. It was a completeness of action that held a never diminishing pleasure. They were doing what it was natural to bird, beast and man to do. Each time that the hawk jumped to his fist for her reward after a kill, he knew his own reward for the days and weeks of patience and training that had brought this moment. He had had better birds, and he would have better birds again, but for the time being this was the only bird.

At the far edge of the wood he called her down by voice and she came, swinging round him twice in a tight circle which was always her habit and then settling to the fist and the meat reward. He hooded her and the three left the wood and went along the hill slope, climbing gradually to the long high shoulder of the downs and to the track that led to home.

An hour later, fed and dressed for school, he stood by the car and said goodbye to his father. Usually his father and his step-mother drove him the fifty miles back to school. Today his step-mother drove him. His father had work to do. Martin understood. His father made his usual joke about the prison gates opening again. He smiled. He liked his step-mother, but his father was the only person in the world that he loved. He got into the car alongside his step-mother and the setter jumped into the back of the car to keep her company on the return journey. His step-mother switched the radio on and he settled back to think about his ferrets. He had to have a new place to keep them because his tutor had put a ban on them. He'd have to find some farm or cottage that would take them. He would bring them home at the end of term. He wanted to try the goshawk with them on some of the hill warrens. That meant he would have to get the hawk used to them otherwise she'd kill them . . . They'd have to go in the mews with her. In a cage close to her where she could see them and get used to them . . .

Edward Shoebridge watched the car's rear lights disappear

around the turn of the drive and went back into the house. He locked the front door and went through the long wide hall to a small oak door at the end which opened on to a flight of stone steps. Immediately at the foot of the steps on his left was the door to his studio. He went in and locked the door.

It was a large room. Part of the wall at the far end was taken up by a projection screen. To the left a low bench ran the length of the wall. It was backed for part of its length by a home-made console system. The right-hand wall was occupied by rows of bookshelves and at the near end by a set of storage cupboards. Behind the cupboards was concealed a door which led to the secret cellar system below the house.

Shoebridge sat sideways to the console and switched on the projector. He ran fifteen minutes of disjointed film, holding it in single frame occasionally while he made a note on a pad at his side. All the film had been taken from some concealed point, mostly from the back of a car or from the safety of natural cover. It had been shot sometimes from quite close range and occasionally through a telescopic lens. In nearly all the shots the same man was the subject, an elderly man in his mid-sixties, a distinguished-looking man, a man with authority written into his manner, intelligence and understanding marking his face. When the film was finished Shoebridge pulled an ordnance survey map, one inch to the mile, to him and a foolscap sheet marked with timings and mileages. He fixed a sheet of transparent paper to the map and, working neatly and without hurry, began to mark out a series of routes. Although he was absorbed in his work he was never completely lost in it. Always some part of him remained detached, aware of his surroundings and alert to catch the slightest sound or sign of the unfamiliar. He did not smoke. His fingers were free of nicotine. His hair was fair, his eyes blue, and his middle-statured body hard and finely muscled beneath his casual clothes. Although he was in his middle thirties he could run the twenty-mile-long crest of the downs on which he lived with ease. He had a deliberately acquired indifference to pain or bodily appetites, acknowledging only his intellect as his master. His personal relationships were confined to two people, to his son and to his second wife. He had been relieved when his first wife had died when the boy was three years old. He had little use for most of the civilization he knew around him. In two weeks he was going to take the last step to free himself as far as possible from it. Nothing was going to stop him. If it meant the taking of human life he would take it. He was the most dangerous of all creatures, an intelligent man with a ruthless obsession for escape; a dreamer who longed for an earthly paradise, and meant to find it. If any outsider could have known this and called him mad, he would have agreed, saying that he preferred to live according to the terms of his madness and to reject the other madness which the world called civilization. What he would never have accepted, which was the truth, was that his was merely another variation among the distortions of the human psyche which kept the prisons of every country in the world overcrowded. Not even the person who featured in his films, with all the compassion and wisdom at his command, could have convinced Shoe-bridge of this.

There had been ten people within the last five years who had been members at some time or other of both the Tiverton Golf Club and the Crowborough Beacon Golf Club. Four of them were women.

There had been sixty-eight people in the same period – not members of the clubs – who had played as guests at both of them. Twenty-eight were women.

For the members of the two golf clubs addresses were available. For the guests there were seldom addresses. Sometimes a town was indicated but more often the name of the golf club of which they were regular members.

Bush passed the information on to Sangwill so that he could detail some of the staff to carry out a private survey of all the joint members and as many of the guests as could be traced. A complete check, Bush knew, would take weeks. He gave instructions that he wanted a daily progress report.

He had lunch in the department canteen and did the *Daily Telegraph* crossword puzzle.

*　　　*　　　*

George had lunch at the Red Lion, bread and cheese and pickles, sitting at the bar. He'd had a very pleasant morning considering his new life while he walked around the Cathedral and its precincts.

He had decided to go into business. The idea had struck him while he was musing in front of the tomb of Sir John de Montacute, who had fought at the battle of Crecy and died in 1390. The worthy knight's effigy lay there almost featureless from Time's attrition, his sword broken and his feet resting on a lion whose tail was missing. Time's wingèd chariot, thought George – it was fast leaving him behind, too, to rot and crumble.

It came to him like a revelation. There were hundreds of new houses going up all over the place. Here, Winchester, Southampton, and in all the towns around. And new houses had to have gardens, gardens that had to be made from scratch most of them. He would become a landscape gardener and do contract work for small householders who were too busy or too lazy to attack the virgin soil. He would need a van, equipment, and a strong lad to help him. Maybe later he would take on more men, buy more vans ... expand, make a real 'do' of it. For the time being he would have to put his back into it alongside the lad. That would do him good. Get some of the old tum down and knock him into shape.

Working it out on the back of an envelope at the bar, he reckoned he could get the whole thing off the ground for five hundred pounds. Second-hand van, second-hand equipment, take no wages himself – there was always his allowance – and operate from the cottage. Good spot that. He had an acre and a half of garden, a wilderness now, but when things were really turning over he could open a garden centre there. Only a few miles from Salisbury, on a good road. He'd make a mint. All he needed was the five hundred to start with. He had a few shares he could sell. Say two hundred pounds. All he wanted was another three hundred. Surely that wouldn't be difficult? Blanche could advance him that without turning a hair. Don't know, though. Sometimes she could be funny about money. Well, if she wouldn't there must be other people. On the back of the envelope he began to make a list of friends who might be good for loans. He wrote down five names, considered them, and scratched out four. He considered the fifth for a while and finally scratched that out. A fiver, maybe, but not three hundred. Undepressed he bought a couple of sausage rolls and went out to his car and gave them to Albert to eat as he drove up to Blanche's place. Blanche it would have to be. For a moment or two he considered the wisdom of waiting until she made her next visit to the cottage. Catch her in the right mood ... No, better to get it over. No point in wasting time. Anyway, spring was coming. That was the best time to get started on gardens. He whistled as he drove, going over the colour he would paint the van, seeing the sign on the side – *Lumley Gardens*? *G. Lumley, Garden Contractor*?

When he got to Blanche's house it was to find that she was engaged with a couple of clients. He went into the kitchen to wait for her to be free and to have a chat with her old mother. Blanche's mother had lived with her for years and although the old girl was broadminded enough, she was the reason advanced by Blanche why George never should stay the night at the house, that and the fact, too, that Blanche felt that strong, earthly sensual vibrations about the place would upset the ethereal atmosphere so necessary to have when her clients called. Personally George felt it was just to avoid neighbourhood gossip.

Mrs Tyler had been born of half-fairground half-gypsy parents. She kept Blanche's house spotless, a spry worker at sixty-eight, but she still longed for the freedom of the roads and the fairgrounds and the joy of sleeping with four wheels at the corners of her home and the old mare tethered outside. She made him a cup of coffee and as he drank it George put a fifty-pence piece on the table and held out his hand. It was a ritual every time he met her alone in the kitchen. George never ceased to wonder at the variety of futures life held for him according to Mrs Tyler.

Today, because he was thinking of his gardening enterprise, he scarcely listened to her trot out the usual predictions. He was going on a journey. He would cross the sea and meet a tall dark stranger who would offer advice . . . bad advice. He was to keep away from horses. They could only bring him bad luck. (George hated horses, anyway, and if he went within a yard of one it gave him hay-fever, and the old girl knew it.) She saw great happiness for him, many children, but one of them would die young. George lit a cigarette and let the old lady drone on. He'd advertise in the local papers, ginger up his chums at the Red Lion and get them recommending him. To-morrow he'd collect some catalogues of mechanical garden equipment and aids. He'd have to find a nurseryman, too, for supplying plants, shrubs, trees. There'd have to be a com-mission in it for him of course. Through his reverie something the old girl was saying came through, half catching his atten-tion.

He said, 'What was that, ma?'

Mrs Tyler grumbled, 'Half I say you don't listen to.'

'I do, you know. I don't chuck a half-a-nicker around with-out getting value. What was that bit about "venture"?'

'I said, you're goin' to start a new venture. Something different.'

'Well, seeing that I've got no venture at the moment, it would have to be different, wouldn't it? What kind of ven-ture?'

'Something like visiting houses. Very busy with people.'

'You don't say? Rent collecting, perhaps? Or selling insur-ance? No thank you, ma.'

'And you keep away from high places. I don't like the look of your heart line; it's there, right above the Mountain of the Moon. High places, you watch them.'

'What kind of high places? Like the Lord Mayor's Banquet or Mount Everest?'

'You can scoff.'

'Well, my hand's the same as it was last week. Why didn't you tell me then? Tell you what – do you see any flowers or gardens in my hand? Or a nice yellow van with green sign-writing on it?'

The old lady gave him a withering look, dropped his hand and pocketed her money. Then her eyes steadily on him she said after a while, 'I can see a van. But it ain't a bright van. It's dark, black almost, and you're a-sittin' in it wishing you weren't there.'

George laughed. 'Could be. The Black Maria.' As he spoke he heard the front door going and knew that Blanche was letting her clients out. He left Mrs Tyler and went through to the hall to find Blanche. He led her into the sitting-room, put her in a chair, leaned forward and kissed her, and said, 'Sit there and listen. I'm going to make over my life, my love. And all I need is five hundred pounds. Strictly on loan – with interest. Or, say, four hundred at a pinch. Now, what I've got in mind is this.'

Enthusiastically George outlined his plan and Blanche listened to him patiently. She liked him when he was just George. She liked him even more when he got some wild idea going and began to talk about it. You could see the boy behind the man. You could see, and be pleasantly warmed with love and tenderness, the pathetic belief in something that would never be more than a dream. Dear old George – he was never going to change. So long as he had that cottage and his allowance he would always be the same. Momentarily she thought, if I get this Temple of Astrodel I might marry him. Look after him ... No, no that wouldn't do. She had to be a priestess. It wouldn't look good with a husband knocking about the place. George on the side, discreetly away, yes. But not a husband.

George finished. 'What do you say? I've calculated that almost from the start I'll be netting an overall profit of around forty to sixty quid a month. That will soon clear equipment and loan charges. After that the sky's the limit.' He kissed her again and she knew he'd had pickled onions with his bar snack somewhere. Probably the Red Lion. If you wanted George between twelve and one-thirty, that's where he would be. 'Just write a cheque, ducks, and I'm on my way.'

Blanche considered him in silence for a while, saw the edge of doubt and the shade of possible disappointment touch his face and felt all her tenderness for him flower.

She said, 'Pass me my handbag.'

George gave it to her from the table.

She took out her cheque book and pen and wrote a cheque and handed it to him.

George saw that it was for five hundred pounds. He saw also – for he was used to scrutinizing cheques carefully because he played such little invalidating tricks himself when pressed – that it was not signed.

As his eyes came back to her, it was a nasty moment for Blanche. She wished sincerely that she had not had to use such a ruse. But she had to think of the Temple of Astrodel and she didn't want to get involved with some stranger. Only George could help her.

She said, 'Georgie, love. You can have five hundred as a gift, not a loan. But before I sign you've got to do something for me. Something you're good at doing, something I wouldn't ask any other man.'

George, putting on a hearty bonhomie to cover his dis-appointment (Oh, he knew his Blanche inside out!) said, 'You already get what I'm good at, love. You don't have to ask any other man.'

'That's not what I mean, George. And also I don't like that kind of talk in this room. This is a place—'

'Okay, Blanche. Okay. What is it?'

'I want you to do some more work on this Miss Rainbird thing.'

'Oh, no! Not that!'

'It's a Christian thing I'm asking you to do, George. The woman's unhappy. I want to bring joy into her life.'

'I want to bring joy in mine, too. Fixing up little suburban gardens. Planting, sowing, weeding. Little rockeries and brick paths.'

'So you can. I think it's wonderful and you'll be a big suc-cess. But if you want five hundred from me – and I don't know who else you'd get it from – then you've got to do some more work.'

George was not ready to give in without a fight. 'It's against my nature, Blanche. Snooping around for dirt.'

'There's no dirt. Just simple, charitable acts. Miss Rainbird is over seventy. I want to make the rest of her years on this earth happy.'

Angrily, George said, 'I can't think why. You're always saying it's a much better place up there. No, you just want your old Temple of Astro-whatever-it-is. Well, get that mealy-mouthed Henry of yours to move his fat arse and do the work for you.'

Blanche sighed. 'George, your aura has gone very murky.' She smiled. 'You're like a bad-tempered little boy who wants his presents before Christmas.' She came over to him and kissed him on the cheek. 'Now let's be sensible about it.'

George shrugged his shoulders. 'I'm sorry, Blanche. But really ... Hell, I don't go for the Mrs Gradidges of this world!'

'Neither do I, George. They are lost souls. But they can be useful. And think of Miss Rainbird, and helping her. That would be a fine thing to do. And it won't take you long. A week, two weeks at the most. All you have to do is to trace her nephew, the child of her sister Harriet. Just find out where he is. And when you've done it—' she indicated the cheque he held – 'well, you'll have what you want. A wonderful new life, and an occupation which will bring colour and beauty to hundreds of people. Yes?'

George was silent for a while. Then suddenly he grinned. 'You're a great girl, Blanche. You could talk the wings off an angel. All right, I'll do it.'

'Thank you, George. I thank you from the bottom of my heart.' Blanche reached forward and took the cheque from him.

'Hey!' George protested. 'That's mine.'

'Yes, George. But I'll look after it for a while so that you won't be tempted to forge my signature and cash it.'

'As though I'd even dream of it!' He broke off, chuckled slowly, and went on, 'Well ... Perhaps I would, seeing the colour my aura is at the moment.'

The next morning George went back to see Mrs Gradidge. His excuse for a second approach had given him a little trouble,

92

but not too much. He had had plenty of experience in finding excuses for himself in his life, and the answer to this one was not long in coming. Already he had warned Blanche that the expenses of this job might run a little higher than normal. Because he was still a little upset at the bargain she had made with him, he had decided to add ten per cent to all the expenses he charged. He might buy a new van instead of a second-hand one. He would get better and longer service from it.

Mrs Gradidge was surprised to see him, but her surprise weakened as he cheerfully asked her if she had any of her excellent tea going and at the same time put a ten-pound note on the table alongside her knitting wool and the *Saturday Titbits*.

As Mrs Gradidge eyed the money bright-eyed, he said, 'There's another ten to come if you can help me. But you've got to understand all this is confidential. Just between you and me.'

Mrs Gradidge said, 'What's all this got to do with magazines and papers, young man?'

'Nothing. That was just a ... well, way of getting to know you. Actually I'm a private inquiry agent.'

'A what?'

'A sort of detective.'

'Here – I don't want no trouble with that kind of thing.'

'There's no trouble. Just the opposite, Mrs Gradidge. Now, why don't you make us a nice cup of tea and I'll tell you all about it.'

Over three cups of her strong, acrid tea he did, and he had to admit to himself that he did it well. When he wanted to he could talk as though he'd kissed the Blarney Stone. And he kept her well supplied with cigarettes and gave her a flattering deference that made her a warm and ready confidante. The young officer who had fathered Miss Harriet's baby boy had been called Megan. Miss Rainbird had revealed this to Blanche. He, George, was engaged by the family – a rich Irish one, so George said – who had long been trying to trace the child. Now a man, of course. Young Megan, before he had

93

died of the wounds he had received in his tank engagement, had confessed to the Roman Catholic priest who was giving him absolution that he had seduced an innocent girl of very good family and fathered a boy on her. It was his dearest wish that his family should take the child and make it a Megan. Unfortunately, the officer had died before he could tell the priest the girl's name.

'Poor young chap,' said Mrs Gradidge.

George agreed and went on to explain that the family had tried years ago to discover the child, but they had met with no success. The matter had been dropped. But in the last year Megan's father, now a very old man with only a few years to go, had begun to be more and more troubled at the thought that his son's last wishes had not been honoured.

'Very strong on that kind o' thing, them Catholics,' said Mrs Gradidge. 'Not that I 'old with this kissin' and' cuddlin' all week and then going to confession and startin' all over with a clean slate. Though, no doubt, it's very handy for some.'

George nodded understandingly. He explained that his firm had been engaged to have another go at trying to trace the child. And they'd been lucky. They'd found an old army friend of Megan's who had known about Harriet and Megan. So naturally ... Well, here he was. But – (It was a masterstroke that had come to him while he burnt his breakfast toast that morning) – when he had reported to old Megan, near dying and longing for his grandson, what Sholto Rainbird had done with the child, the old man had been livid. He wanted nothing to do with any surviving Rainbirds. He just wanted the boy, well, man now, and the Rainbirds were to know nothing about it. The grandson was a Megan and must be found. Wealth and a large estate waited in Ireland for him.

Mrs Gradidge sighed. 'It's just like a story, ain't it? Lovely, really. That old man a-wantin' to see his grandson, afore he dies.'

George agreed. It was a truly lovely story and he had made it up for the old hag. And now – and not a breath of this must ever leak out, ever – he wanted Mrs Gradidge to tell him everything she knew, everything. The smallest detail could be important. Just think, if she helped find the grandson, of the joy it would bring to an old man's heart and — he knew this would appeal to her — it would be one in the eye for people like Miss Rainbird who just arranged their lives selfishly, never giving a thought to others. And, too, he was sure that, if they were successful, the old man would know about her help and for sure he was the kind who would show his gratitude to her. He'd met him in his castle in Ireland and he was a very, very generous sort. The real better type of Irishman.

She took it. Hook, line and sinker. And, George thought as he listened to her, you didn't want ever to think you could live in a village and keep secrets. People like Mrs Gradidge, and old Gradidge her dead husband, didn't need any of Blanche's clairvoyance. They watched points and put two and two together and could spot the coming of events before they happened. Mrs Gradidge gave him every detail of everything she knew, and swore to God that no one in the village should know about George's quest. George had his doubts about that, but he was not worried. If it ever did get back to Miss Rainbird — which he doubted — it would take ages.

Before he left the village he went up to the churchyard to check one of Mrs Gradidge's details. At the far end of the graveyard, near the boundary to the river meadows, was a small, plain headstone. It recorded the death in 1937 of Edward Shoebridge, aged six months, only child of Martha and Ronald Shoebridge, with the inscription — *Suffer the little children to come unto me for of such is the Kingdom of Heaven.*

The next day George (and Albert) drove to Weston-super-Mare, looking forward to a day by the sea and the brisk breezes of the Bristol Channel sweeping across the mud flats — if it happened to be low tide.

And late that afternoon Blanche went by appointment to Reed Court, primed with all that George had so far gathered. On the way up she was considering the exact stage in future meetings with Miss Rainbird (always assuming George would go on turning up information) at which she would introduce hints from Sholto and Harriet that would suggest that Blanche was more than worthy of her hire, that her great gifts merited some suitable, certainly not ordinary, reward. She'd have to watch the old girl on that one. She would wait and take her cue from Henry. He wanted the temple as much as she did and he would know the moment.

Miss Rainbird, she noticed at once, was looking different. As though some enlivening change had come over her. There was more colour in her cheeks and she was wearing a different lipstick, and the brown velvet skirt with a matching jacket over a cream blouse suited her. She must have been a very pretty young woman. It was a surprise she hadn't married, thought Blanche. Fresh she looked, and rested. Certainly no bad dreams for the last few nights.

Without any beating about the bush Miss Rainbird told Blanche exactly what she wanted. She wanted to find Harriet's son and do the best for him she possibly could and, towards this end, she put herself entirely in Blanche's hands. From now on she would have no second thoughts about where her duty rested.

Blanche, inwardly delighted, took the news soberly. Once they came completely over it was easy to deal with and help them.

She said, 'Well, I'm sure that on the other side they will be glad to know that. We'll see if they have anything to say. But I should warn you, Miss Rainbird, that I'd be very surprised if this time or the next few times they would come right out and give you his name and where to find him. They may not know that yet. Remember it's been over thirty years since he was taken away from your sister. But I do assure you he can't be dead otherwise she would never have come to you.'

Miss Rainbird said quietly, 'But why can't they come right out with that information?'

Blanche said, 'Because they won't know. How many people are there in the world, Miss Rainbird? Millions and millions. Your sister and brother will know things you don't know – but they still have to find him. Looking down on this earth, can you imagine, even with their powers, how difficult that may be? People who have crossed over find their loved ones and the ones they have been close to in their lives quite easily because of the sympathetic etheric spirit-waves between one another. But how do you find a stranger in a crowd when you don't know what he looks like and he knows – as I suspect must be the case here – nothing about you? But don't worry, they will be working on it and they will be having Henry's help. Shall we see what the situation is?'

Miss Rainbird nodded. For a moment she had been tempted to question the logic of Madame Blanche's remarks, but had refrained. She had put herself in her hands. It was a bargain which she felt bound now to honour ... at least for a while. The abnegation of her own logical habits and natural scepticism had to be accepted.

Miss Rainbird felt a new excitement in her as she watched Madame Blanche lean back in her chair and begin to go through what was now a familiar transformation. Watching the strain on the woman's face, the change in her breathing and the movement of her hands on her pearls, she remembered her start of horror at the foot of the stairs where Sholto had fallen, and saw in her imagination a small boy with a bird on his wrist or hand ... Inwardly she prayed that she was not being duped. She would be a fool not to broaden her mind sufficiently to accept some extra-terrestrial form of life and communication.

In a slow, heavy voice Madame Blanche said, 'Is that you, Henry?'

'Yes. It's me, Blanche.' The words came in the man's voice, through Madame Blanche, which Miss Rainbird had heard before.

'My goodness, Henry. I don't often see you with such a beaming smile on your face. A real old sober-sides you are normally.'

'I smile,' said Henry, 'because I'm happy. Can't you feel it all around you? It comes through you, Blanche, from your friend, Miss Rainbird. Her mind is at rest, there is a warm tranquillity in her heart, and she knows where her path lies. Tell her we are all happy for her.'

Madame Blanche said to Miss Rainbird, 'You hear that, Miss Rainbird?'

'Yes, Madame Blanche,' replied Miss Rainbird, who with a small part of her mind was not sure whether she liked being referred to as Madame Blanche's friend.

To her surprise Madame Blanche said, 'You must not call Miss Rainbird my friend, Henry. I am her guide. Friendship can only be claimed when it cannot be denied.'

Henry gave a small laugh. 'From here, Blanche, your little social distinctions amuse us. But you will be friends.'

'Maybe, Henry. But we have other things to think of just now. Why have you closed the vista suddenly, Henry? You're standing in the shadows.'

'Because the Word is all-powerful, Blanche. There is no need for light to give it meaning.'

'You mean they are not coming?'

'No, they are not coming, Blanche. Not this time. The true measure of Miss Rainbird's love for them lies now in what she does on her own. Her labours will be a testament of her sincerity. They will help when she needs it but there will be no sudden miracle. True miracles are only simple acts of faith and the long-pursued cherishings of our loved one's desires.'

Madame Blanche laughed. 'That's a bit woolly, Henry. What you mean is they're not sure themselves, but they'll give Miss Rainbird what they know and what they will in future find out.'

'That is true, Blanche. You see,' his voice went solemn, 'neither of them are in the Upper Brightness yet. Many things are still denied to them. But they will arrive. Eventually everyone arrives at the Upper Brightness. Until then they have their difficulties. But Miss Rainbird must not be disappointed. If she will go to them they will help her.'

'Henry!' Madame Blanche's tone was firm. 'Don't start talking in riddles. How can she go to them?'

'To their resting place, Blanche. Not far from it she will find the name of the child, but the child is not dead. In the spring she has placed the daffodils there and in the summer she has strewn the grass with the purity of white roses. Suffer the little children to come unto me for of such is the Kingdom of Heaven. Ask if she knows what I mean.'

Despite the warmth of the room Miss Rainbird felt her body tremble with a spasm of coldness.

Madame Blanche asked her, 'You understand, Miss Rainbird?'

Her throat suddenly dry, Miss Rainbird said, 'Yes, yes . . . about the flowers, yes. But the child is dead. Has been for—'

Henry said sharply, 'One dies and another lives. A body perishes but a name lives, Blanche. Do you see the man, Blanche?'

With an irritation that surprised Miss Rainbird, Blanche said, 'I can't see anything, Henry.'

'Try.'

Miss Rainbird watched Madame Blanche's hands go up to her temple and saw the slight quiver of her fingers as she pressed them hard against the skin. Slowly she gave a small, half-sobbing cry and then said, 'Yes, I see, Henry.'

'Tell Miss Rainbird what you see.'

'It's not very clear, Henry. He keeps coming and going, and there's something beside him . . . Ah, yes, that's better.' She laughed abruptly. 'It's a motor-car, Henry. Looks a bit old-fashioned.'

'Never mind the car. Tell Miss Rainbird about the man.'

'He's in uniform, Henry. A sort of darkish colour . . . chocolate like. And he's got leggings. My, he looks smart. Not much over thirty. And the car's white, all white . . .'

'Ask Miss Rainbird what colour his hair is, Blanche. His cap's off. You can see. Ask her.'

With an asperity which came from memories of long past events, Miss Rainbird said, 'If it's who I think it must be, his hair should be jet black.'

Madame Blanche with a note of anguish in her voice cried, 'What's happening, Henry? The picture's gone and you're going. Henry . . . Henry!'

Almost in a whisper Henry's voice answered, 'As the thundercloud hides the sun and darkens the beauty of flowers and fields, so does anger in the human heart drive out love and understanding ... Love, not anger, lights the road to true understanding ...' His voice faded and was gone.

Miss Rainbird sat there knowing she had been sharply reprimanded and the injustice – as she felt it to be – primed the re-emergence of her own strong personality. Upper Brightness indeed! Well, if there were such a thing, she wasn't surprised that Harriet – and particularly Sholto – hadn't reached it yet. And not to be angry at the thought of that Shoebridge man was an impossibility. True, she did put flowers on the child's grave sometimes. But that was because there was no one else in the village to do it. A simple act of tenderness when she did Sholto's and Harriet's. The whole thing was nonsense. This Madame Blanche, lying back now, eyes closed, pretending exhaustion, was simply a clever trickster. She simply couldn't go on with this. It was an insult to her own intelligence. The woman was getting information somewhere and just feeding it to her. Harriet was dead. Whatever had happened in Harriet's past was dead and there was nothing to be done about it.

As the thought was still with her, Harriet's voice came clearly to her, 'Tippy, dear ... you're making me very unhappy ...' But the words came through Madame Blanche's lips. 'Unhappy for you, Tippy, dear ... Unhappy for you.'

Miss Rainbird had a sense of extreme shock, of coldness striking at her. She stared at Madame Blanche's face, large, and handsome in its vulgar way. It had been Harriet's voice. Oh, God ... was her hearing playing her tricks? Tippy ... how could this woman know that that had been Harriet's nickname for her?

Blanche slowly opened her eyes, sat up in her chair and blew a little breath of relief as she smiled at Miss Rainbird.

'Phew,' she said, 'Henry's knocked me about again. I'm exhausted.' Her eyes moved towards the sherry decanter.

Miss Rainbird, ignoring the hint for the moment, said, 'Do you remember it all?'

'Yes, of course, this time.'

'Do you remember the last thing which was said?'

'Clearly. Henry got poetic again. "Love, not anger, lights the road to true understanding ..." And he's right, Miss Rainbird.

I know you can't help little relapses now and then. It's only human. But it's hard for them always to be patient about it.'

Miss Rainbird said nothing. She got up and went to pour sherry for them both. What was she to think of this woman, what was she to think?

George and Blanche were drinking stout in the kitchen of her Salisbury house. Mrs Tyler had long gone to bed. Albert was sleeping in George's car parked outside. Blanche would not permit him in the house. Terrestrially and ethereally dogs did not rate very high with her. It was late at night and occasional buffets of wind shook the kitchen window. George had a big red-backed notebook on the table before him. He had bought it the day after his first visit to Mrs Gradidge to keep all his notes in about Miss Rainbird and her affairs. Although his memory was reasonable he had long ago learnt that unless he made notes soon after any interview he was inclined to forget some small detail or other. And small details were often more important to Blanche than big ones.

Referring to the notebook now and then, he was giving Blanche an outline of all the facts he had picked up in Chilbolton and more recently at Weston-super-Mare.

Ronald Shoebridge had been the chauffeur to Sholto at Reed Court. He was also rather more than a chauffeur. When his master wanted drinking company Shoebridge often obliged him, and he obliged him in other ways, particularly when Sholto used the car for his amorous forays about the countryside. Shoebridge was not a local man. He had come from London, bringing his wife Martha with him. His closest confidant at Chilbolton had been Gradidge, who travelled in the car when Sholto went shooting and fishing. Two months – Mrs Gradidge had actually given him the day and the hour – before Harriet's child had been born, Mrs Shoebridge had lost her own six-month-old child, a boy, named Edward. A week before Harriet's child was born, Ronald Shoebridge had left the employment of Sholto Rainbird. To his friend Gradidge he had confided that he had had a little money left to him and was moving off to set up his own garage. He hadn't said where.

But a year later he had – prompted by vanity George imagined – written to Gradidge from Weston-super-Mare and said that he was in the garage business there and doing nicely and announced that his wife had had another baby. This last fact had intrigued the Gradidges because Mrs Gradidge had been told by Martha Shoebridge – after the birth of her son, Edward – that there had been complications and the doctor had said that it was doubtful whether she could ever have another.

The Gradidges, who always peered behind all facts, distrusting the appearance of truth, had arrived at the conclusion that Ronald Shoebridge had no more been left a little money than they had, but that Sholto Rainbird had set him up in business well away from Chilbolton on condition that he and his wife took over Harriet's baby and presented it to the world as their own – and probably on condition that the boy was never to be told the truth of his parentage. Ronald Shoebridge was the kind of man who would honour any contract as long as he was paid enough.

George said, 'I found the garage, love. Just looked in the telephone book. Shoebridge Garages Ltd. The original one in Weston, another in Bridgwater and another in Wells. Shoebridge had to go in the army during the war, but his wife ran the original place with the help of a manager who was over army age. After the war he really got cracking and made a go of things ...' Just, he thought, as he would when all this sniffing around was done and he could get down to the gardening lark. 'Eventually he sold out at a nice profit and went to Brighton. There was a nice old chap, storekeeper in the Weston garage, who'd worked there originally with Shoebridge. He hadn't heard from Shoebridge for ages and fancied he must be dead because for years he'd always got a Christmas card at least. Anyway, he knew Shoebridge had gone to Brighton with some idea of starting a hotel, putting a manager in and taking things easy. I've got his last address in Brighton.'

'What about the boy?' asked Blanche.

'Just like you and the Gradidges thought. They called him Edward. Probably used the birth certificate of their own dead boy. There'd only be an age discrepancy of eight months. That wouldn't show by the time he was ten or eleven. He went to a small private school where if he was a bit backward to begin with they wouldn't worry. He was a bright boy, anyway. Good at sports, and mad about the countryside, birds and flowers and all that. The Shoebridges lived over the garage to begin with and then had a small house outside in the country.'

He began to leaf through his notebook.

'You'll have to go to Brighton, George.'

'I know, love. Tomorrow. I want to get this thing finished. Now, what else have I got in the book of words? Don't want to slip anything that you could pass to dear Henry—'

'George, that's enough of that.'

'Give us another stout and let me stay the night here and I'll never mention his name again.' He winked at her as she began to pour him another drink. 'Oh, yes. The boy. He had fair hair and blue eyes. Quick tempered at times. Touch of the old Irish, I'd say. He was fourteen when the Shoebridges left Weston and was away at school. Birth certificate fourteen that would be. Mrs Shoebridge was ambitious for him. Devoted to him and so was Shoebridge. Martha Shoebridge when she was at Chilbolton used to do bits of needlework for the Rainbirds. Garage is near the seafront. What's this? Oh, yes, that's old stuff, about the girls' nicknames.'

'What's that?'

'I told you. The nicknames the two Miss Rainbirds had for one another. Old Mother Gradidge told me.'

'You never told me. George, that's the kind of thing I want. It helps so much in establishing a warm communication.'

'I'm sure I told you. Your Miss Rainbird was Tippy, and Harriet was called Flappy.'

'You certainly didn't tell me. Now, make sure there's nothing else. I want everything. What kind of needlework did Martha Shoebridge do for the Rainbirds?'

'Helped in the linen room. Hell, fancy living in a house with a linen room. Used to hem and repair sheets. Cut 'em down the middle when they were worn and turn them. Old Sholto watched the household expenses.' He flicked more pages. 'No, there's nothing else that I haven't told you. Except my expenses – but I'll save those for when the whole thing's done.' He raised his glass to her, drank and said, 'Well, what about it? Do I stay the night and give the neighbours something to talk about?'

Blanche, looking past him, shook her head and said, 'You know what I think that boy was carrying? I think he was carrying a bird. Yes, he was. Some poor bird that he'd rescued.'

'You're way beyond me, Blanche. You mean you saw this lad?'

'As clearly as I see you.'

'Then he should have had a shotgun. Mad about hunting he was, according to the old storekeeper.'

Blanche's eyes came back to him. 'Why didn't you tell me that?'

'Blimey, Blanche. I can't remember everything. You any idea how some of these people talk? Once they begin you can't stop them. Look, I've been thinking – there might be a quick way out of this. It'd suit you and me. The boy's a man now. There's no reason he'd change his name. If I don't turn him up in Brighton tomorrow all we've got to do is put an advertisement in one of the papers. *News of the World* or something like that. Box number and will Edward Shoebridge, son of Ronald and Martha Shoebridge, last heard of in Brighton such and such a date, please communicate present whereabouts when he will hear of something to his advantage. Yes?'

Very firmly Blanche said, 'No.'

'Why not?'

'Use your head, George. To begin with Miss Rainbird might see. She realizes by now unless she's stupid – which she isn't – that the child was farmed off to the Shoebridges.'

'She isn't the type to read the *News of the World*. A Sunday basinful of sex and sport.'

'Somebody else might see it and mention it to her. One of her friends. "Shoebridge? Wasn't that the name of the chauffeur Sholto used to have?" Can you imagine? But it's not just that – she wants me to find him without his knowing about it.

Love, he could turn out to be the biggest non-starter for the Rainbird stakes in the world. In that case – and I know her – she'd quietly forget about the whole thing. All she wants at the moment is a good excuse for doing nothing about it. You may not believe it, but apart from the Temple of Astrodel angle, I'm becoming very fond of the old girl. I'm not having her life ruined. If Edward Shoebridge is a no-gooder, then she's going to be told that he's dead and she can live and sleep in peace.'

George grinned. 'You're an artful number, aren't you? Either way, you win. Whyn't you take up real crime, Blanche? You could finish up with the Taj Mahal.'

Blanche said stiffly, 'George Lumley – I'll put that down to four bottles of stout and all the other drinks you no doubt had before you got here. Now, you get off home. Brighton for you tomorrow. And if by any chance you do trace Edward Shoebridge there – you keep well clear of him until I tell you otherwise.'

George shrugged his shoulders. 'Okay, me old dear, you're the boss.'

Of the ten people who at some time or other had been members of both the Tiverton and Crowborough Beacon Golf Clubs, four of the men and two of the women had died. That left four men and two women. Of the two women, one was in Rhodesia where she had lived with her husband for the last two years, and the other – a spinster of fifty-four – lived at Crowborough still and was clearly from Bush's angle a non-suspect the moment he had read the report on her. Of the four men, one lived at Tiverton still and was seventy-five and had been a Church of England minister, another was a man of forty who lived at Crowborough, was a member of the Stock Exchange and was married and had four children all below the age of eighteen. (Bush, determined to leave no stone unturned, was having a survey made on him, but knew in his heart that nothing would come of it.) Another man was the master of an Esso oil tanker which at this moment was halfway between London and Bahrein and who had, during the periods of both kidnappings, also been at sea. The fourth was a man in his very late thirties, of slender but independent means, who lived by himself in a country cottage in Wiltshire where he kept a collection of foreign birds, mostly golden and oriental pheasants and budgerigars. His name was George Lumley.

CHAPTER SIX

MISS RAINBIRD WAS was in her small private sitting-room thinking about Madame Blanche, who had just left, and the session they had had. It was a relief to her to find now that she could suspend belief or disbelief. She was content to sit and listen and, whenever it was demanded of her, give her responses and ask her questions. She could remain detached now, she knew, until the moment came when a choice between belief and disbelief would be made in her without volition in the same way as her present state had suddenly possessed her.

While the session – she could not yet bring herself to describe her meetings with Madame Blanche as seances – had been a successful one, it had been a shade irritating to her that Sholto alone had appeared to Madame Blanche to talk to them through Henry. She wasn't happy that Sholto was taking charge of things. Sholto had always been a highly disturbing element in her life. He had to be a long way from Upper Brightness yet, and she could not rule out the possibility that a fair streak of his original dissolute character must remain.

She reached for her telephone and dialled the number for Directory Inquiries. Sholto had said that the child had been adopted by the Shoebridge couple, and that he had given the Shoebridge man – she'd never liked him, there was always something reptilian, she thought, about his eyes and look – a substantial sum to take himself off and establish a business. Sholto said he thought the man had set his heart on a garage business, but he wasn't sure because once the transaction had been made and the cash paid he wanted to know no more of the Shoebridges' existence. And at this point Sholto had signed off, sliding back down his long, glowing vista and out of reach even of Henry. Typical Sholto, washing his hands of the whole thing. But fortunately Harriet had come through. Not in any ethereal form, but handing out the pictures from her album as before. There had been pictures of a garage, of a seaside town, a length of pier, and then others of a small boy and a cottage in the country. Nice pictures, as described by Madame Blanche, Miss Rainbird had to admit. (In Heaven's name why did it take so long always to get Inquiries? That stupid buzzing note boring into one's eardrum!) A boy swimming in a river, bird-nesting, playing with a dog, and finally one of the whole family group standing on a railway platform, luggage around them, obviously going off for a holiday, and in the background the large name-plate of the station. Blanche's voice came back to her. 'I can't see it clearly. It's Weston-something . . . Oh dear, so many people crowding around. Ah . . . now I see it. The man has bent to pick up a case. It's Weston-super-Mare.'

The ringing tone stopped and an operator's voice said, 'Directory Inquiries. Can I help you?'

Miss Rainbird asked to be given the number of Shoebridge Garages Ltd in Weston-super-Mare. The album picture Blanche had described had shown a modern garage.

A few minutes later, Miss Rainbird was given the number. She wrote it down on her telephone pad, looked at it and wondered what on earth she was going to do about it, if in fact she had to do anything. The trail had gone cold at Weston . . . The pictures had faded, Harriet had decamped and Blanche had come round, remembering everything and saying that they could only hope there would be more information next time. At the moment, Miss Rainbird decided, she would be wiser to do nothing. A wait-and-see policy was not ordinarily to her liking, but for the time being she would be content with it.

George's inquiries that day in Brighton took him a long time and produced a little more information, but nothing like enough, he knew, for Blanche's purposes. He had started with a piece of luck and then had run up against a seemingly blank wall. The Shoebridge address given him in Brighton was a modest terrace house set in a small road that lay about two hundred yards back from the seafront out on the Hove side of the town. It was a tall, narrow-fronted house of three storeys, well kept, its green paintwork quite fresh, and the brass fittings on the front door well polished. A woman answered the door and George asked to see the owner or occupier. It took him a few minutes of his charm and blarney to get cooperation, but in the end he was shown into a sitting-room.

Sitting in a chair by the fireplace was the owner, an old gentleman well into his seventies. He had a book on his lap and there was a scattering of daily newspapers about his chair. On a small table at his side was a telephone and on the other side of the fireplace was a large television set. He was a Mr Hanson, a retired butcher, who had once had a small business in the town. He was the thinnest butcher George had ever seen and – the information was soon readily offered – suffered badly from rheumatism and spent most of his days reading, watching television and studying racing form in order to make his daily telephone bets. George told him that he was working for a firm of Salisbury solicitors who were trying to trace the Shoebridge family in connection with a small legacy that had arisen on the death of a distant relative. Mr Hanson, who was lonely and welcomed company, made no attempt to check George's credentials. He told him that he had known the Shoebridge family quite well. After their arrival from Weston-super-Mare, they had lived in the house – which Shoebridge had bought – for two years while Shoebridge was looking for a suitable hotel to buy. Shoebridge had eventually bought a fair-sized hotel on the seafront and he and his family had lived in a suite at the top of the hotel. All the time they had been there he, Mr Hanson, had served the place with its meat and had come to know them well. In fact, when Shoebridge had put up the house for sale, he had bought it and converted the top two floors into a flat which he had let off, and lived himself on the bottom floor.

Shoebridge's hotel was called the Argenta and Shoebridge had pulled it together and made a success of the place. Seven years later he had sold it and moved away from Brighton. Mr Hanson had no idea where he had gone or what had happened to the family. Nobody at the Argenta would be able to help George either, because two years ago it had been pulled down and a block of flats built on the site. Shoebridge, he said, was a good businessman. He'd known him well. They were both members of the Conservative Club and both Rotarians. He'd clearly made a good profit out of the Weston-super-Mare garage sale, and, he guessed, an even better one out of the hotel sale. In addition he knew that Shoebridge had invested wisely in property in the district and had always been quick to take his profit when he felt there had been sufficient appreciation. He was not one to hang on to something too long and then find that he had missed the boat. Where they all were now he hadn't the faintest idea. Probably dead, except the boy, of course. He'd be well into his thirties now.

'What was the boy like?' asked George.

'Oh, he was all right. Bit wild at times, I fancy. Living in a hotel when he was home from school wasn't a good thing. You get some odd types in hotels down here, you know.'

'What did he do when he left school?'

'Worked for his father for a bit, learning the business. Then he went off to do the same sort of thing. First London, I think. And then abroad. I don't really know. I found him a nice enough young chap. But there were others that said he was a bastard when the mood took him. He had an eye for the girls. There was trouble once or twice at the Argenta. I used to get it all, you know, back through the kitchen staff when I delivered. No matter what happens in a hotel, the news finishes up in the kitchens. I've an idea that he got a girl into trouble and married pretty young. Probably had to. Somebody from the Argenta – after Shoebridge sold it – met him once in London casually. I think that was it. I don't know. My memory tricks me these days.'

'Where did he go to school?'

'Lancing College. That's not far away. Along the coast. Old Shoebridge felt it was better for the boy to be a boarder and not kicking round the hotel all the time. They might be able to help you, of course.'

'How?'

'Well, don't they have Old Boys' Associations? Keep in touch and all that business. They could have his address.'

George grinned. 'You should have been a detective, Mr Hanson.'

The old man nodded. 'Have been in my time. You give credit in a shop and you've got to be able to find the odd one or two that scarper leaving a fat bill. Some get away, of course, but that's only because you don't have the time or can't afford it to go after 'em. Nobody can disappear like that!' He snapped his fingers. 'Not in this day and age. Wherever you go you got to leave a mark of some kind. Oh, I could tell you some of the dodges that they used to get up to – all for the sake of a three-pound bill owing.'

And he did, for the next half hour, over whisky and water which was brought in for the two of them by his daily woman who had answered the door. George stayed happily with him, out of charity, out of thanks for his help, and because of the whisky.

Late that afternoon George and Albert drove to Lancing and George saw the school Bursar. He and Edward Shoebridge were much the same age. He explained that he was a friend of Shoebridge's in the hotel business in the South of France, and over on holiday in Brighton. He'd lost trace of Shoebridge and wanted to look him up. The Bursar was helpful and, because of the information he gave, George decided that he had better spend the night in Brighton and pursue his inquiries the next day. He wasn't keen about it, and neither was Albert, but there was no choice. He wanted to clear up this business for Blanche quickly and get on to his gardening lark. The van, he had decided, was to be green and painted on either side would be the head of an enormous yellow, black-centred sunflower with the firm's name running around it – Lumley's Sunshine Gardens Ltd. The notepaper he used would feature the same motif. He couldn't wait.

While George was looking for Edward Shoebridge, Bush was looking for the same man. Reports were beginning to come in from the local police throughout the designated area in the

South of England and were being fed into Sangwill's computer. Some of the local forces did their work conscientiously so far as the pressures of other work and manpower would allow them. Some did it less conscientiously. A few diehard Chief Constables blew their top and did nothing for the time being, content to wait for a sharp reminder from the Yard. Here and there a local constable, bicycle- or motor-bicycle-mounted, balking at the prospect of a wintry round, merely sat down and made some kind of list from memory of his area. The reports that had already arrived numbered hundreds. Their processing for the computer was a slow business, and the minor or major inquiries sparked by them even slower. Bush was looking for a needle in a haystack. He did the only thing that he could at the moment and that was to concentrate on the few names that had emerged from the two golf clubs. He did this out of sheer routine thoroughness and not because he felt that there was the slightest chance of a hard lead emerging.

It was for this reason that while George was on his way to Brighton a member of the Wiltshire CID was detailed to take a look around George's place.

The man, with all the papers and documentation to prove that he was an insurance agent canvassing for new business, drove up to George's cottage two hours after George had left for Brighton. Although he had noticed that the lean-to shed where George kept his car was empty, he rang the bell. There was no reply. He walked round the garden and the small paddock. George's birds were in their long wire run. The food and water hoppers were full. A flight of budgerigars, pale blue, green and yellow, fluttered and perched among the dead branches which George had arranged as perches, and a moulting albino cock pheasant sat sulkily in one corner of the run ignoring the ceaseless up-and-down passage of a belligerent golden pheasant. The paddock was unkempt in places with nettle and dock patches. The small garden around the house clearly was never given more than minimal attention. The cottage was thatched – and would soon need rethatching. The structure itself was built of stone blocks, but whether the stone was limestone the man couldn't tell. Part of the garden wall was made of the same material. He decided to take a piece of it back with him for the experts to decide. One thing was certain, however, the house could have no cellar. The river was less than a hundred yards away. Any digging below the house would hit the water table at once and the man could see that there would be trouble with drainage as there was almost no fallaway at all. For his money this place and its owner could not possibly fill whatever bill it was that had to be filled.

He went back to the front door and rang the bell again. When there was still no reply, he tried the door latch and the door opened. He sighed. Despite all the police publicity people still did it. Walked out and left a house unlocked, wide open to any passing sneak-thief.

He went into the cottage and made a quick examination of all the rooms and checked that indeed there was no cellar. His practised eyes told him a great deal about George Lumley. He already knew, from a chat with the local constable, of George's association with Blanche Tyler. The Salisbury police knew, too, that George sometimes did 'confidential' work for her, but there had never been any complaints from Blanche's clients. As he made his notes he was thinking of the Fraudulent Mediums Act, 1951, which had repealed the Witchcraft Act, 1735. Under it, any person who with intent to deceive purported to act as a spiritualistic medium or to exercise any powers of telepathy, claivoyance or other similar powers, or, in purporting to act as a spiritualistic medium or to exercise such powers as aforesaid, used any fraudulent device, would be guilty of an offence. Trouble was, all proceedings had to be brought by or with the consent of the Director of Public Prosecutions. It was all small beer stuff generally and the police seldom bothered with it. Still . . . he'd been asked to get all he could and felt he had better draw attention to it. The local constable had described Blanche as a 'lively handful who'd keep any man busy and warm in bed'. If the need arose he'd give her the once over. Maybe she could tell him whether he would ever make Detective-Inspector.

Going through the kitchen on his way out, he tried to turn off the dripping cold-water tap without success. It clearly needed a new washer. George Lumley, he thought, was no do-it-yourself handyman.

That day, too, Edward Shoebridge drove by himself some fifty miles from his home, south-east to the small country town of Dorchester, the birthplace of Thomas Hardy. He took a stop-watch with him. He spent some time observing from a distance a country house that lay to the east of the town, and then even more time driving around the neighbouring roads and side lanes. It was the third of such visits he had made well spread out over the last two months. He made no notes of any kind. All that he needed to know he kept in his head. Already the films he had long ago made and recently run through were destroyed.

Driving home he was content that all was now ready. There was no more to do but wait for the day to come when he could act. The next time there would be no publicity. Twice, by not attempting to prevent the news breaking, indeed promoting it, he had made the police look fools. Scotland Yard and the Home Office and many public personalities had all been subjected to heavy press criticism. This time he could safely insist on the whole affair being kept quiet, since he knew he would have the cooperation of the authorities. He would also have, he knew, their enmity and anger, and this would provoke an even greater effort to find him.

The next time he or his wife walked into the hall at the Army Aviation Centre at Middle Wallop in Hampshire, the same people would be there. Grandison he knew by name. He was a publicly recognizable figure. The other two were faces; the man about his own age, plump-faced, mouth edged with a bitter inner anger, and the older man, glasses pushed up on his forehead like an eye-weary clerk. And there would be half a million lying in stones on the table. If they gave any trouble – then his captive would die. They knew that. They would have given their orders to all involved – but there could always be one man to break an order, to take a chance, some unthinking fool who wanted to be an hero. The odds against it were high, but he considered them, and all the way home his mind was

114

exploring all the safeguards he might be able to take against a moment of individual foolishness. Every risk that he could foresee must be countered. In the fast-going light he saw a sparrow hawk swing round the edge of a clump of trees on the roadside ahead and wing low between the tree trunks, pirating for small birds. In the quick glance he recognized it as a female. He thought of his wife waiting for him. She wanted what he wanted, had nourished the want in him almost before he had known it for himself. She had gone to the first collection, not to prove to him there could be no failure – there could always by the turn of chance be that – but to put herself to that risk so that if she failed he would still be free to try again.

George rose late and unrefreshed. He had got a room at a sea-front hotel in Brighton and a strong wind off the sea had smacked and rattled his window all night. Albert had objected to sleeping on a cushion in the small armchair and had twice jumped to the foot of the bed and been repulsed. The third time George let him stay. He was restless himself from a substantial dinner and lay awake for hours wishing he had brought some stomach powder with him and thinking of Lumley's Sunshine Gardens. When he finally dropped off he overslept and woke to find that Albert had cocked a leg against the wardrobe. George before bathing cleaned up and told Albert exactly what he thought of him.

The morning continued to go wrong. At breakfast he ordered coffee and got tea. His eggs were beautifully cooked but he didn't care for them because he liked the yolks hard fried. The bacon wasn't fat enough and all the *Daily Mail*s had gone and he had to make do with the *Daily Express* which made him feel like a lost man. He took Albert to the kitchen for a plate of breakfast scraps and a kitchen boy said, 'What kind of dog's that, then?' George, normally the first to admit or even point out that Albert was of no beauty and no pedigree, resented this. He thought of answering that Albert was a truffle-hound, one of only five in England and worth a couple of hundred quid, but the effort was beyond him. It was one of

115

those days, he recognized, when he was not going to be at his sparkling best until he had had a couple of pints of Guinness or two large gins. There were days like that. Even the thought of Lumley's Sunshine Gardens held little comfort as he drove off to find the address that the Bursar of Lancing College had given him.

Edward Shoebridge had long lapsed as a member of the Old Boys' Association. All the Bursar could do was to give the address which Shoebridge had acknowledged up until seven years after leaving the college – Green Posts, Smallfield, near Glyndebourne. George found Glyndebourne easily enough – it was less than a half-hour run north from Brighton. It took him another half-hour to find Smallfield, and then fifteen minutes to find Green Posts. It was a smallish, red-tiled, red-bricked house in a side lane. A holly hedge ran round the garden which was quite large and well-kept.

The moment the door was opened to his knock, George knew that the morning was going to live up to its shabby start. One look at the woman facing him told George what to expect. He knew the kind. At eleven o'clock in the morning he could catch the sweet smell of gin on her breath. If Blanche knew, he thought, some of the things he did for her! And, if he knew his women, there were things that might be offered here which he would be wise to refuse. Not that the prospect of a large gin was unpleasing. But no more.

She was an ample, dark-haired, slack-faced, loosely built woman in her early forties. She was wearing a white silk blouse, ruched at the sleeves and down the front, and a black skirt that was taking considerable strain over her hips which a small slit up one side did nothing to ease, though every time she moved it showed a substantial slice of thigh and stocking top. She was the perfect finale, George thought, to tea instead of coffee, the *Daily Express* instead of the *Daily Mail* and eggs that ran all over your plate instead of staying put when you cut them. He should have brought Albert in from the car, he at least could have left a visiting card in self-defence. In no time at all she had given George her name and he was invited inside.

116

Mrs Angers, Lydia Angers. Practically every pub in the world, he told himself, had a Lydia Angers type of regular customer. In a moment she would laugh and it would be a laugh he had heard in a hundred saloon bars. He'd hardly got started on his story that he was looking for an old chum he'd known in the hotel business, one Edward Shoebridge, when a large, beringed hand took his hat. He was drawn inside the hall which was decorated with unevenly hung pictures of different roses. A grandfather clock had one of its corners propped up with three copies of the *National Geographical Magazine*. With little time to observe more, he was shepherded into the lounge with its chintz armchairs, a large settee, a pink carpet very worn near the door and the fireplace, and a television set with three brass monkeys on top of it. A small desk was over-flowing with papers, and there was a vase of half-dead chrys-anthemums on a large sideboard that was crowded with bot-tles, decanters and glasses, not all of them clean.

George just avoided being steered on to the settee and set-tled himself in an armchair, a deep and uncomfortable pit of broken springs.

Yes, she and her husband had known Edward Shoebridge well. Her husband better than she had, of course, since they were at school together, and would he like a drink, or a cup of coffee or tea? When he said coffee Mrs Angers made no move to do anything about it. She poured herself a glass of gin and water at the sideboard and, without appearing to hear anything George said, mixed one for him, too.

George held the glass and sighed inwardly. He had got one of the lonely ones again, another of the great Gradidge clan, better educated, better fixed, but still the same loneliness. She lit herself a menthol-flavoured cigarette and George realized what it was that he had smelled the moment he came into the room. There was no need for him to do more than throw in an occasional quick question, smile when she made some flirta-tious move or remark, and dig himself deeper into the safety of the armchair.

Her husband was in the hotel fittings and fixtures trade in London. Worth and Freen Ltd. Terribly busy. Seldom got down to the country and had a small flat in town. (George didn't need to be told anything about Mr Angers. He could imagine the whole situation.) Wild horses wouldn't drag her to London. She adored the country ... the garden and the house and masses of friends around. Edward Shoebridge? Well, that was curious. His father and mother had owned this house once. Moved here from Brighton. Andy – (George marked him correctly as her husband) – had often visited him here. He and Edward were great friends. No, she was sure he didn't know where he was now. In fact, he'd like to know himself. Always talking about the good times he and Edward used to have. They'd been in the hotel business together for a while. Paris, she thought. Or was it Stuttgart? When the old Shoebridges had died (she went within a year of him. Heartbroken. And both buried in the local churchyard) Edward had kept the place going for a few years. Sometimes let it. She and Andy had had it for a year once. That's why Andy had bought it from him ten years ago. Thought it would be a good place for her since she didn't like town and he had to be away so much. ... It was a big house, much bigger than it looked from the outside. She'd show him round in a minute. Did he really want coffee? She helped herself to another gin and George had his glass taken from him and refilled, to which he did not entirely object, but he swore to himself that he was going on no conducted tour of the house. Once upstairs she was the kind, when she fancied a man, who would have no qualms about using force.

Three times she asked him if he were sure that they hadn't met somewhere before and discussed possible places until George led her back to the matter in hand, wishing she would settle somewhere instead of moving up and down giving him generous exposures of broad, quivering thigh through the slit skirt. He decided she liked being on her feet so that it took less time to get to the sideboard – or to take advantage of more susceptible types than himself. If there were many like this when he started his Sunshine Gardens round he didn't know if he would be able to take it. Perhaps he ought to think of something else.

118

Actually, to let him into a secret, she hadn't really liked or got on with Edward Shoebridge much. (Almost certainly she'd never been able to spur him into making a pass at her, decided George.) A funny sort of fellow. Kept things to himself. Oh, clever, brilliant. Made a lot of money. Well, enough. You know, very comfortably off and all that. Kind of icy, never got warmed up type. Really, sometimes, you just felt he was a million miles away in some dream world of his own. A cold fish . . . no fun in him. Wasn't surprised his marriage had gone wrong. Someone in the hotel business, Andy had said. Receptionist or something. After the child was born – no, she couldn't remember whether it was a boy or girl – she'd gone off the rails with other men. Didn't do her much good. He just left her and took the child and Andy said that he'd heard she was killed in a car accident when the boy was about three. No, to be quite frank, she really hadn't liked him at all. Not that she saw him much. Andy used to meet him in town after the house became theirs, and then he just faded out. Andy – what a pity he wasn't here, one of the best – had been crazy about Shoebridge. Right from when they met at school. Hero-worship. Just a straight case of hero-worship.

She headed for the sideboard, although her glass was half full, topped it up and then opened the cupboard door and pulled out a large tattered photograph album. She went back and sat on the settee.

She patted the cushion at her side. 'Come and look at these. Andy was mad about photography. Not now. No time.' She patted the cushion harder. 'Come on. Plenty of Eddie Shoebridge in here.'

Like a man going to the block, George removed himself to the settee, and said, looking at his wristwatch, 'I mustn't take up much more of your time. You've been too kind already and I've—'

She patted him on the shoulder, smiling, wet-lipped, large-eyed, the nipples of her uncontained breasts showing clearly through the silk of her blouse. 'No trouble at all. Always ready to help a friend find a friend. Don't you think friendship is the most rewarding relationship in the world? I do. Not like love.

That can be complicated. But pure friendship and understanding—' she put a hand on his knee, '—now that's something that's worth its weight in rubies.'

In self-defence George nodded agreement and deliberately finished his gin quickly. She took his empty glass and went to refill it. When she returned George had the big album open and spread across his knees. Minor caresses he might have to and could endure, but his virtue at least had some meagre protection.

She leaned across him a little and said, 'Now let me pick out the ones of Eddie. I'm sure they'll interest you.'

With the warmth of her thigh pressed against his leg she began to show him the photographs, her voice now and then breaking into a gin-sparked giggle. George, hot and apprehensive – why was it always this kind of woman, slapping her wares in the shop front without any pretence at window dressing, that Blanche's missions seemed to turn up for him? – tried to take in the Shoebridge pictures and her running commentary while he put up a polite system of defences against her flagrant onslaught. She leant and rubbed against him like a great gin-scented kitten while she talked and laughed her way through the album. *That's me. Yes, really. Would you believe it? God, look at that dress! You wouldn't believe we wore such things. Ah, now – I like this one. Andy and me were on the beach alone. A bit naughty of him to take it, don't you think?* And once or twice she lay back against the settee in her delight, her bosom heaving under a frothy meringue of ruching, her eyes swimming with invitation until she had George laying odds against himself that he would never be let out of the house without committing adultery. Not that he had anything against adultery in its right place. The last pages of the album were coming up and George thought enviously of Albert, sleeping peacefully in the back of the car. He could see it all. She would close the album, slide it to the ground, make some laughing remark and lie back on the settee, arms raised in welcome, her body slewing gently round with a full display of rich hospitality, her eyes melting with dreamy fervour, and nothing that a gentleman like himself could do about it without raising one hell of a row because a woman spurned is a—

At that moment the telephone in the hall rang.

'Now, who the hell's that at this time of the morning?' said Mrs Angers crossly. The bell rang insistently and, exasperated, she got up to answer it. Saved by the bell, thought George, and as he watched her sway into the hall he wondered what it was about a telephone bell that was so compulsive. Pavlovian. No matter what you were doing, you had to answer it. Thank God.

From the doorway, she looked back at him, smiled and winked, and said, 'Don't be lonely, darling. Help yourself to another gin. Do one for me, too.' She gave a dramatic wave of her right arm and almost fell into the hall.

George got to his feet, crossed to the sideboard, passed it and reached the window. As he released the catch he heard her cry, 'Andy! Darling! How lovely to hear your voice … Angel, I was just sitting here quietly, all on my lonely-ownely thinking about you …'

George stepped through the window and, without bothering to close it, ran for his car. He drove away quickly, but when he hit the main road slowed down, not because he feared pursuit but because he was full of gin and didn't want any police trouble. A breathalyzer test after Lydia Angers would top off a perfect morning.

Albert moved to the front passenger seat from the back and pushed his nose against George's arm in one of his rare caresses.

George snarled. 'For God's sake don't you start getting friendly, too, or I'll sell you off to the first bloody ruby merchant I meet.'

Albert settled to sleep and then jerked his head up as George suddenly shouted at the top of his voice, 'Hell – I've left my hat on her bloody hall table!'

At six o'clock that evening Bush in his room overlooking St James's Park read the report that had come in within the last hour on George Lumley. There were fifty others under it wait-

121

ing to be read. The Wiltshire CID man had done a succinct, competent job. Lumley was thirty-nine, a bit of the black sheep of the family, remittance man, worked now and again but not recently. Five years previously he had been employed for a short period by a brewery in Tiverton as a sales representative. A year after that he had become a partner in a small and new coffee bar in Crowborough, but had pulled or been pushed out after six months. He was divorced. No children. Now and again he acted as a private inquiry agent for a medium, Madame Blanche Tyler of Salisbury. Lumley's cottage was thatched, built of sandstone blocks, and had no cellar. In the garden was a wire aviary thirty feet by ten which contained budgerigars, various pheasants, two pinioned mallard ducks and three bantams, two hens and one cock.

As he finished reading it and marked it for transmission to Sangwill and his computer, Bush heard the door open behind him. He turned to find Grandison in the room.

Grandison nodded and moved up to the table. Without a word he picked up the report on George Lumley, glanced through it, and then dropped it.

Bush said, 'They're all like that.'

'Are you surprised? They've all got to be. We shan't get it on a plate.'

'Scotland Yard are laughing their heads off.'

Grandison smiled. 'That's good. It relieves animosities. So, we look like a bunch of fools. But we're not acting like fools. Catching at straws, maybe.' He let his monocle drop and rubbed at his beard. Then he smiled and said, 'Have you ever thought of praying?'

'Praying?'

'Don't deal in echoes, Bush. What's wrong with prayer? A good fat prayer invoking God's help in the overthrowing of evil. We don't consider God enough in this department. You know which God I'm referring to of course?'

'I can't imagine it would be the Christian one.'

'Indeed not. There's only one god who understands and sympathizes – sometimes – with our kind of problems. The god of chance, the disposer of coincidence, the manipulator of time, place and the sought one altogether. It happens sometimes. Statistically it hardly shows on the graph of crime solutions, but it's there.'

'I agree. But it's something you can't recognize until it actually happens.'

'That's just the point. So far we've got nothing at all of any significance. Now is the moment for serious prayer, because I have a strong feeling – which I would only admit to you – that we are not going to get anything except by chance. So pray for it. In the meantime you might go through this—' He dropped a sheet of paper in front of Bush, '—and together with the Home Office and police boys check the security arrangements for all the people listed. The next victim may not be on it. It depends whether our friend has his sights set for a million, a half million or something a little more modest.'

Bush ran through the list when Grandison had gone. It contained over thirty names and many of them were of the highest rank in the order of precedence in England. The thought of a Royal Duke or Prince, or someone like the Lord High Chancellor or the Prime Minister, being kidnapped and the whole thing being hushed up while the country had to pay up secretly, completely pushed out of Bush's mind all thought of an insignificant figure like George Lumley, remittance man, and colleague of some small-time medium called Madame Blanche Tyler.

When Blanche arrived at Reed Court that evening, Miss Rainbird was suffering from a bad migraine. It had come on just after lunch. At moments during the afternoon she had contemplated telephoning Madame Blanche and putting off her appointment. In the end she had decided not to do this. She had been brought up strictly to observe all appointments unless it was quite impossible to fulfil them.

Blanche – who had been telephoned by George from his hotel in Brighton the previous evening, when he had given her the information he had collected so far – had telephoned his cottage before leaving Salisbury in the hope that he might be back and have more to tell her. But there had been no reply to her call. (George had stopped for lunch on the way home and later had pulled the car off the road to take a sleep for a couple of hours. He had arrived at his cottage ten minutes after Blanche had telephoned.)

Syton took her coat in the hall. He was a tall, white-haired, solemn-faced man who had been in service all his life and could make very fine social distinctions instinctively. He had long ago naturally placed Blanche in a lower social order than his own. He quite liked her, having an eye – although he was almost as old as Miss Rainbird – for a fine figure of a woman. He also knew perfectly well what kind of appointments Blanche was keeping with Miss Rainbird, not by the crude method of listening at keyholes or of encouraging other house servants to gossip. Some things he sensed, some he deducted, a few he postulated and with all of them he made what positive checks he could. Madame Blanche Tyler's profession was no secret to him since he had heard Mrs Cookson talking openly about her in this house. Quite genuinely, too, he had a high regard and affection for Miss Rainbird.

As he took Blanche's coat, he cleared his throat and said, 'Perhaps I should mention, Madame Blanche, that the mistress is not feeling very well today. It would be a kindness not to overtire her.'

'That's nice of you to tell me that, Syton.'

'Thank you, Madame.'

He moved away with her coat, not relishing being called Syton by someone who, he was sure, had gypsy blood in her.

Even if Syton had not told her, thought Blanche, she could have sensed and seen that the old girl had a very bad headache. Without the darkness under the eyes, the slight extra wrinkling at their corners and along the brow, she could have known because pain in others came over to her very often. She could pass a man or woman in the street, see their faces and know that there was a disturbance of their health or spirit at once.

She passed a few words of greeting with Miss Rainbird and then moved to her and said, 'Lie back in your chair more and we'll get rid of that headache before we begin, shall we?' She smiled warmly as she saw Miss Rainbird's surprise. 'The body

124

and the human spirit have many voices, you know, to tell us their feelings.'

'You could tell just by seeing me?' asked Miss Rainbird.

Blanche laughed. 'Yes, your pain is a purple and green halo. And anyway—' she knew that this was a good point to score – 'if I couldn't tell, I would have known because your butler out of consideration for you mentioned that he thought you were not quite yourself today. Rest your head against the back of the chair.'

Miss Rainbird dropped her head back and Blanche stood behind her and began to move her fingertips slowly across her forehead. After four or five passes Miss Rainbird felt the pain begin to go and, as it died away, she lay there thinking what an extraordinary woman this Madame Blanche was. There had been no need to mention Syton's comment. Surely, if she were even only partly a fraud, she would have been tempted to hide that fact. And she certainly had some power in her. It was almost as though she were drawing out the pain with her fingertips. It was a wonderfully soothing feeling.

When she had finished Blanche went back to her chair and said, 'You've never had that done to you before, Miss Rainbird?'

'No, I haven't. It's a wonderful gift.'

'It is – if people want me to use it.'

'Why shouldn't they?'

'Because some people are in love with their pain. They won't let it go. I can't do anything with that kind. They are poor, twisted souls whose happiness lies in their own afflictions. It takes a long, long time to do anything for them.' She gave one of her deep, bosomy laughs. 'I'll tell you something which I'd be crazy to do if I were charging you five guineas a cure. The next time you have a headache or migraine – just lie back in that chair, shut your eyes, and imagine that I am stroking your forehead. If you give yourself to the illusion with complete faith you will find yourself cured. Now—' a brisk note came to her voice, '—let's see what Henry and your dear ones on the far side have to say to us today.'

Miss Rainbird watched as Madame Blanche went into her

routine. It was familiar now, giving her no apprehension. She could watch without concern for the strains that seemed to take Madame Blanche's body and – she had to admit this to herself – look forward to the communications from Henry, Harriet and Sholto without any disrupting critical or sceptical overtones of thought. Belief or disbelief played no part now, she acknowledged, in the response of her intellect to this demonstration. Although she could be irritated now and then at some of the turns of the seance, the havering and lack of definition which seized one or other of the communicators at times, she knew that she had come to a point when she really quietly enjoyed it. Like a small girl, she told herself, enjoying a secret and satisfying dream world. And she knew herself to be grateful to Madame Blanche, if for nothing else than giving her a new experience at an age when she had thought the world had little new to offer her in personal novelties.

In a few moments Henry was through. His voice, coming from Madame Blanche, was bouncing and full of vigour and happily – Miss Rainbird realized – free of any of his usual poetic imagery.

'Tell your friend,' he said, 'that her brother and sister can't come just yet. In a little while they will, maybe.'

'Why can't they come?' asked Miss Rainbird. She was well used now, and not at all nervous about it, to putting questions to Henry.

'There is a matter of ... well, I suppose you would call it principle to be resolved. Up here we call it the Double Strand of Kindness.'

Madame Blanche said, 'That doesn't help us much, Henry.'

Henry said, 'You will have to be content for a little while. The Court of Higher Kindness will decide soon. But your friend must not be unhappy. There are some messages for her and some answers to the questions which she has in her mind at the moment.'

Madame Blanche, body limp and relaxed in her chair, her eyes shut and her mouth now drooping in its familiar, almost bucolic gape, said, 'You have questions, Miss Rainbird?'

'Yes, I have. We know the Shoebridge man—'

'Speak not without charity,' said Henry sharply.

'I'm sorry,' said Miss Rainbird. 'We know that Mr Ronald Shoebridge adopted the boy, and that he lived in Weston-super-Mare and became a successful garage owner. But where did the family go from there?'

To Miss Rainbird's surprise, Henry said, 'To a place I knew well. Sammy and I spent a holiday there once.'

'Sammy?' asked Madame Blanche.

'Brunel. Isambard Kingdom Brunel. I always call him Sammy. Yes, they went to Brighton. Looking back through the veils of the past I can see it. First as Sammy and I knew it, and then as it was when the Shoebridge family arrived. I see a large building on the seafront. A hotel. And in great silver letters I see the name across the front. Argenta.'

'Are you sure?' asked Miss Rainbird.

A little stiffly Henry said, 'There is no question of sureness. What I say is or was. Was in this case. The hotel is no longer there.'

'The Shoebridges had a hotel. And then what, Henry? Was it sold?' asked Blanche.

'It was sold and then much later pulled down. Ronald Shoebridge was a good man and a kind father and an honest harvester of his hard work in the fields of commerce.'

In a moment or two Miss Rainbird feared the poetry might start. She reprimanded herself for the thought and said, 'I'd like to know about the boy. About Edward. What did he do at Brighton?'

Henry said heartily, 'He went to college. He grew to manhood.'

'What college?' asked Madame Blanche. 'If we knew we might be able to trace him.'

Henry said sadly, 'Until the Court of Higher Kindness has decided there is no question of tracing him. But the name of the college is not in dispute. It was Lancing College, not far away along the coast. He grew in stature, learning and manliness there.'

Miss Rainbird said, 'Would you kindly explain to me what the Court of Higher Kindness is and what is its particular problem so far as the boy is concerned?'

Henry chuckled. 'The Court of Higher Kindness sits in every human heart. But only after the great crossing over is its wisdom fully operative. Kindness in the human heart is a seed that only comes to full flowering after the world has been left behind.'

It was a typical Henry answer, thought Miss Rainbird. The thought was without asperity or frustration, a purely intellectual comment. Not for the first time Henry through Madame Blanche became aware of her thoughts.

Henry said, 'Your friend is wedded to logic, Blanche. She sees life as a mathematical expression. So did I once. So did my great friend Brunel. Now we know better.'

Surprising herself, Miss Rainbird said briskly, 'How did you first meet Brunel?'

Henry chuckled. 'When he was twenty-five and was designing the suspension bridge over the Avon gorge at Bristol. I worked with him on it for some time. He was a great man. As far beyond me now as he was then. He has passed on to the Bright Circle. Ah—' He broke off for a moment and then said, 'Do you see her, Blanche?'

Madame Blanche said nothing, but a small groan broke from her and Miss Rainbird saw her body twist a little sideways in the chair as though she were in pain.

'Do you see her, Blanche?' asked Henry again.

Madame Blanche sighed, 'Yes ... Yes ... I see her. But she is surrounded by such light. It hurts the eyes to look. Ooooooh!'

The noise Madame Blanche made and a convulsive jerk of her body alarmed Miss Rainbird. This was something she had not met before. Then, overriding her alarm, driving all concern for Madame Blanche from her, she was aware of Harriet's voice coming from Madame Blanche.

'Tippy? ... Tippy, do you hear me? It's Flappy. It's Flappy here, darling ... No, no, don't say anything. Just listen. Tippy, dear, be kind to Madame Blanche ... In the end she will bring you full peace of mind ... the great peace you desire. Be kind, Tippy, for Madame Blanche too seeks peace, seeks the fulfilment of her heart's desire ...'

128

Harriet's voice died away. Madame Blanche was still and silent for a few minutes and then Miss Rainbird saw her stir, her large body moving back from slackness gradually, and then the opening of her eyes.

Madame Blanche looked at Miss Rainbird for a moment or two without speaking and then slowly smiled and fingered the pearls at her neck, and said, 'I have a great feeling of contentment. I'm sure that something good has happened. Tell me about it.'

'You don't remember anything?'

'Nothing. But I have this wonderful feeling of . . . how shall I say? Restful, peaceful exhaustion.'

Miss Rainbird got up and began to pour sherry for both of them. As she did so, without any personal feeling whatever, in a flash of detached lucidity, she said to herself, 'I really ought to have my head examined.' She began to tell Blanche all that had been said during the seance, all, that is, except the last passage between herself and Harriet. That, she felt, was a personal message which it was not necessary to make known to Blanche.

Miss Rainbird said, 'I don't understand about this Court of Higher Kindness, or what problem it has to resolve.'

Blanche sipped her sherry. She was a bit annoyed that she could remember nothing of the session herself. Henry seemed to cut her out in a quite arbitrary way at times. It was annoying because she ought to know everything that was going on. How could she pursue her ministry properly otherwise? Miss Rainbird no doubt gave as accurate an account as she could, but it was quite easy for her to miss something important.

She said, 'It's not difficult to understand. You see, there's a strong possibility that one or other of the Shoebridges has passed over. Maybe both. We must ask Henry about it the next time. If they have, they will know where Edward Shoebridge is. They will know his circumstances and his feelings. So you see, this might cause a conflict. Your sister wants him found and wants you to take him back into the family. But his foster mother and father may consider that this would be an unwise move – from his point of view.'

'I can't see why.'

'But you surely must, Miss Rainbird. Say we find him and you go to him and tell him the truth about his origins. He may be, probably is, a happily married man with children. You arrive and tell him that his life has all been based on a deceit. Not yours, not his. But a deceit none the less. You could find he would reject you instead of welcoming you. You could, in fact, by your revelation of the truth be the means of bringing real unhappiness into his life. I think this is what the Court of Higher Kindness is considering. Your sister's claim to have him acknowledged and possibly his foster-parents' claim for him to be left in peace for his own well-being. You do see that, don't you?'

'Yes, I do now that you explain it. But it seems very odd that it should be a matter that takes any great length of time. I'm quite happy to accept either solution so long . . .' She was going to say 'so long as it shuts Harriet up' but finished, '. . . as the best is decided for the . . . for my nephew.'

'That is the right attitude,' said Blanche, 'and it is all to your credit to adopt it.' Privately she felt that nothing would please the old girl more than to be able to wash her hands of the whole matter so long as Harriet troubled her no more. Well . . . that would have to be seen. She'd known cases before where the Court of Higher Kindness had made the most odd decisions. Human logic was one thing, ethereal logic another.

Before Blanche left Miss Rainbird went to her bureau and came back with an envelope and handed it to her. Blanche, who knew exactly what would be inside, said with a hint of surprise, 'Miss Rainbird?'

Miss Rainbird without any embarrassment said, 'You are giving me a lot of your time and a great deal of help and sympathy, Madame Blanche. It seems only right to do something for you . . . well, some sort of repayment.'

Blanche shook her head. 'There's no question of you paying me, Miss Rainbird. I want no money for myself. The service I perform is made freely and—'

'But please, Madame Blanche. You must let me do something.'

'Only if you genuinely wish to. But don't let's call it a payment. There are causes and desires dear to my heart which call for all the charity the world can spare. I shall regard this as a contribution to them. Some day, I hope, you will let me tell you about them in more detail.'

Blanche left and drove off with the envelope unopened in her coat pocket. She was a shrewd judge of human nature – far more so than she was of her own nature, which had vast areas where she still wandered in a state of mild confusion and half-comprehension. Miss Rainbird at this stage was good for twenty-five pounds, she guessed. When she opened the envelope much later and found the cheque was for fifty pounds, although she regarded it as a good omen for the future of the Temple of Astrodel, she acknowledged that she still had much to understand about Miss Rainbird.

This acknowledgement would have been further strengthened if she could have seen Miss Rainbird at her bureau just after she had left.

Miss Rainbird had written on a sheet of notepaper some headings of things she wanted to think over carefully. They read:

1. *Harriet's voice? Family likeness? Natural mimic.*
2. *Brunel, knowledge of.*
3. *Petnames. Tippy, Flappy?*
4. *Systematic investigation? Who? Lover? Ask Ida C.*
5. *Madame B's financial situation?*

As she read them through and thought about them, Miss Rainbird suddenly remembered how Henry had reprimanded her for speaking of Sholto's chauffeur as 'the Shoebridge man'. *Speak not without charity.* What cheek! It would be a miracle if that leopard had changed its spots. He and Sholto had been a fine pair, and between them they had landed her in this situation and, no matter about *de mortuis nil nisi bonum*, if Shoebridge were dead, the both of them had a long way to go before they would, if ever, reach the Bright Circle with Brunel.

She added to the list:

6. *Faith healing and telepathy. County Library for books.*

131

GEORGE FELT THAT he could easily become bad-tempered. He didn't want to because it was almost time for bed and Blanche had said she was staying the night. She'd come busting in an hour ago full of the joys of spring and floating on some private and invisible cloud of happiness. After a morning session with Lydia Angers and some more drink with his lunch and a two-hour car sleep that had done nothing to help a mild hangover, George felt that happiness and exuberance were out of place.

He'd entered up faithfully all he could remember of his Brighton information in his red notebook and had retailed it all to Blanche, who had listened over a couple of bottles of stout and had seemed in no way daunted by the fact that he considered he had come to a full stop as far as Edward Shoebridge was concerned.

'Two full stops,' he said crossly. 'One, because we're really up against a dead end. This Angers man was his closest friend – and he's lost track of him. And, two, because I've had enough. That's the truth, love. I've served you, endured for you, and faced mortal sin for you – God, you should have seen that woman! And now all I want you to do is sign that cheque and hand it back to me. Hundreds of unmade gardens wait for me.'

'But what you've got, George, isn't enough. There must be lots of paths that lead to Shoebridge. You've only proved that the Angers' one is blocked.'

'Then ask your blasted Henry to—'

'George!'

'Sorry. But I've had enough. Just give me my cheque and let's go to bed and forget it all.'

132

'I'm not going to forget anything, George. Why should I when everything's beginning to move so well? Miss Rainbird is coming round fast. Really cooperative.' Blanche decided to say nothing of the cheque for fifty pounds. 'And Henry has promised more help and the communication between us is really better than I've ever known it before.'

'Look, old girl, don't give me that. I'm fond of you. A bit touched about you, if you want the truth. And I'll admit you've got something which I don't understand. But overall, let's face it – you're running a racket. A nice, gentle racket, full of comfort for a lot of old biddies. But that's all it is. And I've helped you to the limit. And now I want help – five hundred quids' worth. Lumley's Sunshine Gardens. I want to feel I'm doing something in the world that counts, that isn't just for me but for others. Look – if you're really set about this, I'll tell you what. Give me the five hundred and I promise you that I'll find someone, some really good, discreet private agent to carry on for you. That's what you need now. Someone who's a real professional.'

'George – I've explained before why I can't do that. That kind of person could easily be unreliable. Before you know where you are you're being blackmailed or there's talk of going to the police. Not that there's anything wrong in what we're doing. But some types could easily make it look that way. What about the photo album? Wasn't there anything in that?'

George sighed. 'I've told you, Blanche. It was all the usual stuff. School groups, beach snaps. Shots of Shoebridge and Angers doing various things ... sailing, walking in the country, standing together by a car and drinking beer. Most of them, anyway, were of Mrs Angers. She was a good-looking piece when she was younger. No, Blanche – there's nothing. Now, don't get me wrong – but anything you want now you'll have to get from ... well, from higher sources.'

'There's a little trouble there at the moment. I can't go into it. But it means some delay. Anyway, I know how Henry expects me to work. If I do all I can, then he does all he can.'

'You mean if *I* do all I can.'

'Well, love, aren't we one and the same person really? We have this lovely understanding.'

'Then let's go to bed and have a spot of it now and forget Edward Shoebridge.'

You never knew, thought George, how Blanche was going to take a bawdy remark. Sometimes she was with you, giving one of her big laughs and going even further. And sometimes she just went all offended and put on her po-face. This time she gave him a gentle smile and sat back thoughtfully, playing with the pearls at her neck. After a moment she said, 'You're very coarse at times, George. But I don't mind, because there's a real core of goodness in you. And it's there tonight in great force. Your aura's coming over to me in great pulsating waves of iridescent colours . . . all the colours of the spectrum.'

George grinned. What a girl! So, he was all lit up like a Roman candle or a St Catherine's wheel. And he wasn't fooled. Something was coming.

'Let's have it, Blanche.'

Blanche said, 'I'll make a bargain with you. Don't sign off about this Shoebridge thing just yet. Give me two or three more days. You think about it all. Go over everything in your mind and see if anything suggests itself to you. Anything at all that will lead us further. Honest, love, there must be something an intelligent man like you can come up with.'

'But I don't want to come up with anything or go on with it.'

'Not for seven hundred and fifty pounds? It's yours if you can take us a bit further. And what's more, if you go so far as to find Edward Shoebridge, dead or alive, I'll make it a thousand. That's going to give you a much better start with your gardening caper.'

'It's no caper. And, Blanche, since when could you afford to hand out a thousand on a job like this?'

'Since Henry told me about the Temple of Astrodel and I met Miss Rainbird. She's not going to be mean with money once we find Edward Shoebridge. No matter how much she does or doesn't believe in me – she's hooked.'

134

'All right, she's hooked. But there's still me. So, I give you three or four more days. After that if nothing can be turned up, then I want a cheque – seven hundred and fifty pounds, plus expenses.'

'You shall have it, George. Would you like us to have a few moments' silent prayer to ask that for dear Miss Rainbird's sake we shall be guided to Edward Shoebridge? Prayer helps, you know.'

George stood up. 'You do the praying. I'm going to have a nightcap and then take Albert for a turn round the garden before bed.' As he passed by Blanche, he winked at her and reached down inside her dress and gave one of her breasts an affectionate squeeze. She might be a part phoney in some ways, he thought, but the rest of her was good, honest, generous human stuff. If there was going to be a garden around the Temple of Astrodel he'd like the contract for it. He'd bring that up some time, but not just now.

The small portable typewriter which Edward Shoebridge was using was a very cheap one, almost a child's toy machine. It was new. He had bought it at a Bristol stationer's shop four days previously. The sheet of notepaper in the machine was white, a small quarto size, and had been taken from a scribbling pad block which he had bought four months previously in London. He had worn gloves when he had purchased both block and typewriter. He wore gloves now. He had never touched either the machine or the block with his bare hands. When he had finished writing his two letters he would take the machine – ribbonless – from the house and drive west into Devon and drop it over a bridge into the Taunton–Exeter canal, into eight feet of water, there to settle deep into the soft silt of the bottom. The block and the ribbon he would burn before he left the house. He liked to do everything that he could well in advance. It gave him time for any rare after-thoughts to overtake him and changes to be made if necessary. So far he had never had to change anything in his past planning. There was no arrogance in him which made him think that this would always necessarily be so. His first letter, al-

135

ready written, was to go eventually to Grandison at the department. In substance it was much the same as the letters he had previously sent after the kidnappings of Pakefield and Archer. The second letter, not yet finished, would be delivered earlier – when the next kidnapping took place.

He was working at the console table in his cellar studio. A few feet from him on a small screen perch was his saker falcon, an adult female, hooded and belled, its feet linked with a five-inch spread of jesses. Stopping in his typing now to look at her, he remembered an occasion when Pakefield, the MP, had been in the other cellar. Her jesses had been longer then and she was given to sudden bouts of bating. He had switched on the intercom to pass a message and, wings threshing, she had jumped a few inches in the air so that she set her bell ringing sharply. She had come down clumsily on the perch, missing it and straddling her legs across it by the length of the jesses. He had switched off at once. Never again would any bird be in here when he was using the intercom. He remembered it now, thinking of the coming occupant of the cell. A small feather had been found in Archer's clothes, too, before he had been freed. When one played for large stakes success could so often turn on small details. If the falcon had called at the same time in her loud *gaay-gaaey-gaay* cry then the two men could have passed something on – feather, call and bell – which would have meant a lot to a trained ornithologist.

An envelope for the second letter, white, cheap, bought also in London and touched only with gloves, lay by the machine already addressed. The inscription read: *Sir Charles Medham, River Park. By Hand. Highly Confidential.*

Shoebridge typed on. The saker sat dozing on its perch. Outside it was daylight, a warm morning with March fast running out and the rooks in the elms behind the house long engaged at nest repairing and mating. When the letter was finished – copied from the draft that lay by the typewriter – Shoebridge read it without taking it from the machine.

On receipt of this, you will at once telephone Colonel Grandison at the Home Office and speak only to him. Any breach of this or the following instructions will put your guest's life in jeopardy.

Sir Charles Medham was an ex-diplomat. Reaching Grandison would present no problems to him, Shoebridge knew. He had to know. All planning was based on knowledge, success was a combination of time, place and people, all disposed to work for the advantage of the planner.

Your distinguished guest has been taken from you for the same reasons that the Right Hon James Archer and Richard Pakefield, MP were taken, and by the same person. At the moment he is safe and well.
You will – for his safety and reputation – observe the following conditions:
   1. Make known to your household that he has been called back urgently to London.

Sir Charles Medham had no wife to take into his confidence.

   2. Inform Grandison that no publicity whatever is to be given to this affair, and stress that any breach of this whatsoever will endanger your guest's life. Inform Grandison also that some press story must be issued to cover your guest's absence from official duties.
   3. Tell Grandison that as soon as he puts an announcement in the Personal column of the Daily Telegraph, *reading – Felix. All fine at home. Please write. John – a letter giving further instructions will be sent to him.*
   4. Inform Grandison that the ransom demanded is £500,000 to be paid as instructed later. The time period is eight days from your receipt of this. The same conditions as before apply to the return or elimination of your guest.
   On no account will you communicate with anyone else but Grandison. He will appreciate this.

Having read it, Shoebridge took it out of the machine and sealed it in the envelope, wetting the gum with a paintbrush from a glass of water on the console. The letter was no literary composition and he had not meant it to be. Grandison would know exactly the form. The only real risk was that some hint of the abduction should leak to the public. Sir Charles Medham was not the sort of man to need this point over-stressed.

He sat back in his chair, holding the letter in his gloved hand, looking at the saker. She was coming along fast. A desert bird, she was under training, beginning to lose her interest in ground prey, field mice, squirrels and rabbits. There were days now when she would wait on steadily while he flushed pigeon, rook and gull for her. When all this was finished there would be finer sport for her and the others ... heron, grouse and partridge and a great range of land and lake and sky to give them all freedom. It was all there waiting, but although he longed for it there was no impatience in him. Impatience could breed mistakes. One small mistake and his dream could crumble.

For that part of Somerset which lay in the area outlined by Bush the reports had come in quite promptly and had been analysed and processed into the computer by Sangwill. Among the hundreds of similar ones Shoebridge's called no attention to itself. *Edward Shoebridge, aged thirty-six, independent means, married, one son, aged fifteen, boarding school. Address, Highland House, near Blagdon. House, red brick, built 1936, elevated position, no cellars. Shoebridge hobby, training and flying falcons.*

The details were fed into the computer along with hundreds of others for the Somerset areas ... people who lived in brick and stone houses in elevated positions, people who kept ducks, domestic and ornamental, people who kept poultry commercially or for show purposes, breeders of game birds, and owners of game farms, small zoos, public pleasure grounds, and quite a few individuals whose interest in birds ran to the ownership of hawks, falcons, and aviaries full of foreign birds.

The particulars of Shoebridge's house were not accurate. Highlands had been built in 1936 on the site of an old stone house with a large cellar system under it. The house had become derelict and was pulled down by a Bristol builder who had sealed off the cellar system and built a new red-brick house over it. Edward Shoebridge had bought it in 1968 and some time after that had opened up the cellar system, but masking the entry to it so that its existence was not evident.

Edward Shoebridge and the few facts about him and his house became part of a mass of electronically coded information.

Bush, despite Grandison's advice, offered up no prayers to the god of chance. There was no Micawberish optimism in him that something would turn up if you believed it would. He was concentrating, without any success so far, on his list of golf-club names, knowing that with each day that passed the moment for the third strike was growing closer. In effect Bush's department and the whole of the police resources at his disposal had run into a dead end. It was a situation quite common with the police and they were used to dealing with it phlegmatically. However, although cases were pigeon-holed in dead files, the word 'dead' to the police implied that at any time the god of chance might bring the corpse to life. This was a philosophy foreign to Bush. For every problem there was a logic to solve it. Hard work and a strict analysis of detail meticulously collected was the only method which could bring success. The possible intervention of chance held no interest for Bush. He was an arrogant man.

Thinking it over George had decided that he had nothing to lose by humouring Blanche. He was going to get his seven hundred and fifty pounds plus expenses anyway and for a little more effort he might get a thousand without interrupting his plans for setting up Lumley's Sunshine Gardens.

Mrs Angers, he realized on reflection, had fairly thrown him. At any other time and in another mood he might have gone along with her. No good saying he wouldn't, because he might have done. A minor bacchanalia made a change now and then, and she wasn't all that far gone. Good figure in parts still, and they could have had a happy gin session to be topped off by a satisfying romp. Point was, he told himself, he'd still got nothing from her of any importance. She really didn't know much about Shoebridge, nor had she known him well. All her stuff was second-hand from her husband. He was the chap to deal with. He knew the name of his firm in London. He was ready to bet that Mrs Angers would have said nothing about his visit. She had probably gone back into the room, given a couple of curses at a flown opportunity, and then consoled herself with more gin and forgotten him. Anyway, if Angers did know about him, he'd done nothing wrong and he felt he could handle him.

So George decided to go to London to see Angers. While he was there he could see a friend of his in the motor-trade and find out the form about a van.

Two days after his visit to Mrs Angers, George called at eleven-thirty in the morning to see Mr Angers at the offices of Worth & Freen Ltd – Shop Fittings and Hotel Services – in the Tottenham Court Road.

It was a modern office block, full of glass and shiny pine wood. The girl at the desk said that Mr Angers was in, but if he hadn't an appointment would he mind filling in a memo to go up to him, stating his business.

George pondered this one, then wrote on the slip his own name, adding the name and address of a real firm of solicitors in Salisbury (often used by him before, though they had no knowledge even of George's existence) because he knew that shrewd types sometimes made a quick check through telephone directories. Under *Business*, he wrote – *Legal matter re old friend of yours Edward Shoebridge – and to his advantage*. He had no qualms about that. In a way he was trying to sort out an inheritance problem.

He waited fifteen minutes and then he was shown up to Angers' room. George put Angers at a little older than himself, and certainly much less fit. He'd had a plump look in some of the album photographs. Now he was fat, two chins and big paddle-like hands, dark-brown eyes and crisp, short black hair – which, George guessed, must be murder to comb.

George said, 'It's good of you to spare me your time, Mr Angers.'

'Time you can have, Mr Lumley. Money comes harder.' He gave a belly laugh which made the cloth of his waistcoat strain across his stomach. 'Anyway, anything for an old friend. How'd you get on to me?'

'Well ... it's a long story – but eventually through your wife. She was kind enough to give me your business address. Said you might help. It's a matter of a legacy. Can't say more than that, you'll appreciate.'

'Eddie won't say no to money. I'll tell you that.' He paused, eyed George quizzically for a while and then asked, 'You the chap who went out of the window?'

Momentarily George considered a lie, and then decided against it. 'Well ... Yes.'

Angers laughed. 'Don't worry about it. Good old Lydia, tells me everything, and half the time I don't want to know. Compulsive drinker, compulsive confessor. Just compulsive. Lovely girl when I married her. Still lovely in some ways. But a handful. Even if I weren't a Roman Catholic I wouldn't divorce her. Always stick to a bargain, even when it goes partly bad on you. That's me. Thanks for going out of the window. A lot of 'em don't. Now then – Eddie Shoebridge. But first let's have a drink.'

He got up and padded to a cupboard and came back with a bottle of champagne and two glasses. 'Only drink that fits the morning. Clean on the palate, gentle on the head, and sharpens the appetite.'

As Angers began to twist the wire from the cork, George said, 'You were at school with Shoebridge.'

'Eddie? Yes. Also worked with him and his old man at the Argenta – you know all about that? Must do to be here. Lost sight of him. Met up again in the South of France. Then got this job and bought the house his old man left him. He stayed abroad for a while. Hard worker, shrewd with money. Like his old man. The old boy must have been worth a bit when he died.' The cork flew and hit the far wall. 'Here we are then, the stuff that makes girls giggle. Or used to. Knocking back the gin and whisky they are these days before lunch.'

He filled their glasses and they drank.

George said, 'When did you last see him?'

'God knows. Some years ago. Here in London. He'd been back from abroad for about a year. No job as far as I could tell. Fancy, too, he wasn't quite as well heeled as he used to be ... Well, I suppose I'd better be honest. He'd had a lot of money from his old man, but he'd come a bit of a cropper speculating in hotel property and building. Mostly abroad. Majorca. Spain. Tricky places they were in those days. Still can be. Bang went his dream!'

'Dream?'

Angers chuckled. 'Young men stuff. When we were working together. He was going to make a million before he was thirty-five and then clear out. He was mad, you know. Oh, pleasantly mad, but mad. Didn't like people. Not individuals, but people in the mass. Everyone talks about conservation now and pollution of the environment, but he was at it when we were at school. Lydia show you some pictures?'

'Some.'

'Don't be embarrassed. The old album on the settee has trapped plenty of weaker men than you. Anyway, you must have seen one or two of him and me with birds. Feathered of course. Kestrels, sparrow hawks, hobbies, merlin – spent all his money on them and trained them. Mad on animals – and madder still against the way the world was slowly making scores of 'em extinct.'

'What would he have done with his million?'

'Cleared out. Bought himself an island, or some great chunk of land in Ireland, Wales or Scotland, put a bloody great fence round it and kept people out of it – except for the few he could trust. Some dream, but he was going to make it real – that takes money.'

'He probably never made it.'

'Probably. What about your little bonus?'

George shook his head. 'Any man would be glad to have it, but it wouldn't buy any paradise.'

'Well, there it is. We all have dreams. No harm in that. But we've still got to get the eight-thirty in the morning.' He reached over and topped up George's glass.

George said, 'Any idea how I could find him?'

'None.'

'He was married, wasn't he?'

'Was. She was killed in a car accident. Left him with a small boy. He could have married again, but he didn't mention it when I last saw him.' Angers was silent for a moment. 'If he did come a cropper and is kicking around somewhere, your little bit of bunce would be welcome. Tell you what I'll do – I'll make a few inquiries round the trade. Somebody might know something. I'd like to see old Eddie again. If I get anything I'll phone your firm.'

'It would be better if you phoned me direct. You see, I only work as a sort of freelance agent for them and I do most of it from home.'

'Stick it down there, then.' Angers pushed across the memo form George had filled out. George wrote down his telephone number. Angers watching him, went on, 'Must be interesting, your job. Tracing people. Shouldn't really be so difficult these days. We're all down somewhere. Passports, National Insurance Cards. What about sticking an advertisement in the papers?'

'We've done that,' lied George. 'No good.'

'You could go through all the telephone books. Not such a common name, Shoebridge. He'd be on the phone for sure. You might end up with, say, five hundred names. Let's see, at an average of tenpence a call that would be fifty quid. Take a long time of course.'

The idea didn't appeal to George. He finished his drink and rose. 'Well, you've been very good to see me. Won't take up more of your time.' Angers was a dead end. Still, it had been worth a try.

'No trouble. Bit of a slack morning. Always nice to share a drink with someone. If I come up with anything I'll give you a ring. I must say I'd like to see Eddie again. We let our friends go too easily. That's business for you. All good pals, fat smiles and expense-account lunches and order books at the ready. All go. Like a lot of bloody ants. Build it up and pull it down. Make it bigger and better and a different shape so you can't

143

recognize where you are any more. Eddie was right. Give me a million and I'd put in a central heating system and live at the North Pole.'

As George moved away down the passage outside, he could hear Angers laughing still. He'd liked him, but he had no real hope of ever hearing from him. Look up all the E. Shoebridges in all the telephone directories! Well, he could put it to Blanche. Up to her. She paid the expenses. But she'd have to find someone else to do that job. Say there were five hundred numbers (and none of them the Shoebridge you wanted), that would average something like five minutes a call, two thousand five hundred minutes; that was getting on for fifty hours. Fifty hours on the telephone! A man would be dead of frustration and nervous exhaustion!

The report to the department on Edward Shoebridge had not given a telephone number. The police could have supplied it if asked, although the number was not listed in the book. It was ex-directory.

From the County Library in Winchester Miss Rainbird borrowed three or four books on Spiritualism. For a couple of days she immersed herself in them with a great deal of interest. What is Spiritualism? Credulity and the 'Will to Believe'; Trance States, Hypnosis and the Power of Suggestion: Paranormal Phenomena; Spiritual and Faith Healing – she read all the arguments and explanations and theories, being as fair-minded as she could, and eventually ended up, as a lot of people had done before her, with the conclusion that knowledge of these matters from a scientific standpoint was still elementary and that no positive verdict could be pronounced on them. She bought herself copies of the *Psychic News* and *Two Worlds* and wished she hadn't. She found them all vulgar in tone and far too partisan and did not relish reading articles entitled 'Survival is Not too Good to be True', 'Your World could be a Kingdom of Heaven', 'The Grave is not the End', and 'Seances Reveal a Brilliant Spirit Plan'. Nor did she care for headlines such as 'Astral Visitor hears concert in Beyond',

'Spirit World has no Millionaires', and 'I was convinced by my Mother's Spirit Message'.

Reviewing the list of points and doubts which Madame Blanche's seances had thrown up, she decided that so far it was possible to explain them all in non-spiritualistic terms. That Madame Blanche went into a trance and was a highly imaginative and intelligent woman she conceded. It was possible that Madame Blanche was, without knowing it, deceiving herself. And there was every possibility that Madame Blanche had some telepathic powers. There wasn't any doubt at all that she had worldly sources of information. She was prepared to concede her healing powers, but here again the decision was paralleled by the possibility that she, herself, was subject to heterosuggestion. If a child hurt its finger and you said you would kiss it to make it well, it often worked. In fact, in her reading and thinking about spiritualism she found many traces of childishness. But then again, she could hear Blanche – or more likely that old bore Henry – answering this by saying 'Unless we can all revert to the pure white innocence of a child then there is no understanding, no way through the Gates of Higher Understanding.' She had a little giggle to herself about that one. However, so far as the truth of spiritualism was concerned she would admit no more than that no positive verdict could be pronounced.

This did not stop her, though, from making her own personal decision so far as further seances with Madame Blanche were concerned. At the lowest level the woman had been an entertainment. At a higher stage she had undoubtedly tided her over a bad patch of insomnia and the disturbing dreams about Harriet. That she had suffered this period, she told herself, must have been due to a general debility, the body's and the mind's lack of vigour at a dead season of the year. Now with spring on the doorstep, bright vanguard of the summer to come – she could do as well as Henry any day – she felt so much better suddenly that she could rebuke herself for what she now saw as a temporary weakness. Old she might be, but to be old, gullible and ready to lap up false comforts she would not be. So Henry had worked on the Clifton Suspension

Bridge with Brunel in eighteen-thirty-when-ever-it-was. Well, it was all in the encyclopaedia or whatever book Madame Blanche had chosen to consult when she had decided to make Henry a railway engineer.

No, when Madame Blanche came this evening she would let her go through the seance and then tell her, nicely, but firmly, that she had decided to have no more to do with the whole business. There was no need for further payment. The fifty pounds she had already given more than covered all the services rendered. She didn't want to be bothered with Harriet any more – and certainly not with Sholto. The less she thought about him the better. As for her own conscience about Harriet's child ... Really, why had she ever fussed about it? Something that had happened donkey's years ago and was nothing to do with her now. She'd give a handsome donation to the *Save the Children Fund* and forget the whole thing.

For various reasons, the seance that evening made Miss Rainbird slightly bad-tempered. To begin with, Madame Blanche was wearing a ridiculously short skirt for a woman of her age and figure and a very tight silk sweater that came up under her plump chin in a little rolled collar from which in one long loop her pearls swung down into her lap. She was made-up rather more than usual and Miss Rainbird suspected that she had been drinking. Blanche had. She had dropped George at the Grosvenor in Stockbridge and had had a couple of gins with him before coming to Reed Court. Later they were going to dinner at the Pheasant on the way home along the Stockbridge–Salisbury road.

And then, irritatingly, Henry was at his most poetic. He'd described Ronald Shoebridge prospering not – as Miss Rainbird would have thought – like a green bay tree, but from industry, intelligence and wisdom, and the boy burgeoning into manhood and taking his place alongside his father, his eyes alight with a fervour to be worthy of his parents. Harriet had sent a second-hand message about the young man – in typical Harriet terms, Miss Rainbird had to admit. 'As a young man he was so handsome. Like a young god. Fair-haired, and brown-skinned and strong, Grace. What a pity neither of us could have known him then. He would have given us so much happiness, so much to look forward to on his behalf. Thankfully, he really took after me in looks.' And thankfully a little later Henry had gone on to describe the last resting place (of their earthly bodies only) of Ronald Shoebridge and his wife ... a small graveyard in a Sussex village close to the downs where the larks hymned their praise to all creation in the cerulean deep blue above (if there was one thing that Miss Rainbird couldn't stand it was tautology in speech or writing), and where yews and larches cast their sweet shade across the greensward and the moss-dappled ancient headstones.

She must have been mad, Miss Rainbird told herself, to have put up with this nonsense so long. Anyway, it was a relief to know the Shoebridges were dead – she hoped Madame Blanche's information on that point was accurate. Alive, they were still capable of trouble if it suited them. Henry fluted on in his lyric voice, slightly touched, Miss Rainbird realized now, with something of Blanche's own accent, describing Edward Shoebridge, the young man, drawing other young men to him like bees to the honeysuckle bloom. Miss Rainbird, who, though a spinster, was fully aware of the varieties of now permissive relationships, thought that Henry's description was close to ambiguity, but she forgot about it as Henry said that the Court of Higher Kindness had now reached a decision. Ronald Shoebridge and his wife had appeared before it and had said that as far as they were concerned it would only increase their ethereal happiness if Miss Rainbird found their darling Eddie and led him back into his rightful inheritance, into the bosom of his true family, to warm, comfort and enrich the remaining years of his dear aunt's life. He had travelled far, but the days of his wandering were numbered. Reed Court would ring with the sound of happy laughter and young feet, for when he came he would bring a son. It was a prospect that at the moment held no pleasure for Miss Rainbird. A boy about the place would upset everything, mud tracks on the polished boards and the great stairway, bicycle marks over the lawn, branches broken off her shrubs, and probably speaking with some dreadful accent as the sons even of some of her well-connected, wealthy friends did these days ... and all looking like gypsies even though they went to Marlborough and Wellington, and worse still when they went off to University ... living with equally disreputable girls, taking drugs and spending half their time marching up and down protesting against this and that when they should be studying. 'They will come,' Henry had finished, 'as the swallows, parched and made homesick by the African sun, follow the mysterious highways of Heaven and turn northwards and homewards in spring to claim the shelter and sanctuary of the places that saw their birth.'

Madame Blanche came out of her trance and said that she could remember nothing. For a moment or two Miss Rainbird was undecided. It was going to be an awkward moment telling the woman that she did not want her to come again. Treated as a private entertainment it had its refreshing as well as irritating moments, but to continue with the seances for such reasons would be in distinct bad taste. She poured them both glasses of sherry, sat down, sipped, and then decided to be quite straightforward.

'Madame Blanche, I think I—'

Blanche gave a little shake of her head and interrupted her quickly. 'No, no – you don't have to say it, Miss Rainbird. All the time that Henry was using me, I could feel it. I was standing away from my own body, leaving it for Henry to use, hearing nothing that he was saying. I was only hearing you.'

'But I said nothing, Madame Blanche.' Miss Rainbird was puzzled.

'Oh, yes, Miss Rainbird, you did. You said everything to me. In words and in feeling. It began the moment I came into the room.' Blanche drained her sherry and put the glass down, smiling at Miss Rainbird. 'Your mind was an open book. You don't want me to come any more. I won't give you the reasons because you know them.' Blanche stood up. 'I've told you that I can't do anything for those who don't want me to. I'm very sorry, not for myself but for you and for those who belong with you. I shall go now and you need say no more on the subject.'

148

Touched by Madame Blanche's tact, and impressed, too, by her prescience, Miss Rainbird said, 'I am very, very sorry. But my mind is made up.'

Blanche rose and said, 'The mind is only part of the spirit, Miss Rainbird. And our spirit is something we only hold in trust until the moment of true revelation comes. You have chosen to resist the unknown. I am happy for you because that is the way, the only way, some people can find their comfort. Please don't look so unhappy.' Blanche laughed. 'This has happened to me many times. I have failed. Not you.'

Sitting in the room by herself, Miss Rainbird heard the sound of Madame Blanche's car driving away. For a moment or two she felt a deep sense of loss.

Lying in bed the next morning, waiting for George to bring up her toast and coffee, Blanche considered Miss Rainbird. She had a slight headache which she knew would go with her coffee. Now and again she and George liked to have dinner out and do themselves well. It had been one o'clock before they had got to bed and finished a splendid evening together. She liked old George. In different circumstances she would have married him long ago and then set-to and made him make something out of himself. So far she had not told him that Miss Rainbird had signed off. This was principally because she knew that there was a high probability that Miss Rainbird would call for her again. She knew the type.

On the table in the sitting-room when she had entered last night there had been a pile of library books – these wealthy old lady types never bought books, they went to the free libraries – and the title of the top one had been *Spiritualism: A Critical Survey* by Simeon Edmunds. Just seeing it had opened up all Miss Rainbird's thoughts to her. She could almost list the explanations Miss Rainbird had accepted ... mental telepathy, auto- and hetero-suggestion, the discreet collection of information presented as revelation from the life beyond and so on. She'd been through it all before. She knew her gifts and she knew all the approaches and reactions. She'd had a few Miss Rainbirds in her time. And, to be honest, some of them had

never come back. But most of them did, and she knew that
Miss Rainbird would come back. Henry had led her to Miss
Rainbird, Henry had put the dream of the Temple of Astrodel
in her mind, Henry would never fail her. Yes, Miss Rainbird
would come back. She was the kind who, ill, shouted for a
doctor, and then, well, kept him waiting for his bill. At the
moment she suffered no bad dreams, no qualms of conscience
... but something would happen. Sooner or later she would
call for her. Until then she was content to wait. The only thing
that would make her, Blanche, go to Miss Rainbird was if
George turned up the address of Edward Shoebridge and she
could give him a quick look-over quietly and decide what line
to take with the old girl. But at the moment that seemed more
and more like a long shot. She had a group meeting at her
house at three. When it was all over and her clients gone, she
would go back on her own to Henry and have a talk with him
and see what he had to say about the position. Already she
knew he would be working on it. Henry was an engineer and
an architect. He loved building and she knew he couldn't wait
to see the beginning of the Temple. Of course, he would want
to have a say about its layout. She could see that she would
have to be firm about that with him. The Temple of Solomon
was more his style.

George appeared in the doorway in his dressing-gown and
pyjamas, carrying the breakfast tray. He looked worn out and
ten years older than he was. As he put the tray down on the
edge of the bed and groaned at the pain in his head, Blanche
grinned and said, 'You never learn, do you? It's always that
last large brandy when you get home that's the killer, Georgie,
love. Come here and I'll fix it for you. Coffee won't touch
what you've got.'

He sat down on the bed with his back to her and she began
to run her fingers over his forehead from behind. After a moment or two his body slumped gently at the beginning of relief
and he said, 'Whatever else you may fake, you've really got
something in your fingers.'

'Well, we can't have you moping around all day, can we?
You want to be fit for the day's work.'

'What day's work is that?'

'Those telephone numbers. You're going to go into Salisbury to the General Post Office and go through all the telephone directories you can find—'

'I'm bloody not!'

'You bloody are. You'll find all the E. Shoebridges you can and make a list of them. Just make a list of them and let me have it. That's all. And when you get back you can have your seven hundred and fifty.'

George swung round. 'You mean it?'

'I gave my word.'

'Blanche – you're a great girl.' He turned to put his arms around her and the breakfast tray tilted and the pot fell over, spilling hot coffee across the bed.

George went off at ten o'clock and Blanche stayed behind to tidy up the cottage and to wash out the coffee-stained bedcover and sheet.

At half-past ten the telephone rang. Blanche answered it.

A man's voice said, 'May I speak to Mr Lumley, please.'

'I'm sorry, he's not here at the moment. Can I take a message?'

'Oh . . .' the voice was hesitant and disappointed.

Blanche said, 'Who is it speaking, please?'

'Well, this is Angers – Worth & Freen Ltd. He came—'

'Oh, yes, Mr Angers. He told me all about you. Is it in connection with Mr Shoebridge?'

'Well, yes it is.' Angers' voice brightened, and went on, 'Excuse the question, but the matter's rather confidential. Who am I speaking to?'

Blanche laughed. 'You needn't worry, Mr Angers. I know all about it. This is Mrs Lumley. I do all George's secretarial work for him.'

'Oh, I see. Well, that's all right then. Sorry to be cagey, but you never know, do you? Solicitor's stuff and all that.'

Blanche took the chance, knowing she was risking nothing. 'Well, if you'd rather speak to him—'

'No, no. If you'd give him a message. Tell him I've got the

address. It's Highlands House, near Blagdon, Somerset.'

'Hold on a minute, I'll just write that down.' Blanche wrote the address down on the telephone pad and said, 'He'll be most grateful to you, Mr Angers.'

'Well, tell him it was no trouble. Just thought it over and had a brain wave. Eddie and I were both keen on falconry. He still is. I suddenly remembered we had both joined the British Falconers' Club years ago. Must say I let my membership go, but it struck me Eddie might still be a member.'

'That was very clever of you.'

Angers laughed, 'I'm a bright boy sometimes, Mrs Lumley. Anyway, I phoned the secretary, told him I used to be a member – he was cagey and checked this, I must say – and wanted to trace my old chum Edward Shoebridge. He gave me the address at once. Not keen on handing out addresses, some of these societies. Quite right too. All sorts of types around. The secretary didn't have a telephone number. Said he thought it was ex-directory. Sounds like Eddie – keep the world away from his door. Tell your husband when he sees Eddie to mention me. Tell him to look me up. Or give me a ring. Like to see him again.'

'Of course. I'll do that. Thank you again, Mr Angers. George's firm will be very pleased about this. And so, of course, will Mr Shoebridge eventually.'

Angers chuckled, 'Tell him not to spend it all on wine, women and song. Not that he's likely to. Probably buy himself a golden eagle.'

When they rang off, Blanche looked at the address. It was amazing how things turned out. Henry hadn't waited for her to approach him that afternoon. He had known and acted. In a way, of course, it had been George's doing. But who had put the thought of the falconry club into Angers' mind? Why ... Henry, of course. Already foreseeing and controlling events.

As she tore the page off the pad and put it in her bag, another thought came into her mind. Technically George could claim that he had earned the thousand pounds. If she told him she'd got the address he certainly would claim it and make a terrible fuss if she didn't pay. But having the address didn't necessarily mean that the Rainbird situation was resolved. She would have to wait and see about that when she'd looked Edward Shoebridge over. In the circumstances it would be better to say nothing to George yet. She'd pay him his seven hundred and fifty pounds, and then, eventually, if things turned out right, she'd pay him another two hundred and fifty. But, until she had seen Shoebridge and had further direction from Henry, it was better to keep things to herself. What George didn't know wouldn't fuss him. Thank goodness Shoebridge didn't have a telephone number. George might have come roaring back with it!

CHAPTER EIGHT

REMEMBERING WHAT HAD happened the first time she had decided not to see Madame Blanche any more, Miss Rainbird was prepared for some form of self-induced dreams again about Harriet and perhaps even for an onset of bad migraines. If they did return she was prepared to resist them until they went of their own accord.

It was refreshing to find that after four or five days she had had neither bad dreams nor headaches. In fact she felt much better in herself than she had done for many months. Spring was on its way and there was a lot of garden planning to organize, and she felt, too, that it was time the large sitting-room and her own small room were redecorated. While she was having the rooms done she decided that she would furnish them with new curtains. That gave her a good excuse to spend a night in London and do some shopping at Harrods. Perhaps, after all, this whole stupid affair had arisen because she had let herself go, fallen into a recluse-like state and hadn't been taking enough interest in outside things. At seventy-plus the mind and body had to be kept active. But between bullying the gardener and exhausting the patience of shop assistants at Harrods and changing her mind two or three times with the builder over the colour schemes for the new decorations, she did find some moments when she thought of the Shoebridge family.

It was quite clear that Ronald Shoebridge had become a success of a kind. Perhaps it was charitable to assume that there always had been some good qualities there. Probably the man while at Reed Court had only followed the tune which Sholto had called. Anyway, they were all dead now, Harriet, Sholto, and the two Shoebridges. They could not bother her any longer. But Edward Shoebridge and his son, and possibly a wife, still remained. It would have been less than human of her not to have had a natural curiosity about them. Strictly speaking, when she died, Edward Shoebridge as her nearest relative should inherit her estate. At the moment, as her will stood, she had left very large bequests to half a dozen charities, but these did not make very much impression on the bulk of her fortune. She had at first been very concerned about the disposal of this, but in the end, after consultation with her solicitor, she had decided to leave it all – including Reed Court – to the National Trust Fund. The house was very old and very beautiful and full of fine furniture and paintings. It was pleasant to think that it would all stay exactly as she had known it. It was less pleasant to think of the troops of visitors who would be admitted to the house and grounds. Lumping great children with their vulgar parents picnicking in the gardens, moving through the rooms and, she had no doubt, making facetious remarks ... However, she personally would be spared that. In fact – she played with the idea – if this Edward Shoebridge and his family were really the right sort of people (and let's face it, he carried Harriet's blood partly, and the Irish side of him was, she had always understood, very well connected), it would be much better if Reed Court could go on as a real family home. Museums were all right in their place, but the continuity of line, the attachment of one family to a house, was vastly preferable ... Perhaps what she ought to do now was to get her solicitor to engage a thoroughly reliable man to trace Edward Shoebridge and – without Shoebridge knowing – submit a confidential report so that she could make a decision one way or the other without incurring any unpleasantness. Really, why had she ever taken up with Madame Blanche? She must have been thoroughly run down. Well, that was finished. As for doing it on her own, through her solicitor, she would think it over for a while. At the moment she had quite enough on her hands. The builder simply had no idea of how she wanted the rooms. She would have to get a good interior designer who would understand at once what she had in mind ...

*   *   *

It was the week-end before Blanche could go to Blagdon. She had various appointments and meetings which could not be cancelled. It was a Saturday when she went. She said nothing to George. Whenever she wanted to see him she just turned up at the cottage, or dropped into the Red Lion to find him. And at the moment – since he was free of his Shoebridge inquiries for good – he was immersing himself in the arrangements for setting up Lumley's Sunshine Gardens Limited. It might be very *limited*, Blanche thought, as she drove the sixty-odd miles west to Blagdon. George usually took off like a rocket on any new project and then gently fizzled out and came down like a burnt stick. With burnt hands, too, often; ending worse off than he had started. Poor old George. She really hoped he would make things go this time. Maybe he would. It was at least a more promising idea than all the others. They had been get-rich-quick stunts that had never stood a chance. This one at least meant putting his back into some hard work. Though if he wanted the cottage to be any advertisement for his new venture he ought to do something about the garden there first ... a wilderness of weeds and tall grass and those precious birds of his still hanging on. They were the last that remained of his previous grand scheme. Breeding cage and aviary birds. She smiled to herself as she drove, hearing him say 'Every home needs a bird in a cage. What boy or girl doesn't pester mother for a canary or budgerigar? Talking mina birds, parrots, African finches. In time I'll put in electrically heated cages and runs, breed, import and sell retail and to the trade. It's a gold mine!' With George it was always a gold mine. But in the end it always came back to the same thing. George in his cottage with his monthly remittance cheque. He'd get older and older, shabbier and more untidy but the last thing to change would be his optimism. When he was seventy he'd be still having bright ideas.

It was a fine morning. The sun cast a mildness over the windless day, and the sky was as blue as a hedge-sparrow's egg. There was the faintest touch of green in places along the hedgerows and now and again in some village the pink and white explosion of cherry and almond blossom. Blanche liked

156

driving. She liked travelling. She was after all the child of travellers. She'd come a long way from her early caravan and fairground life, but the countryside and the changing towns and villages still pulled at her as she passed through them. You never got it out of your blood, she thought. Her old Mum at home now, comfortably settled, wouldn't think twice of going back even at her age. Breaking the ice on the water buckets. The town or village children staring at you, full of envy, as though you'd come from outer space. Dogs, horses, shining brass, painted wagon-sides and the smell of wood smoke ... They had posh jobs now, modern caravans and trailers. Shiny cars in the place of horses, but the life was the same. Bunching up wild daffodils and primroses to sell around the houses. Her old Mum with a red scarf drawn tight, gypsy fashion, over her head, big gold earrings, staring into the crystal ball or reading a palm. That's where she'd got it, of course. She was one of the *fascino* people, right down the female line. She'd done well. Made herself what she was by her own efforts. Always reading and improving herself. Snotty-nosed Blanche Tyler, now Madame Blanche Tyler who was going to have the Temple of Astrodel and bring comfort, consolation and happiness to hundreds.

She sat at the wheel of the small car, driving expertly and carefully, a large, amply-endowed woman wearing a small fur hat, sheepskin driving coat and gloves, and a red jacket and skirt, the string of pearls tight around her neck like a collar above the green silk blouse. On the back seat was a little zip-fastened plastic bag with her lunch in it. A leg of cold chicken and a slice of breast, salad, a roll, and half a bottle of vin rosé. When she was out on her own she liked to find some picturesque spot where she could park and eat, feeling and seeing the countryside around her. George would head for the nearest pub. Not her. Just as the inner eye was rested and refreshed by the vast perspectives of eternity, so was the physical eye cleansed and awakened by the wide sweep of woods and downs.

Somewhere Henry was watching her. Somewhere ahead in time destiny was shaping already the foundations of their

Temple. People would flock to it to hear her services and to wait for the messages that would come flowing through her. 'You Madame ... No, the one on the outside of the back row. Yes, you. I have someone here ... I get the name Bert or is it Bill? ... He passed over not long ago and he wants you to know...'

She came down the hill to the lake at Blagdon and pulled the car off into a small layby among trees where she could look across the wide stretch of the waters. Ahead of her the road ran across the dam. The village straggled on the steep hillside beyond. She put two or three tissues across her lap and began to have her lunch, watching the water. It was a trout fishing lake, she knew. All watchfully preserved. If her father had come down here in the old days he'd have had a few night lines out. Fat trout for breakfast. Rabbit, hare, pheasant and partridge ... the flavour went from food when you cooked it under a roof. She was completely happy and relaxed. It was good to have a day out by yourself – even if she did have to do a little business. But that was no trouble. The moment she had found out a few things about Shoebridge she would know how to handle Miss Rainbird. She mustn't overlook the fact, either, that if the circumstances were right this Edward Shoebridge might well be good for a contribution towards the Temple ... After all, the bearer of good news deserved some measure of thanks.

A heron flapped lazily across the lake and Blanche poured herself some vin rosé and watched the sun sparkle of the waters glow pinkily through the liquid as she raised the glass before her in a silent toast to a happy day.

As Blanche was having her early lunch, Edward Shoebridge and his wife were leaving their house. They travelled together in a small closed van which they had owned for a couple of years. Before they reached their destination they would stop and put false plates on the van. There was little talk between them. They both knew exactly what they had to do. In the past they had always had to use a stolen car as well as the van. This time there was no need. When the kidnapping had been done

158

and the letter delivered to Sir Charles Medham there would be no alarm raised until Grandison had been spoken to. There would be no police checks, no road cordons. Only the very highest echelons of the police service would ever know what had happened. Their security lay first of all in Sir Charles Medham's discretion, which they knew would not fail them, and then later in the official conspiracy to avoid all publicity. This time their operation could be simpler and would involve less risk. The victim had been studied for two years quietly and unobtrusively. Three times a year he spent a weekend with his old friend Sir Charles Medham and the visits were almost rituals, fixed by habit and accepted customs. No hunter could hope for success unless he knew the movements and habits of his prey. Habit dominated largely the life of man and beast, habit arising from need, from sentiment, from custom. The barn owl made its forays, and the fox worked field, down and woodland at night to a close set of patterns.

It took Blanche some time to find Highlands House. It was about three miles from Blagdon, standing on the high rolling plateau of the Mendips with a view north and west to the Bristol Channel and the wide marsh plains below. From a small side road, a rough, stone-walled drive about two hundred yards long led to the house. On two sides it was surrounded by a narrow clump of elms through which the drive passed. On the other two sides the back quarters of the house looked out over a steep slope towards the east and south and the distant Blagdon and Chew Lakes. It was a red-bricked house with a stone stable and garage block to one side, these part of the older house which had once stood there. At the back of the house were two grass paddocks, enclosed by stone walls. In the front the driveway ran up between two long, wide strips of grass lawn, each with a rose bed in its centre. It was an ugly, unwelcoming house, isolated, wind-swept, and the two rose beds the only attempts at giving it any attraction. Nesting rooks were busy in the high branches of the elms.

Miles from anywhere, thought Blanche. Perched on top of the world. Driveway and grass well-kept and the doorways and window-frames well maintained. It was a house which would not have appealed to many people. Perhaps only to someone who wanted to keep away from the modern world and its people.

She drove past the front door and parked the car close to the garage block. In gathering information some of George's best cover stories had been suggested by Blanche's fertile imagination. She was working for a travel agency in Salisbury who were making a registry of landowners who would be interested in letting summer caravan sites to a very high class of clientele. She would not need more than five or ten minutes' talk with Shoebridge to decide which line she would take with him eventually. But most certainly she would not divulge the real reason for her visit at their first meeting. All she needed at first was to know what kind of man she was dealing with. Before she got anywhere near the truth with him she would have to decide how she was going to handle Miss Rainbird.

The front door was sheltered by a red-brick porchway with deep seat recesses at either side of it. She rang the doorbell but got no reply. She waited a while and then rang again. Saturday, she thought. It wasn't the best of days to call. They were probably out shopping somewhere. Well, it was the first day she had been able to manage. She certainly wasn't going back to Salisbury without talking to Shoebridge. She would have to come back later in the afternoon. She rang the bell a third time without any answer. She walked back to her car, past the stables and along a small path through a shrubbery to a large flagged yard at the far side of the house. There was no sign of life anywhere. Then, as she turned to go back to her car, a dog began to bark in the house. She went back to the front of the house and tried the bell again. Nobody came.

Blanche shrugged her shoulders. It was a nuisance, but there it was. She consulted the map she had brought with her and saw that Cheddar with its gorge and famous caves was not a long way off. None of the attractions would be open at this time of year, but she decided to drive there leisurely, have tea and then come back again. During the drive, the temper of the day changed. A cold wind moved in from the north, the sky rapidly clouded and, while she was having tea, the first spots of heavy rain began to smack against the window panes. Blanche helped herself to a third cup of tea and a second slice of cake and resigned herself to the fact that she was going to have a rainy drive home.

On the three occasions a year when he stayed at River Park with his old friend Sir Charles it was his habit after his after-noon nap to walk the few hundred yards down through the well-kept gardens to the large lake below the house and then along its banks to the Medham family's private chapel. It was a very pleasing little chapel which had been built in the Reg-ency period in a small rhododendron dell at the head of the lake. His walk was always the same. Around the lake as far as the chapel, then a few minutes' visit to the chapel where he usually knelt before the altar rail and said a quiet prayer or, sometimes – since his visits to Sir Charles were rare oases in a very busy, appointment-ridden life – he just knelt and let his mind wander, soaking in the peace of solitude and quiet, his memory often going back nostalgically – he was now in his mid-sixties – to the days he had passed on vacation here when he and Sir Charles had been young men. He was far from being a recluse but such moments of escape from the world as these were rewardingly refreshing. Leaving the chapel he would move on round the lake, knowing that nothing would disturb him. Sir Charles knew his habit and, being Saturday, none of the estate staff were around. Halfway along the far side of the lake he would take the small paper bag of bread pieces from his pocket and feed the water fowl. The paper bag was always waiting for him on the hall table when he came down from his rest. He knew almost to the minute the time he would arrive back at the house, where Sir Charles would be waiting in the study and they would have tea and then play their game of chess ... all part of a well-organized, unbur-dened weekend. There were few such in his life.

As he went down to the chapel the rain started to fall. It gave him no concern for he was wearing his overcoat against the cold wind. The afternoon was darkening quickly. As he entered the chapel he was sorry there was no sunshine outside. The stained-glass windows were very beautiful. Today he would not see them at their best. He walked slowly up the aisle and knelt on the carpet in front of the altar rail. Oddly, as he knelt and before he began to pray, he remembered one of the few disagreements he and Sir Charles had had in their long friendship. Three years ago one of the staff had been approached by a London journalist who had wanted material for an article on how he spent his weekends here. The man had outlined his routines. There was nothing offensive or unpleasing in the way the journalist had handled his material. In fact he'd done it very well. But Sir Charles had been furious at the breach of confidence by one of his staff. He had dismissed the man. Nothing he could do would make Sir Charles alter his mind. Well, well, that had been Charles ... proud of him, joying in their friendship and always ready to protect him. He had been touched when the dismissed man had written him a letter of apology and said that Sir Charles had been quite right to dismiss him. He stayed a few minutes, head and hands resting on the rail, and then got up and left the chapel. As he entered the gloomy porch he was surprised to see a man and woman standing in it. Their backs were to him and they were examining a marble memorial plaque let into the wall. There was a pathway at the side of the church which led for a few yards through a clipped yew garden to the road-bordered estate wall. The gateway to the road was usually kept locked unless there was a service in the chapel to which the neighbourhood and villagers had been invited. Moving past the couple, who seemed unaware of him, he presumed the gate had been inadvertently left unlocked and that they had wandered in. At the precise moment that he was just past the two, he felt himself gripped powerfully from behind. The collars of his coat and his jacket underneath it were pulled roughly backwards and, before he could turn or protest, he felt something prick him through his shirt in the upper part of the arm.

The wooden doorway in the estate wall leading to the small country lane outside had not been unlocked by any key. It had been forced.

Although he was a big man they carried him easily and quickly between them the few yards to the van outside. He was put in the back on a couple of blankets, the door closed and they drove off.

Shoebridge's wife drove. She took the van down the road, following the line of the estate wall, turned left into a larger road, waiting for a car – its sidelights on against the late afternoon gloom and rain – to pass and then drove three hundred yards along the wall to the main drive entrance. The tall iron gates were open. To the left of them stood a small greystoned lodge house. Fifty yards past the gate the van stopped. Shoebridge got out, wrapped his scarf around the lower part of his face, pulled up his coat collar, and went quickly back to the lodge house. With his gloved hands he pushed the letter to Sir Charles through the letter box and gave the bell a quick ring. There was a light coming through the curtains of the room to the right of the door. He pressed the bell once more and then turned and ran back to the car. By the time the lodge-keeper had come to the door to pick up the letter, the van was a quarter of a mile away.

His wife drove in silence for ten minutes. There was an unspoken understanding between them. They had been under strain for a long time. Now, for a little while, the tension had slackened.

She said quietly, the words a breath of relief from her, 'He's got a very fine face.'

Shoebridge nodded. 'This is the true beginning. All the rest was setting the trap. It's taken time and patience. I couldn't have done it without you.'

She smiled. She was content. He had no need to say it, but she was glad to hear it. His words of love were always disguised. The boy was like him, too. Their affection and love were rare gems, hard to mine at first, but now, polished in her hand, were more than any other treasure life could show. She wanted what he and the boy wanted, wanted it not because there was a lust in her for it herself, but simply because it was his dream and the boy's. The man in the back was civilized. The man at her side was a savage. Mad the world would call him – and without knowing it would be right, but it was a madness that rested on logic and a true compassion for the life and beauty of this world. The world was overwhelming itself with its own litter and lunacy. To save some small part of it was a beginning, a holiness in which he believed and for which, if the fates decided against him, he would willingly die. If he went, she told herself, then she would go too. They were nothing without one another.

It was a very dark afternoon. He said, 'Watch for the wood. It's coming up soon. Run in and I'll change the plates.'

Sitting in the car, lights out, the engine silent, she waited for him to change the plates. He worked in the gloom silently, swiftly and surely – as he did most things when his heart as well as his brain was with them.

They had an hour and more of driving before them. She drove all the way. Only now and again did they speak.

Fifteen minutes after its delivery to the lodge house, the letter was brought by his butler to Sir Charles. When the butler had gone he read it. He had served in the diplomatic corps too long to let his face show any surprise, even when he was alone. He got up and went to the telephone. As he dialled he was already working out how he would discreetly cover the absence of his guest. There would be little trouble in a bachelor household. His butler had been with him for thirty years at home and abroad.

An hour later Bush sat in his flat, reading the evening paper and wondering whether he should summon up the will to go out into the Saturday London evening and find himself a meal or make do with what food was in the flat. So far all the hard work, investigating and processing, had produced nothing. If the god of chance was ever going to take a hand, he thought wryly, then he was long overdue.

At that moment the telephone rang. He picked it up. Grandison's voice at the other end said, 'Bush. Get over here at once. It's happened.' The line went dead.

*　　　*　　　*

It was almost six o'clock as the van came along the narrow road that followed the crest line of the hills. The wind was much stronger and carried great gusty showers of heavy rain with it. Some fifty yards before the drive to Highlands House Mrs Shoebridge switched off the dipped headlights and drove on the side lights.

As the van went down the drive Shoebridge leaned over the back and with a small torch checked the condition of their passenger. The big man lay slackly on the blankets, breathing quietly, his eyes closed. The van bumped down the long drive, windscreen wipers working against the rain squalls, and then turned in through the house gates and moved up between the narrow stretches of bordering lawn to the gravelled sweep in front of the house. As it pulled up at the bottom of the low flight of steps that led up to the wide porch of the set-back front door, Mrs Shoebridge switched off the side lights. The house was in a high and exposed position. They wanted no unnecessary advertising of the time of their return.

Entirely occupied with the task in hand, knowing exactly what had to be done, the Shoebridges got out of the van. The back doors were opened and, using the two blankets under their passenger as a loose stretcher, they hauled the man out and carried him through the rain up the steps and into the shelter of the dark porchway. They laid the man down on the ground. Shoebridge, who was leading, straightened up, took his key from his pocket and felt for the lock of the door. As he did so Mrs Shoebridge reached to her right and found the outside switch for the porch light. It came on, a faint, low-powered light.

For a moment or two neither of them was aware of the presence of Blanche. She was standing back to one side of the porch, where she had been waiting for them, sheltering from the wind and rain. A few moments before she had seen their side lights coming down the long drive to the house and had got out of her car and run through the rain to the porch. She had been waiting for half an hour in her car parked by the garage and had almost decided to give up her vigil and come back another day.

As the light came on Blanche had a sideways view of Mrs Shoebridge. All she could see of Shoebridge was his raincoated back. In the few seconds before she spoke she looked down at the man resting on the blanket. His face was turned up to her. Without any sense of surprise, for a moment all thought or emotion or speculation suspended in a frozen spasm of existence, she looked at the man's face and instantly recognized it. She had seen the face often enough in the newspapers, on television and in life itself. Three times over the last few years she had gone with George to hear him preach in Salisbury Cathedral.

Shoebridge unlocked the door and pushed it open, and then turned to see Blanche. At the same moment his wife saw her. The shock inside them was a blankness on their faces. They were statues, the world starting to crumble slowly beneath their feet.

Blanche, misinterpreting their reaction, said, 'I'm sorry. Must have made you jump. I was waiting here for you to come back. Almost gave you up.' Then, her eyes going to the man on the floor, concern moving through her, she went on, 'What's the matter with him? Has he had an accident? It's the Archbishop, isn't it? Yes, of course it is. Come on, I'll give you a hand.'

She was moving to help them when Shoebridge's hand came from his pocket. He was himself again now. But his world had altered. It had moved into a different orbit. A dangerous orbit, but not a disastrous one. It would need a little time, thought and care to restore it to its old track.

Shoebridge. gun in his hand, said evenly, 'Just go inside.'

Blanche looked from the gun to his face, and his face told her more than the gun. Violence was locked in it. She could sense it, stirring in him, contained and controlled. There was no aura of evil about him but she could sense almost physically an emission of dark, pulsating waves of bitter coldness.

Mrs Shoebridge said, 'Do as my husband says.' For a moment her hand touched Blanche's arm. Without a word Blanche went by them and into the hallway, lit only by the reflected light from the porch. With the flow of movement came also the slow upsurge of fear in her. Halfway down the hall the light came on.

Shoebridge closed to her side, stopped her movement with a touch of his hand and then opened the door of a room.

'Wait in there.' He turned to his wife and handed her the gun. 'Stay with her. I can manage all this. See that she doesn't take her gloves off.'

He saw the two women into the room, locked the door and went back to the Archbishop. He wrapped the blankets around him. He was a big man. Shoebridge went on one knee and hoisted the body over his shoulder and then rose slowly and carried him into the hall. He kicked the door shut on its catch and switched out the porch light with his free hand. At the far end of the hall, he pressed the switch to swing back the concealed door that led down to the cellars.

Grandison said, 'I'm due at 10 Downing Street in fifteen minutes. At the moment only the Prime Minister knows. I've asked for the Home Secretary and the Commissioner of the Metropolitan Police to be there. Sir Charles Medham is on his way there, too. He's promised to fix everything at his end. That's a copy of the letter.' He handed Bush a carbon copy. Bush knew that he would have typed it himself, that the top copy would be in his pocket now. He knew, too, that when they got the original, there would be nothing on it or in it to help.

Bush said without emphasis, concealing the anger and frustration that had lived with him for so long, 'He's flown high.'

'We always knew he would.' Grandison shrugged his shoulders and smiled. 'The whole thing has been beautifully built. So simple. Unless he's made a mistake somewhere we shan't turn him up, barring some bolt from the blue. You know what it means if he gets away with it?'

Bush nodded. 'All against us will draw their knives. This department will go.' He didn't add, because it was unnecessary, that if the department went Grandison would not suffer. But he would. There would be a mark against him for the rest of his career.

When Grandison had gone he read the letter through. It was a crude piece of composition. Almost certainly deliberately so. There was nothing crude about this man. To the bottom of the letter Grandison had added some notes he had taken from Sir Charles. His Grace, a very old friend, had been staying the weekend. Disappeared during his afternoon walk around the park. Always called in at the family chapel on the walk. Visited River Park three times a year, always the same times of the year within a week or so. Regularity of habit helped, Bush knew. Almost certainly there'd been some folksy magazine article or newspaper feature which would have started a train of thought in someone like Trader. The rest was easy.

He rang the map department and had them send up the six-inch-to-the-mile sections for the area. River Park had two lengths of roadway running around part of it. The private chapel was marked to the north of the lake. It was only a few yards from a small side road. Instinct backed by experience told Bush that it would have happened there. The Most Reverend, His Grace the Lord Archbishop – one of the two Primates of England, York and Canterbury, taking precedence after the Royal Family with the Lord High Chancellor – bundled up like a sack of potatoes and hauled off to some car or van. Half a million pounds in ransom. The ecclesiastical authorities and the Church Commissioners would be delighted about that. They would have to find some of it. He pulled a reference book from his shelf and checked. From stock exchange investments, land and property, mortgages and loans and beneficiaries the Church had an annual income of over twenty-four million pounds. Over twenty million of that was spent on clergy stipends and pensions and the maintenance of clergy houses and other Church property. Not much left. But a discreet word to a few wealthy old ladies that the dear Archbishop was in danger and the half-million could be raised in an hour. Trader had picked well. There would be no publicity. God, what a thing the papers would make of it! And the heads that would roll! Against this a kidnapped Ambassador was nothing ... And he, Bush, had to sit here, doing what? Twiddling his thumbs. Perhaps Grandison was right. It was the time for prayer.

It was seven o'clock. Blanche sat in a high-backed chair on the fireplace side of the table. It was a dining-room. The table and chairs were old-fashioned mahogany. There was the gleam of silver and glass from the sideboard under the red-tinted shades of the wall sconces. One or two oil paintings hid murkily in the shadows of the far wall. Against the window rain and wind beat in violent gusts. Mrs Shoebridge sat near the door. She was a tall, dark, pale-faced woman, a long, brooding, still face. She gave no hint of any of her feelings. Shoebridge sat opposite Blanche. He had gloves on and was going through her handbag.

They had given her a glass of sherry, but would not let her take her gloves off. The contents of the bag were on the table. Shoebridge was going meticulously through her diary, reading it page by page. Blanche was frightened, but there was no panic in her. That she had walked into trouble was evident ... bad trouble. She was quick enough to be able to put an explanation to many things herself. The man had been the Archbishop. She had made no mistake about that. Except, perhaps, by revealing she knew who he was. No, they would have held her just the same. She knew about the Trader kidnappings. She guessed that Edward Shoebridge could be the same man.

Mrs Shoebridge had kept her in the room, holding the gun and watching her in silence, cutting short Blanche's first attempt at talk with a sharp gesture of her head. When Shoebridge had come back Blanche had been angry and indignant, not from feeling but from policy. But it had not helped her. Genuinely not knowing what line to take, she had given Shoebridge the explanation that she had come to see him about caravan sites. He had heard her without interruption, and then had taken her handbag and told his wife to serve her with some sherry.

He sat there in silence now, the diary put aside, leafing through her address book. He pulled out the slip of paper on which she had written his name and address when Angers had

169

telephoned her. He laid it on the table and went on examining the address book. Thought and observation running in tandem with her fear, Blanche watched him. All his movements were neat and deliberate, a kind of slow sureness which possessed his whole body. He was of middle height, wiry ... that deceptive wiriness which masked strength. His face was tanned, weather-hardened. It was a still, inexpressive face. Once when she started to say something, to protest, to take some comfort just from the sound of her own voice, he had looked at her and shaken his head, his expression unchanging. She had stopped, cut off short by the cold, spiritual blow of his personality. It was then that a brief stir of panic touched her. This man, she thought, could easily kill her if he felt it necessary. She fought back fear, overwhelming it with a silent flood of disbelief. For God's sake, Blanche, she told herself, keep your head and don't act like a fool.

Slowly Shoebridge sat back in his chair and looked at her thoughtfully. Unexpectedly he suddenly smiled, but the smile Blanche felt was not for her. It was for himself. Something had happened inside him. Something had suddenly changed. It came to her clearly, just as now and again with other people their thoughts inexplicably became hers. This man had made up his mind. Not only had he made it up, but he was happy with his decision, was no longer worrying about her presence here. So far as he was concerned the whole matter was finished.

He said, 'So you came to see us about this caravan business? And when we were out you went and had tea in Cheddar and then came back here later and waited for us?'

'Yes. But I should explain now—'

He cut her short with that quick shake of the head which was almost like a blow.

'There is no need to explain. You are not interested in caravans. That was merely to see me. To get you into the house. You wanted to know something about us first so that you could decide how to handle your true business.'

Curiously because of his matter-of-fact way of talking, his

tones holding neither anger nor anxiety, Blanche was suddenly comforted. She would be silly to make too much of this, she thought. Maybe things weren't as bad as she had imagined. Maybe she had imagined everything the wrong way round. Imagination could be a bad ally.

With a smile, one gloved hand going up in nervous reflex to touch her pearls, Blanche said, 'It was silly of me. But sometimes it's best to know first when ... well, when very confidential matters are concerned.'

Shoebridge returned her smile briefly. He said, 'You keep a very bare diary, Miss Tyler, but it's easy to read between the lines. You're from Salisbury?'

'Yes, and I—'

'I only want you to give direct answers. Your emotions are of little interest. I can read them anyway. You're a professional medium?'

'Yes.'

'With a little terrestrial help on the side in some cases?'

'There are truths in this world as well as the other. It is part of my ministry to reveal them.'

'Professional jargon.' He reached out and picked up the address book. Without opening it, he said, 'You're here because of Miss Rainbird of Reed Court, Chilbolton?'

'Yes.' She longed to do more than give straight answers. There had to be safety somewhere, somehow in a cloud of words. But she knew he would cut her off.

'It's a pity my telephone is ex-directory. You could have telephoned me and our business could have been settled in a few minutes. That would have left us both in peace. How did you get my address?' He held up the slip of paper.

'Through a friend of yours. A Mr Angers.'

'A past friend. How did he know it and how did you find him?'

'He remembered your interest in falconry and got it from the British Falconers' Club. Look—' she made a quick bid to get away from his control '—why don't we come straight to the point? What are you doing with the Arch—'

171

'We are coming straight to the point.' His voice rose a little. 'By the route I know as straight.' He smiled.

Blanche stood up. Neither of the two moved. She forced anger into herself to drive out fear and said, 'I've had enough of this. I insist that you let me leave at once.'

Shoebridge said, 'Sit down.'

Blanche faced him across the table. He cocked his head a little to look up at her. Quietly, from the far side of the room, Mrs Shoebridge said, 'You're not a fool, Miss Tyler. We have kidnapped the Archbishop. You have seen him. You can see that it is not possible for you to leave . . . yet.'

There was no comfort in that lingering *yet* for Blanche. Slowly she sat down. Keep your head, Blanche, she told herself. Keep your head. You're in a mess, but there must be a way out. Compromise. Some agreement. God, there had to be something.

Shoebridge said, 'How did you find Mr Angers?'

'Through a friend of mine who does that kind of work for me sometimes.'

Shoebridge flicked the diary with one finger.

'George Lumley? The one whose expenses and payments you list?'

'Yes. Look, what you don't understand is—'

'I understand everything, Miss Tyler.'

'No, you don't! And just you let me speak! No, I won't be bullied. You just listen to me. So you've kidnapped the Archbishop. Obviously for money. Well, all you have to do is to turn him loose . . . anywhere. Forget him. There's plenty of money waiting for you. That's what you don't know. And I'm prepared to help you, to forget anything I've seen here. If you've got any sense that's what you will do.'

Shoebridge smiled. 'You really would do that? Go away and forget everything?'

'Of course I would. And there's the money, too. You can be a rich man without this . . . this Archbishop thing. Oh, please, don't you see that?'

Shoebridge studied her, and then slowly shook his head.

'I'm sorry, Miss Tyler, but it won't do. You see, I know all about Miss Rainbird of Reed Court. I've known it since I was sixteen years old. I know who my real father and mother were – and I am not interested. They rejected me and I was very happy with the people who took their place. I know all about Miss Grace Rainbird. She has money, but I am not interested in it. I have no wish to go to her to make any claim, or to be welcomed because that would ease her conscience or put anything right. Everything was put right when Ronald Shoebridge and his wife became my mother and father years ago. Miss Rainbird is probably worth two hundred thousand pounds. She could live for another ten years. The time is too long and the money not enough, Miss Tyler. So let us get back to the real problem. Does George Lumley know you were coming to see me?'

Quickly Blanche said, 'Of course he does.'

'I am sure you are lying. But it makes no difference. So you came and told me a story about caravan sites. And then you went. That is all that I have to tell anyone who might question me.'

He picked up the diary, the address book and the piece of paper with his name and address on it. He put the diary and the address book back in her bag. He looked at the sheet of paper and then across at Blanche. He said, 'It may be true that this George Lumley knows my address and knows you are coming here today. But there is always the possibility that he knows nothing. You haven't entered my name in your address book, and you haven't made any note in your diary about getting it from Angers. I don't think you told George Lumley about it. But, as I said, if you did it makes no difference.' He picked up the slip of paper, crumpled it in his hand and put it into his pocket.

The action filled Blanche with rising panic.

Shoebridge stood up and tidied the rest of her things into the handbag. Blanche, her throat dry, and her heart beginning to pound fast, said hoarsely, 'What are you going to do? For God's sake, what are you going to do?'

Shoebridge looked round at his wife. Mrs Shoebridge gave a little nod as though she had agreed to some unspoken question. Shoebridge turned back to Blanche. She saw Mrs Shoebridge rise from her chair and begin to move.

Shoebridge said, 'What can I do, Miss Tyler? I have worked for years for this day. I have a dream which I mean to turn into reality. You mean nothing to me. The fact that it may be known you came here puts me to no risk which I cannot face with confidence. I have to go on, Miss Tyler. You are in my way.'

Blanche stood up, panic coursing through her, destroying all but one thought. 'No! No . . . Oh, no!' she cried and turned to run for the door.

Shoebridge put out an arm and caught her. He swung her round and held her with both hands, clamping her shoulders up against his chest. As Mrs Shoebridge came in front of her Blanche began to scream. Neither of the Shoebridges took any notice of the scream. Mrs Shoebridge reached out and pulled the lapel of the open lambskin coat back. She unbuttoned the front of the red jacket and slid a hand under the loose silk blouse neck, exposing part of the right shoulder, the flesh pink and soft.

Blanche screamed again, long and with animal fear, and the Shoebridges did nothing to stop her. Mrs Shoebridge raised the hypodermic syringe. Blanche's scream was cut to a long wailing sob through which she called, 'Henry! Oh, Henry . . .' Mrs Shoebridge inserted the point with great care, her hand steady. As the point went in Blanche screamed again, and kicked out with her feet so that Shoebridge had to hold her upright. Then she slowly slumped in his arms and he lowered her gently into her chair.

He stepped back, looked at his wristwatch – it was half-past seven – and then said to his wife, 'We've got plenty of time. You take her car. I'll drive her in the van. We've got to take her back to her own part of the country. I'll give you the route. It's got to be done half an hour before she's due to recover. We'll find a place. Until we do we are at risk but it is unavoidable.' He stood looking down at Blanche and reached out with

174

his right hand and took his wife's arm, his fingers clamping hard on the flesh.

A little after nine o'clock that night, George switched off the television in his cottage and got up to make himself a nightcap. He was pleased with himself. The gardening thing was coming along. He'd got a good secondhand van lined up and had agreed the price for repainting it. Next week he would be going after equipment and have an advertisement out for a strong lad as help. Handposters were being printed. They'd be ready in a few days. By the end of next week he would be ready to distribute them. He and the boy could do that in the van. Lumley's Sunshine Gardens. As advertised weekly in the local press. Before he knew where he was he would be expanding all over the place. Work it up into a real concern and – who knows? – end by selling it lock, stock and barrel and with the cash go on to bigger and better things. He looked across at Albert, who was sitting on the window-seat. Outside the wind and rain sweeping down the river valley were slashing and shaking at the window.

As George poured whisky into his glass a particularly vicious storm squall beat against the window, shaking the loose frame, the hammer of rain and wind like the great surge of some elemental force outside assaulting the house, determined on entrance. Albert jumped to his feet and, raising his head towards the window, its curtains flapping in the draught, began to howl, and went on howling until George threw a cushion at him.

At that same moment, too, in Reed Court, Miss Rainbird, who was sitting reading a book in the solitary light from her table lamp, happened to look up and her eye fell on the chair, deep in the shadows, which Madame Blanche had always used during her sessions. Just for a moment through a trick of light and shadow disposed over its cushions and the shawl which Miss Rainbird had thrown over the chairback on coming in, it looked as though someone were sitting there. So vivid was the impression as Miss Rainbird flicked her eyes to relieve them from the strain of reading that she was sure someone was there. She felt the skin at the back of her neck creep. A moment later she realized that the chair was empty and she gave a little snort of self-disgust at her imaginative nonsense.

And at that moment in a little wood high on the barren lands of the western part of Salisbury plain, Blanche died.

CHAPTER NINE

GRANDISON'S DIRECTIVE FROM the conference at 10 Downing Street was as Bush had expected. The kidnapper's terms must be met. There was no question whatsoever of any action being taken which would put the Archbishop's life in jeopardy. The code message would be put in the *Daily Telegraph* on the Monday and the department would then await instructions giving the terms and method of release. There would be no publicity either now or after the release of the Archbishop. No publicity at the moment was imperative for the safety of the Archbishop's life. No publicity later was equally imperative to protect the professional and public reputations of the high-ranking members of the government and the police. If in years to come the story should leak then it could easily be claimed that secrecy at the time had been the wisest policy and by then there would be no threat to anyone's reputation.

The Archbishop's family was told the truth and so also were a few members of the hierarchy in the Church who had to know. A press release was put out that the Archbishop was suffering from a severe chill and would be confined to his bed for the next few days. All his public engagements were cancelled.

The whole affair, Bush had to concede, was running exactly as the kidnapper had planned. If by some stroke of fortune he were to find out within the next couple of days who the kidnapper was and where he was hiding the Archbishop, still no action would be taken until the ransom had been paid and the Archbishop was safely back in the bosom of his family. Grandison's brief was explicit on this point. Not the smallest move was to be made which would even for a few minutes expose the Archbishop to danger.

The Archbishop had taken his afternoon stroll around the lake at River Park and had been seized either as he was going in or coming out of the private chapel. The lock of the wall door on to the roadway had been forced, and the letter for Sir Charles Medham left at the lodge gates as the kidnapper drove away. Except for the Commissioner at Scotland Yard there was not a policeman in the country who had any idea that the Archbishop had been kidnapped.

When Grandison had explained the position to Sangwill and himself, Bush had said, 'It's so simple I wonder it hasn't been done before.'

Grandison shook his head. 'It's not only simple. It's audacious and arrogant. We shall be sitting in that damned hallway again, and the man or woman will come and collect a half a million. He or she will walk out and that will be the end. They will never bother us again.'

'Unless?' Sangwill pushed his glasses up and rubbed his eyes.

Grandison shrugged his shoulders. 'You know the answer to that one. You've run all your computer combinations. You've fed the big brain everything you know. The oracle refuses to utter. Prayer is the answer. I told Bush that ages ago, but he refuses to go down on his knees, refuses to sacrifice a couple of chickens to some heathen god. The man behind all this is prepared to sacrifice himself if the gods desert him. They won't desert him, not unless you or someone bribes them with richer offerings than his own arrogance and audacity.'

Humouring Grandison's extravagant mood, knowing that it covered a frustration greater than his own because Grandison would never have accepted the kidnapping terms, would have refused and put the Archbishop at risk, Bush said, 'What is there to offer? What have we got?'

Grandison smiled. 'There's always something we can find that will please the dark powers that control time and chance. Some simple little donation that catches their imagination or a sincere appeal to their sense of irony.'

Sangwill laughed. 'I really think you mean it.'

'Of course I mean it. What we should pray for is the moment of chaos, the small sideslip in time, the million to one chance, the mutation which makes a nonsense of normality. If it doesn't happen, then we aren't going to be anything but witnesses to a man or woman collecting half a million and disappearing into the night for ever.'

The following day, which was a Monday, the *Daily Telegraph* personal column carried the item—*Felix. All fine at home. Please write. John.*

That same day at ten in the morning a farm labourer walking through a wood on the downs a few miles from Salisbury found a car parked between the trees a hundred yards from the road. Behind the wheel was a dead woman. All the windows of the car were closed except for a small triangular vent in the offside back window. A length of rubber piping had been wired to the exhaust pipe and led into the car through the vent.

The farm labourer called the police without opening the car. When the patrol car arrived one of the policemen recognized Blanche. She was slumped behind the wheel, wearing her lambskin coat and gloves. The gloves were marked with rust and dirt stains acquired presumably when she had wired the rubber tube to the exhaust pipe. A pair of pliers from the car tool kit lay on the ground by the exhaust pipe with a small piece of loose wire. It had rained hard during Saturday evening and for most of the Sunday. Blanche's shoes were mud-covered where she had stood on the wet ground fixing the tubing. The flushed red colour of her face was no surprise to the two policemen. They had seen deaths by carbon monoxide poisoning before. The tracks of the car into the wood from the road, and the footprints at the back of the car, were all badly obliterated by the rain.

Over the weekend George had not missed Blanche. Her visits to his cottage followed no fixed pattern. She sometimes telephoned and said she was coming, or just turned up. To go a whole week or more without seeing her when he was not professionally working for her was nothing unusual to George.

Blanche's mother had not missed her either. She had gone off on Saturday morning saying she was going for a drive in the country. Blanche never discussed her clients or professional work with her mother. When she did not return Mrs Tyler assumed that she was staying with George. The Salisbury police informed Mrs Tyler of Blanche's death at midday and she went in the police car to identify the body. A routine autopsy was performed on Blanche that evening.

That evening the Archbishop prepared himself for his third night in his cellar quarters. So far he had seen nothing of the people who were keeping him captive. He had followed the routine dictated to him over the loudspeaker. He knew why he was being held because he was already familiar with the kidnapping cases of Archer and Pakefield. He had, in fact, met Pakefield socially once since the man's release and had been given an account of his experiences and had been quietly amused at the low payment demanded for his release. He had a mild interest in the actual amount which might be asked for his own release as a measure of his own importance, but he was distinctly upset by the thought that the money – no matter whether a large or small amount – could ill be spared from the Church's funds. He had no personal concern for his own safety. He was in God's good hands and was certainly being afforded ample time in which to practise his devotions and to find comfort and strength in the power of prayer. The food he was given was very good and the wine which he had been brought on his second evening was one which he would have served with confidence at his own table. Before settling to bed now, he said his prayers and included his captors in them. He had no doubt of the plurality. That he had been abducted by the man and woman in the chapel porch was beyond doubt. It was a strange and violent world that he lived in. But then, of course, it had always been a strange and violent world ... without faith and belief it would be difficult to make any sense out of it at all.

*　　*　　*

180

That same night, Miss Rainbird slept badly. When she awoke at five o'clock in the morning it was to find that she had one of her bad headaches. She could remember nothing of her dreams except that they had been disturbing and that they had concerned Madame Blanche. She lay back against her pillows and told herself that it was really going to be too much if she had to cope with Madame Blanche in her dreams as well as Harriet. It was enough to give anyone a bad headache. And it was a bad headache, throbbing away in her skull. She remembered how Madame Blanche had cured her once and had told her that she could cure herself if she really tried.

She shut her eyes and lay in the darkness and began to imagine that Madame Blanche was at the head of the bed behind her, that her fingertips were stroking her brow. She told herself that the woman was there, the string of pearls swinging as she moved her hands, the air touched with the scent of the strong perfume she used. She could feel the fingertips, incredibly light, moving across her skin. For all that the woman was clearly quite mercenary minded, there had been something about her, some gift, some quality which could not be rationalized away. An extraordinary woman.

Miss Rainbird fell asleep. When she woke an hour later her headache had gone.

Mrs Tyler telephoned George early in the morning and told him the news about Blanche. When he put the telephone down, George stood staring through the window. Outside, snowdrops and daffodils were showing in the rough grass of the paddock. Spring was touching the earth with colour and stirring the wild life. There was a blur of blue and yellow wings from the budgerigars in the aviary. It just could not be, he told himself. Not Blanche. Blanche was life. All robust and warm and earthy. Full of it. For all her spiritualism and ethereal ideas, the last thing Blanche would have wanted to do was deliberately to leave this world before her proper time. It was just unbelievable that Blanche was never going to come here again, that he was never going to burn the toast for her and take up her breakfast again. Never going to see her sitting up in bed, waiting for him, a gorgeous, generous woman, or hear her shout at him to keep Albert out of the bedroom. He would never hear her laugh again, or see the sudden odd withdrawal from the world around her as she went off into one of her spells of talk with the other world ... Henry and her Temple of Astrodel. Poor Blanche ... she was never going to get that now, not in this world.

He sat down slowly and felt tears begin to wet the corners of his eyes. He was a simple, uncomplicated man. He had no sophistication or philosophy in him which helped to meet grief. Perhaps, he thought, he really had loved her. Theirs wasn't just one of those loose arrangements which some men and women have. Perhaps, too, she had really loved him. He ought to have recognized it all, taken charge, and married her. It would have taken some bullying, but he could have done it ... made her want it. If they had been married this couldn't have happened. And now it had, he still couldn't understand it. Of all the people he knew, Blanche was the last one likely to do a thing like that ... mucking about with bits of wire and rubber piping, sitting up there on the plain with the rain belting down, and just waiting calmly for it to happen. In God's name why? Why?

He stood up, suddenly angry. How could you ever tell with people, he thought. You never knew where you bloody well were. You never got right across to them and they never really got right across to you. Part strangers all the time. What on earth had got into her? Had she been to see a doctor some time and been told she had cancer? She wouldn't say anything if she had. She wouldn't want to go through all that, not when she knew that she could always pass over ... Cancer? For God's sake, that was nonsense. She was as fit as a horse.

The telephone rang. It was the Salisbury police. They would be obliged if George could make it convenient to see them at half-past twelve that morning.

Before going to the police headquarters George went to the Red Lion and had a couple of glasses of Guinness. The first one he drank for Blanche, a silent, farewell toast. She'd loved a glass of Guinness.

George was interviewed by a detective sergeant, a big, fatherly figure. The man knew George fairly well and quite liked him. But quite liking people was something that was never allowed to interfere with duty. He told George of the circumstances of Blanche's death and said that since George – after her mother – was the closest person to her, they felt that anything he had to offer might be of help to them.

The sergeant said, 'We've had an autopsy and, of course, there will be an inquest. I don't want to embarrass you, Mr Lumley, but I should make it clear that we know something of your relationship with Miss Tyler.'

'That's all right. Scores of people knew. What I want to know is why the hell she'd do a thing like that?'

'That's what the coroner will want to find out too. Do you mind if I ask you a few questions?'

'Of course not. Anything I can do—'

'When did you see her last?'

'Wednesday last week. She was full of the joys of spring. Sorry, I don't mean to be ... Well, it's a fact. She was on top of the world.'

'You didn't see her or hear from her after that?'

'No.'

'Did she tell you what her movements were going to be over the weekend?'

'No, she didn't. But I told her I was going to be busy. I'm trying to set up a small business. I must say all this has taken the steam out of it a bit now.'

'She left home fairly early Saturday morning and she took a picnic lunch with her. When she was found the lunch had been eaten. No idea where she might have gone to?'

'None at all. Except ... well, you know she was a spiritualist. Professionally. Sometimes she just liked to go off. Get into the country to be by herself. Think things out. Meditate, maybe. I know a lot of people think it's all fake and nonsense. But it's not. She'd got something.'

'You helped her professionally sometimes, didn't you?'

'Now and again. There was nothing wrong about it. She didn't go in for faked seances and all that caper. But now and

183

then I'd look up a few facts. Trace someone. Get information which would help her.'

'She paid you well for this?'

'Sometimes. If she was feeling generous.'

'When did you last work for her?'

'I finished a job for her about a week ago. Well, more or less finished it. Came to a dead end as a matter of fact.'

'Can you tell me about this job?'

'If it's absolutely necessary, yes. But it does concern someone quite important in the area. I really feel I would have to mention it to them first. To be quite honest – for Blanche's sake – I'd rather not have to do that. I can't see that it would have anything to do with her committing suicide. Just the opposite, I'd say.'

'Well, let's leave that for the moment.' He went on, 'Have you any idea at all why she might do a thing like this?'

'Not a bloody one. In fact the opposite. She was as fit as a fiddle and full of life. She'd got plans and ambitions for the future. The whole thing's a mystery to me.'

'Was there ever any question of marriage between you?'

'Not really. We had a good relationship. Apart from that, she wanted to be on her own and so did I. I've been married once, you know. It didn't work out.'

The sergeant leaned back in his chair, considered George for a moment or two, and then said quietly, 'Did you know she was pregnant?'

'What?'

It was clear at once to the sergeant that George's surprise was genuine.

'The autopsy shows that she was carrying a two-months foetus.'

'Good God – why the hell didn't she tell me?'

'She was a big woman, Mr Lumley. She might not have known herself. But if she had, what do you think her reaction would have been?'

'She would have wanted me to marry her and I would have done. And I wish to God she had known and it had been like that. She might have been an odd bird in some people's eyes,

184

but she wouldn't have played around with any abortion stuff. Life was precious to her. All life.'

'If she'd had to marry would it have affected her professionally?'

'Of course not. Plenty of mediums are married. In many ways it helps. But I can see why she might not have known. She was a big girl and she always was skipping a monthly now and then. I always did the proper thing by her, of course. But it used to scare us at first.'

'Scare?'

'Well, you know what I mean.'

'Yes, I think I do. Tell me, did she ever discuss her financial affairs with you?'

'In what way?'

'Well, how much money she had. How she'd got it invested and that sort of thing?'

'No, she didn't. She was fairly well off, I knew that. She paid me seven hundred and fifty pounds for this last job, even though I didn't pull it off. Quite frankly, she knew how I was fixed and she was generous.'

'We saw her mother again this morning, Mr Lumley. Miss Tyler made a will a year ago. One copy is with her solicitor, and another copy was in the house. Her mother knew about the will. I mean she knew what was in it and where it was kept. Mrs Tyler is the principal beneficiary. I have her permission and also her solicitor's to disclose one item of the will to you.'

Suddenly George was aware of the change of mood in the man. He said, 'Look, what are you getting at?'

'I'm asking you a few questions, and you're being very co-operative, Mr Lumley. That's all. We're inquiring into a case of suicide, and want to know the reason. Any help you can give us will be welcome. Did you know that you are mentioned in Miss Tyler's will?'

'No. I didn't.'

'She left you five thousand pounds.'

'Five thousand what?'

The sergeant smiled. 'Pounds.'

'I don't believe it.'

'It's quite true. I can tell you that she wasn't a rich woman, but she was not in need for a penny or two.'

'I don't care what she left me. I'd rather she was here alive. And if you want my opinion, I don't believe that she was the kind who would ever commit suicide. And I can see quite clearly what you may be thinking – and that's damned wrong too. That I killed her because the baby would be a nuisance and I'd get a nice five-thousand-pound bonus.' George stood up, his face tight with anger. 'Jesus Christ, what kind of man do you think I am?'

The sergeant waved a placatory hand at him.

'Nobody is suggesting anything. We're just having a chat and I'm giving you some information and you're giving me some, in the hope that we can clear this matter up. If you want my personal opinion, I am quite sure that you would have married her if you'd known about the baby. And equally certain that you wouldn't kill anyone for the sake of five thousand pounds. You're not the type, Mr Lumley.'

'But what you are suggesting is that it might not have been suicide. That it was faked? That someone might have killed her?'

'You're talking to a policeman, Mr Lumley. Our job is to get at the facts. Miss Tyler might have committed suicide for reasons, good ones in her view, which we shall never know. On the other hand, she might not. What I would like you to do is to go away and think about it. I don't want you to discuss it with anyone else. But think about it. If anything occurs to you, then let us know.'

George went back to the Red Lion and had a bar lunch and two large whiskies and soda.

At police headquarters after George had gone, the sergeant was joined by the CID man who had checked George's cottage in the past and sent a report on him through Scotland Yard to Bush's department.

He said, 'Well?'

The sergeant shook his head. 'I'd stake my life on it. He doesn't know a thing. He didn't know she was pregnant and he didn't know he was due for anything under the will. And he can't think of a damned reason why she should go off for the day with a nice picnic and then commit suicide.'

The CID man picked up the autopsy report from the desk and glanced at it.

'Slight superficial bruising top of left arm?'

'You could do that just getting in and out of a car. Knocking yourself accidentally. There's no question that she died from CO poisoning. You don't need much more than a few minutes in a car like that before the atmosphere is lethal. I think she committed suicide and we'll probably never know why.'

'What does the Chief think?'

'Well, you know him and suicide. Especially when it's a car lark. Despite what the old girl, Mrs Tyler, said, he's asked for a further test. Blood, internal organs for any trace of drugs or toxics. She wouldn't be the first one to be slipped something and then set up to look like suicide, would she?'

'Nor the last. You know we reported this chap Lumley under that Trader inquiry?'

'Yes. He's first a kidnapper and then a murderer, I don't think. We sent in about a hundred names under that business.'

'I think we should let them know about this. You never know what line they're working.'

'All right. But I should wait until you get the doctor's second report. Should be here tomorrow. Anyway, the Trader thing is a dead duck. He's away comfortably with his loot by now. Just a memory that's always going to be a thorn in the side of the big boys. If you think Lumley has any connection with that then you could believe that Jack the Ripper is alive and well and living in Blackpool.'

Edward Shoebridge saw the code announcement in the *Daily Telegraph* that day. There was no elation in him. That would come much later. At the moment the signal was no more than he had expected. He sat down at his cellar console with a small child's printing set and filled in a blank date space which he had left when the Grandison letter had been typed at the same time as the one to Sir Charles Medham. He gave it to his wife

187

to be posted. She was going to drive to Southampton to do this.

As he stood by the car before she left, he said, 'While you're in Southampton get a copy of the evening paper. It's the *Evening Echo*, I think.'

'Miss Tyler?'

'Yes. There may be a report.'

'You're not worried about it?'

'No. Even if they find out that she was here it can make no difference. We don't know she has committed suicide. We don't know the real reason for her visit. She came inquiring about caravan sites. That's the truth. She would never have told us about Miss Rainbird if she hadn't been frightened. She just wanted to have a look at us before she made up her mind. If anyone knows she came here, then we may soon get a visit from the police. We just tell the truth up to a point. If they know about Miss Rainbird and the connection with me, I tell the truth. I'm not interested in Miss Rainbird. When you get the paper just check if there is a report and then throw it away.'

'It's a pity it happened.'

'We've always known that there could be a random element any time. Either it would be disastrous or we could deal with it. It happened and we've dealt with it.' He gave a rare smile. 'We know the stakes and we know the risks. We've always known that there's no such thing as infallibility. The gods gave us a little bad luck, that's all. Just to be sure that we could deal with it.' He leaned forward and kissed her through the car door.

She said thoughtfully, 'She looked the wrong type to commit suicide.'

He smiled again. He knew it was no weakness in her. There was no weakness or fear in her. He said, 'So many of them do. People are always saying, "I can't believe it. She just wasn't that kind." '

When his wife had gone he went to the mews and took out his son's goshawk. While the boy was at school he exercised her. He went up through the elms at the back of the house.

The unhooded hawk, seeing and hearing the birds in the rookery above, began to bob, to spread her tail, and her head twisted as she followed the flight of the birds above.

He took her through the stand of elms and walked half a mile along the down. Lower down the slopes were the first fields, green now with young corn shoots. There was always a passage of rooks from the fields to the elms. Sometimes they moved in company, but now and again there would be a solitary one flying back to the trees. After a while a single rook came winging up the slope. He slipped the goshawk and she went upwind after the rook. It saw her coming and with no trees or cover below began to climb in clumsy circles dropping downwind as it did so. The goshawk ringed up after the rook. The rook was a strong bird and it was some time before the hawk was high above her.

Shoebridge stood watching, remembering the first time his son had flown the goshawk at a rook like this. With the really good things, he thought, one always remembered the first time, and every time after that was still good but there was the smallest edge of magic gone from it. One's first pheasant taken coming downwind like a rocket, the first salmon running out line to burn inexperienced fingers ... Life was full of good things. But these days so many of the good things were going. There was a natural balance between life and death. But there was no balance in nature that could control man's fast spread of filth and pollution. He was turning the seas and rivers into sewers and the land itself into poisonous rubbish heaps. Nothing could stop it. The only thing to do was to find some uncontaminated place and ring it round with a defence against the world's slow stain.

The goshawk fetched the rook, hanging a hundred feet above the bird, and then made two quick feints, false stooping to drive the rook lower. The rook went sideways down the wind, dropping fast for the shelter of the hedges that lined the fields far below.

The goshawk turned over and went down after the bird in a close-winged dive and Shoebridge could hear the hiss of the air as she cut through it. She hit the rook a hundred feet above ground without binding to it and there was an explosion of black feathers as the goshawk threw up and the rook tumbled clumsily towards the ground. It was death, thought Shoebridge, and it was beautiful.

Walking back to the house he thought of the boy. School-term was coming to an end. He would be home soon. They would take the car and go off, the three of them, a close trinity, to Scotland and Ireland ... If they couldn't find what they wanted there, then they would find some place abroad. Norway, Sweden or Canada. None of them had any conservative feeling about this country. They all knew what they wanted and would recognize it when they saw it. All he felt the boy knew and understood. Their desire was not poetic or philosophical, they wanted neither Thoreau nor Robinson Crusoe as guides. Their desire was physical. They wanted a place with bastions against the world where in twenty, a hundred or five hundred years they or their spawn would have lived as close to their true nature as they could and where they would fight the last fight against the final overwhelming of the world by man's pollution. It was a project at which many would have laughed and then called him mad for having such a dream, and madder still to want to make it real. So let them – but the desire in him was iron-hard.

When his wife came back she said that there had been a small paragraph in the *Evening Echo* reporting the discovery of the body of Blanche Tyler. She cooked the Archbishop's dinner, giving him smoked trout and a tournedos Rossini with broccoli spears. When she came back she brought with her the copy of the *Daily Telegraph* from the cellar. Across the top of the front page the Archbishop had written – *I would prefer the Times to this*.

Shoebridge took the paper and burnt it. The paper would not be changed. Although he treated the Archbishop with all the consideration that was possible, the man did not exist as a personality for him. He was an object of value which very shortly would be sold.

George sat in the kitchen with Blanche's mother drinking

whisky. He had brought in a bottle with him. The old lady accepted it, although she preferred tea. But a death in the family made things different for a while. They drank it from cheap tumblers. The house was hers now and there was good glass in the dining-room, but for the time being habit held her, restrained her almost as surely as if Blanche were alive and still mistress at Maidan Road.

George was adjusting now to the tragedy, moving slowly back into a pattern of normal behaviour and thought, doing what thousands do every day somewhere, absorbing shock and accepting that life must go on. 'You think she ever had any idea she was pregnant?' he asked.

'No. Head in the clouds too much for that. She thought she was safe. You never are. No matter what you do, lad. Life finds ways of creepin' in.'

'I'd have married her. Like a shot. Poor old darling.'

'You wouldn't. She weren't the marryin' kind. Not our Blanche. I don't mean she'd have got rid of it. She'd have had it, done right by it, found a home or kept it here. I weren't never married to her father. In our life sometimes you did and sometimes you didn't. Church didn't mean much. A man took a woman to live with him, got her kids and stuck by her or didn't.'

George poured more whisky for them. It had been a bad day, but with its ending he was beginning to feel better. Not the same. Better. It was the way life went and you had to go with it.

He said, 'When you phoned this morning the bottom dropped right out of things. It was the last thing I would ever have thought of. Blanche sitting up there in the car with the rain belting down . . . doing that. I still can't believe that part of it. She's gone, yes, I can face that. But not the way she did it.'

'It weren't no surprise to me.'

'What do you mean?'

'Well, in the way it was to you. Oh, yes, it was a shock. Just as it would have been if she'd been knocked down. But not the other.'

'I don't get you.'

191

'Why should you? Like I told them at the police station. It's in the family. I never told her, mind. Though she might have guessed. You can't keep things from kids. But Old Tyler was the same.'

'Her father committed suicide?'

'He did that. Walked out one night. Strong man. Not a care in the world, you'd say. And they found him in the river next morning. Old Tyler that could swim like an eel. One of his brothers was worse. Only forty. Sat on a railway bank and waited for the train to come. Put his neck on the line when it was fifty yards away. Weren't a thing wrong with him. He'd just bought a new horse and had the caravan repainted all outside. Both of 'em cheerful, normal men, you'd say.'

'Good God. They just did it? For no reason?'

'That's right. 'Cepting there's got to be a reason inside somewhere. Old Tyler, you'd say, didn't have a care in the world. Four hundred pounds we had in the Post Office bank. Gave me a kiss and a cuddle afore he went out and they brung him up to the fairground the next morning on a hurdle. Smiling, he was, like it was all some joke. It's in the blood. No, it weren't no surprise to me what Blanche done. Shock, yes, and a mother's grief. But no surprise. She must have got it from his side of the family. What you going to do now, without her?'

George didn't answer. He sipped his whisky and shook his head. Blanche had been more part of his life than he had realized. What was he going to do without her? Do what everyone else did. he supposed, when they lost people ... let time and chance fill up the gaps, wait for memory to lose its sharp outlines. die away.

He said, 'I don't know. Just get stuck into something I suppose. Like this little business of mine. Make a go of it. She'd want me to do that.'

'Well, the money she left you will help. She wouldn't have left that unless she'd been real fond of you. Always careful about money was Blanche.'

So far as he was concerned, thought George bitterly, the money could all go down the drain if it would bring Blanche back. Lumley's Sunshine Gardens Ltd. How could you put your heart into something like that now? He'd wanted to do it for her. To show her that he could really make a go of something, and then to know her pleasure and the pride she would have had at his success. Christ Almighty, the things life did to you, and right out of the blue. You got up smiling, the sun shining, and – wham – life gave you a damned great smack in the face.

Outside, the morning was golden with sunlight that sparkled on the waters of the lake in St James's Park. A cock pigeon strutted up and down on the window sill, crop puffed up, aggressive, rumbling with courting calls to the hen pigeons on the roof.

Bush had Trader's second letter on the desk in front of him. It had been posted in Southampton the previous day. Already Sangwill had had the letter itself checked for fingerprints. There had been none. Trader had written that he wanted the same arrangements as before. The ransom was to be paid in diamonds, and he had specified the types and qualities. When the letter had been typed blank spaces had been left for the day, time and place for the hand-over of the Archbishop. These had been filled in by uneven purple letters and figures from some cheap child's hand-set printing kit. The typeface of the letter was the same as that on the letter to Sir Charles Medham. Bush guessed that the man had typed both letters at the same time ... He could imagine him typing them, and then going out, driving away in a car to ditch the typewriter somewhere. The sureness and arrogance of the man irritated him more than ever this morning. His mind went back to the hall of the Officers' Mess of the Army Aviation Centre at Middle Wallop. The slim wiry figure coming up the steps from the night, the grotesque mask, and the cab driver grinning from his car ... all that, thought Bush, he would have to go through again. There was no stopping it. The fiat had been issued through Grandison. There were to be no stratagems, no deceptions, not the slightest move which might in any way impede the smoothness of the hand-over or prejudice the safety of the Archbishop. The man would walk in from the night, take the diamonds and go. He, Bush, was going to stand there again and watch it all happen. And after it had happened, no matter what future was decided for the department – and there was no escaping the conventional pressures building against it already – there would be a black mark against his own name that would follow him in his record wherever he went. There would be other jobs for him, but none of them would ever be the ones he craved. And this Trader man would have done it to him, marked him before he was as developed and mature as Grandison, who already bore too many scars of past failures and triumphs for any further defeat or success to be able to touch him.

The previous evening his wife had returned unexpectedly from Norfolk. With a calmness and self-confidence he had not known in her before, she had said that she was going back to Norfolk to begin living with her lover. She had given the man's name – adding that she intended to change her name by deed poll to the same – and said that she was quite content to sit out the necessary time period before getting a divorce. She was happy and determined and saw clearly the way ahead of her. Her sureness and happy self-confidence were irritants to him that carried over into the Trader case. Nothing he handled was going his way. Thinking of it now, he wondered if the gods of chaos were laughing their heads off as they watched him – a man who wanted to trap and destroy Trader, their darling of the moment, a man who could not even create a moment's unease for a wife who meant nothing to him.

He got up and walked to the window. In a moment of human weariness he suddenly thought, what the hell did it matter? Let Trader have his diamonds, and let his wife have her divorce. It really didn't matter. By next Sunday morning it would all be over, the Archbishop back and Trader successful. All right – and then he would walk out, let ambition die, rid himself of his wife legally, and accept whatever life offered him. Standing there, watching the young green of shrubs and trees, the colours of daffodils and crocuses in the park, his mood was one of true despair.

It was at this moment that Sangwill came in. He handed Bush two sheets of paper.

'We had this from the Yard a little while ago. It came from the Wiltshire police. The second sheet is the print-out from the computer.'

Bush sat down and read the top sheet. It was a CID report from Salisbury on the suicide of one, Blanche Tyler. It gave all the relevant details, and a summary of her known movements on the Saturday prior to her discovery in the suicide car. It also mentioned that there was a family history of suicide. An autopsy had revealed that she was two months pregnant, death had undoubtedly been due to CO poisoning, but further examination and analytical tests on internal organs had revealed small traces of a compound of sodium theopentone and chlorpromezathine. It was possible that she could have been drugged first, placed in the car and then killed by carbon monoxide poisoning, the whole act being arranged to look like a suicide. She had a lover – one, George Lumley – who could have been responsible for her pregnancy and who inherited five thousand pounds under her will. Lumley's movements over the weekend had been cleared. Blanche Tyler's death had occurred between nine and ten o'clock on the Saturday night. Lumley had spent the hours between eight and ten o'clock in the Red Lion Hotel bar, Salisbury. He had been interviewed by the police and it was considered highly unlikely that he had had any connection with her death. The report was forwarded as a routine matter because Lumley had already been reported to the department in the Trader inquiries. Instructions regarding any further action with regard to Lumley or the case in general were requested. The Coroner's inquest had been fixed for the coming Friday.

The computer print-out gave all the Lumley details already reported with a cross reference to the sodium theopentone and chlorpromezathine traces found in the blood test of the Right Honourable James Archer, MP.

Bush, his mind reaching forward and assessing possibilities, his frustration lifting a shade in him, said, 'This theopentone stuff was used on Archer. It's a fair bet it was used on Pakefield. It could have been used on the Archbishop on Saturday. Trader used it each time. Now we have this woman on whom it has been used – on the same Saturday. By Trader?'

'Well, that's what the computer doesn't want us to ignore. Let's face it, it's not the kind of stuff you can walk into a chemist's shop and buy ready to use. But it could be made up by anyone who had the necessary chemical and dispensing knowledge.'

'Which George Lumley certainly doesn't appear to have.'

'Assuming for the moment that George Lumley is innocent of her death, and assuming, too, that he has no connection with Trader, and assuming also that this might be the million-to-one chance we've hoped, if not prayed, for. What kind of connection could there be between Trader and this woman Blanche Tyler which would make him kill her?'

Bush leaned back in his chair. In the past he had known truth to travel strange byways to reach them, and he had gone down many byways after truth and been disappointed. But the implications here – if truth was making some faint call for recognition out of the maze of computer data in which it had been lost – were elementary. He said, 'The Archbishop was kidnapped between four and five o'clock. Four or five hours later Blanche Tyler dies. Well?'

Sangwill shrugged his shoulders. 'Assuming Trader used the sodium theopentone on her, it's not hard to invent a reason. The most obvious one is that she got in the way, somewhere along the kidnapping line. She became more than a threat. She was a positive danger and he had to get rid of her. Or perhaps she'd been working with him all along and for some reason he found he had to murder her. Her description is nothing like that of the woman who collected the first lot of diamonds. But we have no proof that only one man and one woman have been involved in the kidnappings.'

Bush said, 'There's only one assumption we want to put our money on. That there's a connection between Trader and Blanche Tyler. Whether it was a long-established connection or a random one – something that happened that Saturday – doesn't matter. We've got to assume that what we want to be true is the truth. So where did Blanche Tyler go on that Saturday? Wherever she went we've got to believe that she found or met Trader there.'

'Nobody knows where she went. She packed up a picnic lunch and took off. Her mother doesn't know and Lumley doesn't know. All he can offer is that she sometimes went off to commune with nature.'

Bush stood up. 'We're going to find out. But we've got to be more than circumspect about it. Grandison will be in soon. I'll speak to him about the line we should take. But I can tell you one thing. Even if we could put our finger on Trader at this moment, we wouldn't be allowed to do anything about it. The exchange goes through. There is to be no smallest move that might put the Archbishop in jeopardy. That really would send up the balloon.'

'Well, that suits us. The Archbishop comes back. He's recovered from a bad chill and takes up his duties. Nobody knows a thing. And then we deal quietly with Trader – *if* all these assumptions are right and *if* we can trace him. Tracing him is the problem. You've got a dead medium and a happy-go-lucky remittance man. Big help.'

Bush shook his head sharply. This was the first scrap of hope ever offered. Now was the moment for an act of faith. Now was the moment for chaos to resolve itself into a revealing pattern. Perhaps the gods had turned against Trader at last. He said, 'Wherever she went, there must be some way of tracing her movements. I'll have to see how Grandison wants it handled.'

When he saw Grandison an hour later, the directive he was given was straightforward.

'You don't do anything. The Archbishop is going to be handed over on Saturday. Until that happens *all* inquiries by us or the police are taboo.'

'But this may be the lead we want!'

'I hope it is. But we do nothing about it now. How do you know Lumley or this Blanche Tyler's mother is not connected in some way with Trader? That's an assumption that mustn't be overlooked.' Grandison began to polish his monocle with his silk handkerchief. 'Blanche Tyler could have been working with Trader, too. It may be a long shot – but assume it's true. And then you turn up, making inquiries. That always makes people edgy, suspicious. So far it's a plain case of suicide. The Wiltshire people have got to keep it that way. The Coroner's inquest must go that way and a finding of suicide be brought in. I'll have a word with them and fix that. *Nothing* must be done that might at the longest stretch of imagination reach back to Trader and make him think the game is going against him. But once the Archbishop is back we can go to work. Until we get him back, Trader, whoever he is and wherever he is, has got to be absolutely certain that he is in no danger.' Grandison smiled. 'Would you like to take any step that might lead to the death of an Archbishop? Something that couldn't be kept quiet. The papers would explode! And a lot of heads, including ours, would roll. Don't worry. I mean to get Trader. But not until the Archbishop is safely back in his pulpit.'

'That may be too late. He may give us the slip.'

Grandison shook his head and slotted his monocle into place. 'I don't think so. I've been praying too hard. Prayer is often answered. The trouble is we sometimes don't realize it. But this is plain enough. The Archbishop is kidnapped between four and five. A woman dies between eight and nine the same day. Suicide it looks. Woman pregnant and with a family history of suicide. The police are busy people. Most forces would accept that. And why not? But the real answer to the prayer is that the Salisbury chief just doesn't take routinely to suicides. He asked for a further examination and it has brought out this theopentone stuff. If that hadn't been in their report neither you nor Sangwill would have been interested. You're not a betting man, are you? No. Well, if you were, you would know that there are a few rare moments in a punter's life when he picks a long shot and knows that it is going to win. This is a long shot and every nerve in my body tells me that it is going to turn up. So, just let's sit back and wait until after Saturday. The gods are working for us. They don't want us interfering just yet.'

*　　*　　*

Miss Rainbird put down the telephone and stared out of the window. Across the gardens by the lake some contractor's men had felled a diseased elm and the air was full of the sound of their mechanical saws as they trimmed it. She hated to see trees go. The elm had been there as long as she could remember ... had been standing there for years and years before she had been born. Now it was dead. There was a beginning and an end for everything.

She felt quite shaken by what Ida Cookson had just told her. Very shaken. She turned away from the window, poured herself a glass of sherry and sat down in her chair, the chair in which she had always sat when Madame Blanche had come here for her seances. And now Madame Blanche was dead. Had committed suicide, so Ida had said. Gassed herself in her car. It was unbelievable. A big, strong, capable, intelligent woman, that you only had to look at to know she enjoyed life ... loved it and as clearly loved what she did professionally. How extraordinary. What on earth made people do that? Just for a moment, while Ida had talked on, she had wondered if it could possibly have had anything to do with her rejection of the woman; but after a moment's reflection she had dismissed that. Madame Blanche had been used to rebuffs and to failures. She had stood here in this room and said so ...

And the dream, too. It was very odd that only last night she should have dreamt about the woman. Thank goodness Harriet didn't bother her at night now. But Madame Blanche had been with her last night. As clear and real as though she were sitting in the chair opposite now. She'd even been wearing those ghastly artificial pearls. In some odd way Madame Blanche, in the dream, had been on very different terms with her. As though they were old friends, reunited after a long parting. It was curious how you remembered some dreams so well. The memory persisting through to wakefulness with astonishing clarity. Madame Blanche had been wearing the lambskin coat which she had often seen Syton take from her on her visits, and she had been showing her around the house.

They were chatting and laughing like old friends. In the upper hallway at the top of the great staircase they had stood and looked out of the window, right down across the gardens to the lake, and she remembered there had been someone by the lake. It was a youth or a young man. She couldn't make him out very well because her sight was not so good for distances. But he was fair-haired, she knew. Knew, not only because she could make that much out, but because she knew the youth, though in her dream she had no name or reference to give him. She just knew him, accepted and loved him. She recalled now that she must have loved him because in the dream it had been clear enough that he was using a fly rod from the lakeside. Not in forty years since Sholto had stocked it with brown trout had the lake been fished. The trout were her pets, fat and lazy with daily feeding, some of them five and six pounds. And in the dream the youth had caught one. She could sense from his stance and movements the bow-like bending of the rod, and had seen the smooth water surface broken by the struggles of the fish. If anyone else had invaded the lake it would have been sacrilege. She would have been furious and would have rung for Syton at once. But she had just looked at Madame Blanche and the both of them had smiled, nodding happily to one another, sharing some unwordable pleasure at the sight of the youth fishing.

And then they had both turned out of the shaft of sunlight towards the gloom at the top of the stairs. There was no break in her memory of the dream at all. For her the head of the long staircase held bad memories, too. It was from here that Sholto had gone down to his death ... a death which had brought her freedom although she had had to struggle with her conscience against the sense of relief and happiness when she had known he was dead, that at last she was free and alone in the house, no longer to be plagued and bullied and humiliated by his ways.

Madame Blanche, pausing with her at the top of the stairs, had looked at her smiling and had said, as though all the family history and all her own thoughts were clear to her, 'Poor Sholto ... an unhappy man. You have no need to reproach yourself for your feelings, Grace.'

Grace. Yes, she had called her that. And she had replied –

how extraordinarily clearly the dream memory persisted with her – 'He would drink so much. I'd warned him. Asked him to be careful. But I must confess, now the years have passed, that it was a great relief for me.'

And Madame Blanche, beginning to move down the stairs, had said, 'All wrongs are redressed in time by those above who control the balance of life and death.' Then she had laughed and said with that heavy, jocular girlishness of hers, 'Come on, Grace, I want to see these new decorations and curtains of yours.'

She had walked on down the stairs with Madame Blanche and out of the dream. And now, Madame Blanche, the real one, not the friendly dream one, was dead, and it was very hard to believe.

She helped herself to another sherry. As she did so she realized that she drank rather more of it these days than had ever been her habit before. Well, old age, she thought, excuses a few indulgences. She sat there, thinking about Madame Blanche's death, and then going back to those moments as they had looked out of the window at the fair-haired youth, recalling the intense sensation of happiness there had been for her in those moments. She had had the feeling that something had come full circle, that life had been restored to its true pattern again. Extraordinary. What extraordinary things dreams were. She sipped her sherry and came slowly to the decision that it would not be out of place for her to send a wreath to Madame Blanche's funeral. She must find out when it was to take place. Perhaps it might be better not to put her name to it. Mark the card simply from 'a friend'. After all, just for a few moments in the dream they had been friends.

CHAPTER TEN

GEORGE COLLECTED HIS van on Wednesday morning from
Salisbury and drove it back to his cottage. He parked it outside the shed and with Albert at his heels walked slowly round
it, admiring it. Albert had not taken too kindly to the new van.
He clearly preferred the old car which George had traded in.
All the way back he had sat stiffly on the spare front seat and
growled to himself until George had cuffed his head and told
him to shut up.

It was a beautiful van, George thought. The green was the
shining green of the brightest, rain-washed spring grass, and
the yellow sunflower heads on each side were like great round,
golden shields. Exotic. Aztec. Eye-catching. George gloated
quietly and let his eye wander over the trade inscription –
Lumley's Sunshine Gardens Ltd, and below that his address
and telephone number. Beautiful. And he already had his first
contract. A man he had met in the Red Lion bar had moved
into a new bungalow and wanted his front lawn made up and
seeded and a square of paving stones laid at the back surrounded by a small rockery. He was going to start next week.
With luck he would have a boy by then because his advertisement was appearing in the local newspaper today.

It was a pity, he thought, that Blanche couldn't see the van.
A real eye-catcher. It would have appealed to her. Maybe the
old darling could see it. Looking down from up there and
enjoying the sight. Well, he hoped so. Poor Blanche. It still hit
him hard at times. Coroner's inquest on Friday. He had to be
on call for that, the police had told him.

Albert cocked a leg against one of the back tyres and
sprayed it. George swore at him. Inside the house he heard the
telephone bell begin to ring. Some early bird, he hoped, who

had read the newspaper advertisement, some bright, hard-working lad keen to get on in the world, green-fingered, broad-shouldered and with a reasonably short hair-cut. He wasn't taking on any hippie, freak-out types, no clock-watching, bead-wearing drop-outs.

He went inside and picked up the telephone and said, 'George Lumley here.'

A man's voice said, 'And how are things, then? All bright and shining in the legal world? Fees and briefs coming in? Wills to be willed and conveyances to be conveyed, trusts to be trusted and widows to be wept with?'

George recognized the voice at once as that of Mr Angers and, since it was twelve o'clock, he guessed that a bottle of champagne had already been opened with some customer.

George said, 'Angers, isn't it?'

'Dead right. Thought I'd give you a call about Eddie. What happened when you looked him up at Blagdon?'

For a moment George was lost.

'Blagdon?'

Angers laughed. 'Come on, lad, you're slow this morning. Late night lethargy? Eddie. Eddie Shoebridge. Remember? I phoned and gave your wife his address. Was just sitting here thinking about him. Wondered what had happened and how the old boy was and then said to myself I'd give you a ring and find out.'

'Oh, that Shoebridge thing.'

'Spot on. How did he take it? I mean, I don't want to have you break any professional confidences – just give me the newsy stuff around the edges.'

George's mind worked fast. Angers had called his wife and given her Shoebridge's address? That wasn't difficult to put in its place. He said, 'Well, as a matter of fact the thing's still in the air a bit. You know . . . these things take time and—'

'All right, old boy, I don't want you to tell me anything you can't. Just a friendly inquiry after old Eddie. Thought I might pop down to Blagdon one of these days and see him. Just wanted to know what the form was. Did someone go and see him or did you write?'

George now could picture Blanche driving off that Saturday with her picnic, knew exactly where she had been going, and could see her standing at this telephone at some time while he was out ... Clever, shrewd Blanche, keeping things to herself.

He said, seizing the help from Angers, 'Well, as a matter of fact we wrote to him. The firm felt that was the best first approach. Trouble is ... Well, so far we've had no reply.'

'Could be abroad, what?' suggested Angers. 'And why not? If you've got money who'd want to spend a winter in this country?'

George was on easy ground now and his mind found improvization easily. 'Well, he might be. But it's funny you rang because the firm felt perhaps my wife had got the wrong address. I was going to check with you again if we didn't hear in a couple of days. You're sure it was Blagdon?'

'Absolutely. Highlands House, Blagdon, Somerset. That's what the secretary of the Falconers' Club gave me.'

'Highlands House, Blagdon. Yes, that's what we've got. He must be away. I think I'll have to take a run down there and check it over. If it had been anything dead serious, of course, we'd have done it before, but there's no urgency about this matter.'

Angers laughed. 'If there's money in it, it's urgent, old boy. You show me the man who doesn't believe that – no matter how much he's already got. Well, when you see Eddie give him my love.'

'I will. And thanks for calling.'

George sat down on the settee and lit a cigarette. He stared across the length of carpet at Albert, who was sitting in the doorway. That Blanche. She was a quiet one. He would like to have asked Angers when he had telephoned but there had been no opportunity for that. In fact, he'd been damned lucky to get what he had. Quick as a flash he'd been about writing a letter. Well, he wasn't so dumb that simple things had to be spelled out for him. Blanche had got the address, and he knew exactly why she hadn't told him. There was an extra two hundred and fifty pounds involved. If she went and had a quiet chat with Shoebridge she'd know at once whether he was going to be acceptable to Miss Rainbird. If it were thumbs down ... well, that would be that and she'd have saved herself some money. Anyway, that didn't matter now. She was gone. The point was, what was he to do, if anything, about Shoebridge? Blanche *must* have gone to Blagdon. Once she had the address nothing would have stopped her except her regular appointments through the week. But Saturday she always kept free, and on the Saturday she'd gone off. He'd like to know what had happened at Blagdon that day. It might give some clue to her state of mind. It was all very well saying that suicide was in the family, but it must take some outside thing to spark it off. Some big disappointment, perhaps? Perhaps Shoebridge had turned out to be a hopeless proposition so far as Miss Rainbird was concerned. That would have been a blow for Blanche and her Temple of Astrodel. She really had been dead-set on that.

The more he thought about it, the more George felt that he would like to see Shoebridge. In a way, just to check for his own satisfaction. It was only two hours away at the most. He could pop down there this afternoon. Give the new van an airing. Show the flag. And maybe pick up some information that would make a little more sense out of poor old Blanche sitting up there in the wood, finishing it all off.

Half an hour later George was on his way to Blagdon. It had only briefly occurred to him to give the police this new information first, but he knew that if he had they might easily have told him not to go, that they would interview Shoebridge. He felt strongly that it was something he wanted to do. To see Shoebridge himself, a duty to Blanche to get a little closer to her and the way she had felt on that last Saturday. Dear old Blanche ... why in hell had she done it? Why? God, you could never tell with women, could you? Making out she was Mrs Lumley to Angers, too. Well, it was a pity she hadn't been. They should have been married. They were both blind not to have known it. Then none of this would have happened.

The Archbishop was by now well accustomed to the limited routines of his captivity. He was reasonably comfortable and certainly well fed. He also enjoyed a concession which had not been made to either Pakefield or Archer. He had been provided with writing paper and a supply of pencils. For this he was grateful. Prolonged time for thought and writing had been little enough in his public life. Now, whether he wished it or not, he was being given a period of meditation and privacy which he valued highly. He was a monk in a cell, a hermit in a cave. God gave strange gifts and worked strange shifts in the pattern of men's lives, and he acknowledged that for certain aspects of his captivity he was grateful.

The previous day, over the loudspeaker system, the man's voice, distorted but comprehensible, had told him that he would probably be released within a few days, and that the ransom being paid for him was a half a million pounds. The Archbishop had been distressed at the amount of money involved. It could have been used so much more usefully in the Church's business. He was, however, glad to be told that while the news of his kidnapping had not been made public – which he knew anyway from his reading of the *Daily Telegraph* – all those nearest to him knew the truth about his disappearance. In the paper today was a brief note that he was still confined to his bed with a severe chill.

Spending much of his time in prayer, meditation and writing, he found himself somewhat naturally concerned with the moral and practical attitudes which should be taken against evil – particularly current aspects of evil. Aircraft were hijacked and the lives of passengers and crew held against various exorbitant demands. Ambassadors and men in high public positions were kidnapped and equally outrageous demands were made either for pecuniary reward or political concessions. And always at risk in all the negotiations was human life. If demands were not met then men, women and children would die. Life was a gift from God which was to be treasured, but he wondered now whether it was not, too, a gift which men and women should be prepared to sacrifice in order to combat evil. The most foul-mouthed, irreligious private in a regiment accepted that premise. Every soldier contracted to give his life if it were necessary. Did people in high places make less solid contracts, underscoring them with saving clauses, or letting others write in saving clauses for them without protest? Of course they did. Sometimes, he thought, there was a purer conception of the true value to be placed on life, and the duty to offer it in sacrifice in the fight against evil among the men and women of the fighting forces. Why should his life be worth half a million pounds, which should have been spent in God's urgent work, not only to succour but in some cases to save other lives? Against evil there should be a bold, Christian statement of no compromise no matter what sacrifice it entailed, and he was very concerned that, perhaps, until this philosophy was accepted there could not be any true beginning to a real victory against evil. Evil, he thought wryly, kept pace with these modern times. It renewed its armament and its strategy. The Church possibly was still fighting a medieval war.

He wondered how he would feel if at this moment the choice could be given to him, the decision put absolutely in his hands to say or not to say 'pay no ransom, let them kill me'. The saints and martyrs had never had any doubt. Against evil there is only one true answer. No compromise, no matter what the cost. Evil thrived on men's fears and vanities. Until the day came when evil had that power stripped from it the battle had not really begun. Satan picked his people well. They were all ready to sacrifice themselves and gave no house-room to compromise. This man who held him, he guessed, would, if things went wrong for him, sacrifice himself or accept all the consequences of his act without flinching.

If the decision were his now to reject all compromise, what would he do? He knew the answer in his heart immediately.

From their sitting-room window Edward Shoebridge and his wife saw the van turn into the driveway and come up to the gravelled space in front of the house, a green van with great yellow sunflower heads on its sides.

'Lumley's Sunshine Gardens,' said Shoebridge. 'George Lumley.' There was little concern in him. When the stakes were high you expected moments of strain. He and his wife had gone through many such moments and with each one their confidence in their own powers had grown.

'Miss Tyler's man,' said his wife. She looked at her watch. It had just gone four. 'Be nice to him. I'll get some tea.' She turned and left the room as George began to climb the porch steps.

George rang the bell and it was answered by Shoebridge. George said, 'Mr Shoebridge?'

'Yes.'

'My name's Lumley. George Lumley. I wonder if you could spare me a little time? It's about a friend of mine, a Miss Blanche Tyler who, I think, must have called on you last Saturday. Did she?'

Shoebridge nodded. 'She certainly did. Come in, won't you.'

George was led into the sitting-room and offered a chair. He liked the room. It was comfortably furnished and not too tidy. Shoebridge seemed all right. A little younger than himself, perhaps; middle-height, wiry, thin fair hair, blue eyes crinkled at the corners and a tanned face, comfortable in corduroy trousers and a green sweater. Outdoor type he looked, easy-going George guessed, but no fool.

George said, 'I don't quite know where to begin with all this ... Let me say that I knew Blanche very well. Used to work for her on and off and – you haven't heard, of course, what happened to her?'

'Happened to her? What do you mean?'

'She's dead.'

'What!' Shoebridge's face registered his surprise.

'Yes, dead. You see that's why I had to come and see you. She committed suicide ... in her car ... you know, gassed herself. In a wood near Salisbury. It happened last Saturday night. They didn't find her until Monday morning.'

'Good Lord – what on earth did she do that for?'

'God alone knows. In a way, that's why when Angers telephoned and gave me your address I felt I had to come and see you and—'

208

'Angers? Oh, I remember – so that's how Miss Tyler got my address originally?'

'Yes. Only she didn't tell me she'd got it. She was a bit close, poor darling, at times. If Angers hadn't phoned me this morning I'd never have had any idea that Blanche had come down here. So I thought I'd just pop down and have a word with you about her.'

'Naturally. Poor Miss Tyler. Why should she do a thing like that? That's terrible.'

'I know. It just gets me. Blanche of all people. Did she act at all odd while she was here?'

Shoebridge was silent for a moment. It was quite clear that a readjustment of strategy was needed. Then he said, 'You know, of course, why she came to see me?'

'Yes, of course. I worked for her. She wanted to trace you and I did most of the work. Found old Angers and so on. But he phoned my place while I was out and she took the address and said nothing to me. He got the address from some falconry club. By the way, he'd like very much to hear from you. She came straight to the point with you, did she?'

'Well, not exactly. At first she pretended she was looking for a caravan site.'

'She would. That was one of her acts – until she'd made up her mind. She wanted to have a look at you first, size you up before she got down to the real business. What time did she get down here?'

'About half-past six. She'd called earlier but my wife and I were out. So she came back. Were you two engaged?'

'Not exactly. Good friends, you know. Knowing what you do now, how did she strike you?'

'Well, certainly not as the sort of person who would commit suicide. Unless she was more disappointed than she showed.'

'How come?'

'You know about Miss Rainbird and the true facts of my mother and father?'

'Yes I do. Blanche was dead keen on finding you and restoring you to the bosom of the family. Don't get any of this wrong, though. Blanche had her funny little ways, but she really believed in herself as a medium. She'd go the long way round sometimes to get what she wanted, but she was never dishonest. She had Miss Rainbird lined up for a fat donation to a crazy plan she had for building a temple. Sort of spiritualistic church. Finding you must have put her on top of the world.'

Shoebridge shook his head. 'I'm afraid it didn't. You see, Mr Lumley, I've known for years and years the truth about my birth. I knew all about Miss Rainbird of Reed Court. My foster parents made me their own child. They gave me love and a good life. *They* were my mother and father. I told Miss Tyler all this. And I told her also that I wanted nothing to do with Miss Rainbird. Nothing at all. I didn't want to see her, or hear from her, or accept anything from her. She was a stranger to me and I wanted to keep it that way. I'm afraid Miss Tyler was very upset about that.'

'I'll bet she was.'

'She tried to persuade me to change my mind – but without success.'

'Poor old Blanche. That must have been a blow for her. Good Lord, what with that, and if she had known she was pregnant . . . perhaps that accounts for it.'

'She was pregnant?'

'Two months – by me. Police autopsy showed it. We'll never know if she knew. But if she did, even though she knew I would do the right thing by her, it might have been enough to set her off. It runs in the family, you know. Her old man and one of her uncles, they both committed suicide.'

'I didn't know that, of course. But it all begins to make sense now, doesn't it? I hadn't realized just how disappointed she must have been at my attitude towards Miss Rainbird. It must have been quite a blow.'

'Knocked the stuffing out of her. Yes, I suppose that accounts for it. She was really counting on something big from Miss Rainbird if she had brought home the long lost nephew.'

George could see her, sitting in the car with the rain drumming down. She'd missed a couple of periods and could guess what had happened, and the foundations had been knocked clean out of the Temple of Astrodel. Poor old love, sitting there and then, maybe, remembering how her father and uncle had gone . . . The whole thing had been too much for her.

Shoebridge said, 'When is the inquest?'

'On Friday. I'm sorry about the trouble it may give you, but now I've found you and know she was here and what went on . . . well, I've got to tell the police.'

'Of course you have. If they want me to attend or to make any statement then naturally I'll do it.'

Half an hour later George was still in the house. Mrs Shoebridge had brought tea in and had been shocked when she had heard the news about Blanche. George liked them both and found them easy to get on with. They were the last people who had had any contact with Blanche and what they had told him had eased his mind a lot. He could give credibility now to Blanche's act. It was no longer the puzzle it had been. Clearly she had been backing on this Shoebridge discovery more than she had shown to help her set up her temple. He had two cups of tea and a large slice of excellent Dundee cake and slowly the talk drifted away from Blanche and he found himself telling them about his business venture and his hopes for it. They were interested and full of encouragement. They had no doubt that it would succeed. To George their enthusiasm was heartwarming. It was good to be told you were on the right lines, that with proper care there was a bright future ahead. Yes, he liked them both. A nice, easy-mannered couple, the kind you could easily have as friends. In a curious way he almost felt that they were friends, felt – from his researches for Blanche – that he had already known Shoebridge for a long time.

Before he left, he said to them, 'When I tell the police about this, you realize that I'll have to go into this Miss Rainbird thing. They'll ask you about it anyway – but there's one thing that bothers me. I think I ought to go and see Miss Rainbird.'

'Why?' asked Mrs Shoebridge.

'Well – she ought to know that Blanche found you. Blanche would have gone to her. I'd like to do it for her. I mean, unless you get in touch with her and tell her your feelings, she may go on looking for you and you'll have it all in your lap again some time later, maybe. Of course, if you want to see her, then that's fine and it lets me out.'

Shoebridge said, 'I'm quite happy for you to see her. There's no need for any bad feeling about the thing. The Rainbird family didn't want me when I was born. Now – no matter what Miss Rainbird might feel she could offer me – I don't want the Rainbird family.' He smiled. 'You tell her. I think you'll find she will be relieved. She's been suffering, I imagine, from a bad conscience on her sister's behalf. Now she's got absolution. We want nothing from her.'

Driving back, George felt that although Miss Rainbird had got absolution from Shoebridge, he wasn't so sure about from himself. Indirectly she had been the cause of Blanche's death. In fairness it wasn't Miss Rainbird's fault, but the fact remained that Blanche could have still been alive if she had never started this Shoebridge lark. And it was all to no point anyway. Shoebridge wanted nothing from Miss Rainbird. And he didn't blame him. The man had a proper pride. Well, he'd go and see the old girl and put the record right. Then there was the inquest to come and then the funeral – and after that he could really get down to his new business. By God he was going to make a success of that. For the first time in his life he was going to do something and make it stick. In a few years – if there were any truth in Blanche's beliefs – then she'd be able to look down and be proud of him.

Half an hour after George had left the Shoebridge house the telephone rang. It was their son calling from school. He rang them every Wednesday evening, talking first to his mother and then his father, giving and receiving news. School term finished the following week and he would be home for the holidays. Listening to his wife talking to the boy on the telephone, Shoebridge told himself that by the time the boy was home the Archbishop would have been returned. A new phase of living would begin for them.

At eight o'clock that evening, George called at the Salisbury police headquarters and gave a full account of his visit to the Shoebridges. Shortly after George had left the headquarters the new information was being passed on to Scotland Yard for transmission to Grandison's department. George, himself, was on his way to see Miss Rainbird. He wanted to get everything cleared as quickly as possible. If the old girl was out, well, he would be unlucky and have to see her the next day. He had not mentioned to the police that he was going to see Miss Rainbird. He regarded it as a piece of personal business between himself and Blanche which had to be finished. Anyway, the police knew all about Miss Rainbird and the Shoebridge search now. He was doing nothing unorthodox. If they had not wanted him to see Miss Rainbird they could have said so. They had not, so he saw no good reason why he should not go. He stopped in Stockbridge to have a drink and bought a pork pie for Albert.

At nine o'clock Syton came in to Miss Rainbird's drawing-room where she was reading after dinner and told her that there was a Mr Lumley at the door who would like to see her on behalf of Miss Blanche Tyler. Miss Rainbird, after a moment's hesitation, said she would see him.

After George Lumley had gone Miss Rainbird poured herself a large glass of sherry and sat down to think over the things Lumley had told her. She'd known a little of George's relationship with Madame Blanche from Ida Cookson. George himself had been quite frank about it. She couldn't say that she liked the man. His breath had smelt of gin and he had a seedy, slightly run-down look backed by a common sort of affability which she knew would have appealed to Sholto. In fact he was just Sholto's type. Still there had been no doubt about his distress over Madame Blanche's death. And he had been frank about her pregnancy and his responsibility. That he had been equally frank in revealing his part in tracing Edward Shoebridge did not surprise her. She had long ago guessed that Madame Blanche, no matter what genuine powers she had, must support her work with some kind of investigation in cases like hers. And now the police knew all about it. The thought of that was very irritating and she knew that she could easily become angry about it. The next thing would be that they

213

would be in touch with her and she might have to go to the inquest and the whole affair would become public.

The thought of publicity did upset her. To begin with she didn't want her family affairs the subject of newspaper reports and, even more, she in no way welcomed the thought of what her friends would think – that she was a stupid, gullible woman who had been on the point of being taken in by a medium. It was what she herself would have thought of anyone else in similar circumstances. Really, the whole thing was too much. And all stemming from those stupid dreams about Harriet. All her life Harriet had been a worry and a responsibility to her ... a soft-headed, stupid creature, no backbone, no steady character. In many ways she and Sholto had had much in common. It had been a relief to her when she had finally found herself alone and mistress of Reed Court. Years of peace and tranquillity had stretched ahead. And now – because of Harriet's whining dream appearances and her own weakness in taking notice of them – she could easily become the laughing stock of the county. Tomorrow she would have to get on to her solicitor and see what could be done about it. Her solicitor was a conventional, afraid-to-say-boo-to-a-goose type, but she would have to bully him and insist that he use his influence with the authorities to make sure that she was not called at the inquest if it were at all possible. Surely the authorities would understand the undesirability of such an appearance for a woman in her position?

And as for the Shoebridges – well, there was the final answer to any further whining demands on Harriet's part, though she was happily free from them so far. Her sleep and her dreams had become her own again. So Edward Shoebridge had rejected the Rainbirds. He had looked on Ronald Shoebridge and his wife as his real father and mother, even though he'd long known the truth. Finishing her sherry and helping herself to another, she could find it in herself to be annoyed about that. All along she had seen herself – if Edward Shoebridge were traced – as the one who would do the deciding. It really was quite unforgivable of the man not to come and make his feelings known personally. That was Harriet's blood in him

214

all right. If there was anything unpleasant to do then you got someone else to do it for you. Well, if that were his decision then it absolved her from all further concern. But any real man would surely have come himself and made his position clear in a private conversation. Apart from all this nonsense of regarding the Shoebridges as his true parents, the man must be an idiot not at least to have had the common courtesy to see her and to find out what she had to offer. Perhaps if he had he might have changed his mind. She was Miss Rainbird of Reed Court and at the last check of her properties and investments she had been worth nearly a million pounds. One didn't advertise it, of course. But if she had liked him, she might have hinted at it. After all, he had a wife and a son – about fifteen the Lumley man had said – and a responsible father would have considered their welfare. No, all she had had was a curt dismissal through an intermediary. Cheek! Pure, arrogant rudeness!

So strongly did emotion overcome her at the thought that her hand shook and she spilled sherry over the brocaded arm of her chair. If she had the man here now she would tell him exactly what she thought of his way of behaving. Perhaps, she thought, the correct response from her would be to write and tell him in frank terms what she thought of his rudeness and to point out that, if at any time in the future he changed his mind, it would be quite useless to make any approach to her. No, she wouldn't do that. She would do nothing. Absolutely nothing.

She finished her sherry and could feel her head swimming a little. Not much, but just that much which she knew now was enough to send her to sleep the moment her head touched the pillow, to sleep without dreams. As she went up the grand staircase she remembered the dream she had had of Madame Blanche visiting her, Blanche the old friend. Ridiculous. And the lad, youth, young man, whatever he had been, seen fishing through the landing window? Who had that been? Shoebridge's son? Certainly not. His father had rejected her, rejected everything concerned with her. And thank God for that. She turned and looked down the stairs, remembering Sholto's

215

drunken fall ... Harriet disgracing them ... pestering her, still bothering her after death ... and Sholto disgracing her, too, with his women and drink ... But for them both she might have married and had her own family ... Well, she hadn't. And she wasn't the kind who wasted time crying over spilt milk.

Just for a moment as she looked down into the half-lit hall-way below she fancied she could see Sholto's form lying crumpled at the foot of the stairs. Poor Sholto, what a fool he had been to himself. Like Harriet he had been wrapped up in himself. From no one in this house or elsewhere, Miss Rain-bird thought, had she received real love and affection.

Bush went into Grandison's room. It was ten o'clock in the morning and he had spent the night in the department. At midnight the department had received the additional report from the Salisbury police containing the information about Blanche Tyler's visit to the Shoebridges' house. The report had been passed on to Grandison at once. Elation was in Bush like a slow, smooth current, flowing easily and with a deep strength. The pleasure that this moment brought him had come from little that the department had done. Its work was now only beginning. Time and chance had run for them, and there was a certainty in him that it would go on running.

He sat down opposite Grandison. His chief was in heavy tweeds and there was a green silk cord to his monocle – always green or red. Bush felt there was some hidden rhythm or sig-nificance in the changes of colour. One day he would give it thought – correlate it to mood or weather conditions. He smiled. He was feeling good and could indulge in the occa-sional side fancy now.

Grandison said, 'You look like a cat that's been at the cream.'

Bush shrugged his shoulders. 'You know we've got him. There's no room for doubt in my mind.'

'There's always room for doubt. But, I agree, little here. What have you got?'

'I've been in touch with Salisbury and with Somerset. The

only approach that Somerset will make – on a request from Salisbury – is to visit Shoebridge, acting on information received through this Lumley man, and take a statement about Miss Tyler's visit. He has no record, but they know something about him and we know more now. His birth and his foster parents and so on. It's his second marriage. His wife – his second – was a doctor. Gave up practice when she married him.'

'She'd manage the theopentone stuff?'

'Yes. He was never thrown up by the computer because there was no cellar to his house. They made a mistake there. It's a house built on the site of an old one which did have cellars. Could still have.'

'Must have if we're going to be right.'

'I'd bet on it. One of your long shots which are certainties. He's mad about hawking. That's how the Lumley man got his address. An old friend remembered he was a member of the British Falconers' Club.'

'Lumley seems to have done all our work for us.'

'Unwittingly. The noise Pakefield heard could have been one of the birds. Falconers carry them around with them a lot. He could have been working the intercom system and it became disturbed. They have these little bells on their feet. The house is high. Well-drained. He and his wife were out of the house last Saturday when Miss Tyler first called. They didn't get back until around six-thirty.'

'She walked in on them at the wrong moment? Probably saw the Archbishop, is that it?'

'Something like that. They had to fix her. They must be cool customers. First they get a visit from her and then one from the Lumley man. They handle both without turning a hair. Lumley told the Salisbury police he was a nice chap. He liked them both and they were helpful and quite prepared to go to the inquest.'

'We don't want that. I'll get in touch with Salisbury and arrange it. The Coroner will be satisfied with a certified statement from Shoebridge through the Somerset people. Lumley can be called. This Miss Rainbird – I think she should be kept out too. A statement from her will be enough. We want the whole thing quiet and unobtrusive. The Salisbury people will understand that. I'll explain the position to them. If Shoebridge is our man we don't want the slightest thing to ruffle him. The inquest must go through smoothly. Woman pregnant, big disappointment over this medium business with Shoebridge, family history of suicide ... the Coroner won't want more than that. And after that the exchange of the Archbishop goes through with the same smoothness. Nothing is ever going to make the headlines. Only a few people are going to know the truth and then lock it away. We want no checks, no watch on the Shoebridge couple. They must be left alone.'

'Until Sunday. Then what?'

Grandison smiled. 'Then this department does something it was created to do – if the Shoebridges are the right couple.' Grandison stood up. 'There's been no credit in this for us. We've been lucky – if the Shoebridges are our people. All we can do is to tidy up at the end. I want one man down at Blagdon on Saturday. At midnight. They'll have left by then to return the Archbishop. Our man stays until they return and then lets us know.'

'They may take off. We ought to warn all ports and airfields.'

'If it is them they'll return. They're not going to abandon the house. It's full of birds. The cellar is there. No, they'll go back and just go on living normally for some time. My guess is that they haven't even sold the diamonds they've already collected.'

'What are they after? Money. The good life?'

'If the gods are really going to be kind to us, then we'll have the pleasure of asking Shoebridge. I've an idea what he'll say already.'

'The good life?'

'Yes. As he sees it.'

Bush stood up. 'It'll be good to have it all finished.'

Grandison shook his head. 'Nothing's ever finished. It's an endless pattern.'

*   *   *

218

George went to the inquest with Blanche's mother. Neither Miss Rainbird nor Edward Shoebridge was called, but statements had been submitted on their behalf. It was all over very quickly and a finding of suicide while the balance of her mind had been disturbed was brought in on Blanche. The next day, Saturday, he went to the funeral at the crematorium with Blanche's mother. There were quite a few wreaths, many of them from Blanche's clients including Miss Rainbird. (Miss Rainbird, since her name had featured at the inquest, had decided against sending an anonymous wreath.) Blanche's mother cried a little on the way back to the house, and they sat in the kitchen and had tea with whisky in it. Mrs Tyler decided that she would have a rose planted in the crematorium grounds in memory of Blanche. She brightened up a little as they discussed what kind of rose and George, burgeoning now as an horticulturalist, said he'd get some rose catalogues for her so that she could choose. Personally he felt that neither the rose nor the little pot of ashes had anything to do with Blanche. When the coffin had sunk slowly out of sight within the marble platform it had been like a log disappearing through melting ice and he had been incapable of connecting Blanche with it. Blanche had gone days before. She was over on the other side, happy with her Henry, and he sincerely hoped that it would be all that dear old Blanche had wanted it to be. He doubted it. Disappointment was the lot of humankind. When he left Mrs Tyler he went to the Red Lion and had three or four whiskies as a private farewell to Blanche and, not wanting Albert to feel neglected – though Blanche had never been very fond of Albert – he took the dog out two meat pies to have for its supper when they got home.

Driving home he was a little tight and turning into the narrow lane entrance to his cottage he lightly grazed the side of his beautiful van on one of the posts. He was furious at his clumsiness and decided that Albert should have only one meat pie.

In the cottage he poured himself another whisky and began to go through a small pile of applications he had had for the post of assistant. The illiteracy of most of them made him

219

angry and he had another whisky to show what he thought of modern education and the youth of his day. He put the whole bundle of letters on the fire and by the time he went up to bed he was very drunk.

The last thing he remembered was standing in his pyjamas and casting his eyes up to the badly papered bedroom ceiling and calling heavenwards, 'Send me a sign! Blanche, send me a sign!' and then collapsing across the bed before he could know whether Blanche had obliged. In the morning when he went out, badly hung-over, to his van to inspect the damage he found that he had left the headlights on all night and the battery was flat. At that moment he came very close to abandoning his project.

CHAPTER ELEVEN

FOR THE THIRD time they were in the large hallway of the
Officers' Mess of the Army Aviation Centre at Middle Wallop. It was fifteen minutes past midnight. Outside, the driveway lights were on and a warm wind was blowing from the
west. The bowl on the centre table held dwarf, crimson-
bloomed tulips. Alongside it lay the washleather bag of diamonds, a jeweller's optic and the set of balances. The diamonds were genuine, a half a million pounds' worth. Trader's
letter of instruction had stated that he wanted blue whites, fine
whites and whites and none of them were to have a clarity
value of less than vsi (very slight inclusions) and that among
the blue whites – the most valuable of all the colours – there
had to be at least fifty per cent which were flawless. If the man
himself came this time, Bush thought, then he would closely
examine at least some of the diamonds. On this third sortie
nothing would be taken on trust.

Grandison was reading a pocket volume by the fireplace.
Sangwill sat by the hall telephone. Here they all were as they
had been twice before. But this time things were different.
Bush had no doubt in his mind that Edward Shoebridge was
Trader. It had become an article of faith with him. That they
were going to be successful because they had been lucky would
be known to very few people. All frustration was gone from
him now. There would be no mark against his name. From the
department he would go on to higher appointments. Well, in
every man's life there came a time when luck joined him. He
accepted that now, but still wished that their success could
have come from their own efforts. Tonight luck was with him
and against Shoebridge. Tonight everything was against Shoebridge, thanks to the heavy-handed sleuthing of George Lum-

ley, a George Lumley who would never know anything about the part he had played, and thanks to an impressionable old lady whose conscience had finally troubled her over her dead sister's illegitimate child.

The telephone rang. Sangwill answered it, speaking briefly. When he put it down he said, 'She's coming up now.'

'She?' Bush's voice showed his surprise.

Grandison put his book into his pocket and stood up. 'Naturally. Both Archer and Pakefield were smallish men. She could handle them from the van alone. But the Archbishop is heavy. The man would have to work that end this time.'

'It's a car. She's driving herself.'

Grandison nodded. 'That fits. All the world knows about the first two times ... a masked woman and then a man with a carnival mask. They wouldn't risk having to deal with some long-memoried, heroic cab driver. It'll be a stolen car, taken somewhere locally. A hospital probably. She was a doctor once.' He flipped a finger towards the door for Bush to meet the woman.

Bush went out, angry with himself. It was an unimportant deduction which Grandison had kept to himself. But he should have made it for himself. (Four hours later it was confirmed that the car had been taken from the Andover War Memorial Hospital a few miles away. The hospital was five minutes' walk from the station.)

He went down the steps as the car came up the drive. As the car stopped all its lights were turned off. Bush stood there, the warm, unseasonal wind washing against him, blowing strongly across the open playing field where the waiting helicopter was parked.

The woman was dressed as he had seen her before, her face swathed to the eyes in a black silk scarf, a raincoat belted closely around her, and a dark beret pulled close over her head, hiding all of her hair. For a moment it was possible to imagine she was some close-cropped man.

She crossed from the car to the steps, paused and looked at him and then gave a little nod. She went up the steps past him and pushed open the door with a gloved hand. Bush went in after her.

Watching her and her movements was like experiencing some familiar dream sequence. But there was no satisfaction in it. He had wanted it to be the man. He had wanted to have the man here, to stand and watch him and know within himself that the man was doomed, that bad luck had marked him. The woman was nothing. The man was their real prey. Bush felt that he had been cheated. The gods who had worked for them should have seen that this scene was played with proper irony.

The woman tipped a scattering of stones free from the bag and began to examine them through the optic. She made three small piles and then weighed each pile on the carat scales. None of them spoke. She examined and weighed another sample of diamonds and then carefully put the diamonds back into the bag. She slipped the bag into her coat pocket, nodded at Grandison, and then moved towards the door.

Bush followed her. The first time he had escorted her he had led the way. Now she kept ahead of him. She went down the drive and turned right-handed along the little shrub-lined path that led to the helicopter field. In the helicopter was the same pilot who had flown the mission twice before.

A few moments later the rotor blades turned, their wind flattened the grasses and buffeted against Bush. He watched as the machine went up into the windy, cloud-pocked sky. The navigation lights were turned off and the machine was lost in the night while the sound of its flight was still with him. She would be sitting up there writing her directions on her note-pad. There would be triumph in her. Let there be, he thought. Let her be full of it. She and her husband had almost sent him into limbo, marked for life. But the gods had said no. They had wheeled Miss Rainbird, Miss Blanche Tyler and George Lumley on to the scene and the whole pattern of the play had altered in his and the department's favour.

He went back into the hall and helped himself to a whisky. The others were already drinking. Grandison had his book out. Grandison, he knew, regarded this night as a routine matter. Grandison would be a different man tomorrow.

223

Just over an hour later the helicopter returned. It landed on the playing field. The three of them met it. With them now was an ambulance with a driver and a doctor. The Archbishop was still very heavily sedated. They lifted him from the helicopter to the ambulance. The doctor made a quick examination, nodded his head, and within minutes the ambulance was on its way to London with Sangwill and the doctor in the back.

Bush and Grandison took the helicopter pilot into the mess hall and gave him a drink. He had flown south-west on a line which would have taken him to the coast at Bournemouth. He knew the whole area well. They had landed in a clearing of the New Forest surrounded by trees which had a small road running close by. He had seen no car but the man had flashed them down with a torch. He had been waiting with the Archbishop, blanket-wrapped, on the grass and had helped load him aboard while the woman covered them with a gun. The man had worn a raincoat, cloth cap and gloves and the lower half of his face had been scarf-wrapped. The pilot was sure that it was the same man that he had seen before, the same height and the same build. When the Archbishop was aboard the man and woman had backed away into the trees. The pilot had made no attempt to search for them from the air.

When the pilot had gone Bush spread the map of Southern England on the table. From the New Forest point to Blagdon would take a car anything between two to two and a half hours. The time could well be longer if the pair deliberately took a roundabout route which they might do because they would assume that once the Archbishop was safely back there would be a police call out to check cars in the area. If the Shoebridges were the kidnappers then there should be a call from their man at Blagdon reporting their return to the house within the next three to four hours.

The call came at a quarter to five that morning. It was made from a telephone box in the village of Blagdon. The Shoebridges had returned in a small van at twenty minutes past four.

Bush, no doubt at all in his mind now, turned to Grandison. 'They're back. Half an hour ago.'

Grandison nodded. 'We'll leave here at eight o'clock. That'll give us two hours' sleep and time for breakfast. Eleven o'clock is a civilized hour to call on a Sunday morning.'

'Just you and I?'

'Yes. It now becomes our private business. No publicity, no police, just a simple adjustment – meeting violence with violence. It's the only way until men realize that you gain nothing by compromising with evil, that there are times when life must be sacrificed to make other lives safe. If it had been necessary Shoebridge would have killed the Archbishop. To be able to kill, you must already have accepted death for yourself as the due consequence of failure.'

'We just drive up to the front door?'

'Why not? The house is isolated. Visitors don't come on foot. And they won't know the car. We drive up and walk in, Bush. It's a moment you must have thought would never come.'

'Well, yes, that's true.'

Grandison smiled. 'Prayer and luck, they're two good horses to back. I did the praying and luck favoured you. A fair division. We'll end it that way, too.' He took a coin from his pocket, spun it and trapped it on the back of his hand. 'Heads you get the woman, tails you get the man. Agreed?'

Bush nodded.

Grandison uncovered the coin. 'Tails. Your luck is holding. You wanted him, didn't you?'

Bush nodded again.

Sunday morning, the first Sunday in April, the sixth Sunday in Lent, and Palm Sunday, puffballs of cloud racing over a blue sky, young green showing on the hawthorns and the wind tolling at the heavy heads of the daffodils, and George whistling contentedly to himself as he put out fresh food and water for his birds in the aviary. Albert sat outside and watched him. George was happy. Early that morning a village mother had come to him with her son, a big, strong, cheerful boy of sixteen whom George knew and liked, a neat, tidy boy who wanted to work for him. The scratch on the van could be fixed as good as new for a couple of pounds, and on Monday morning he started his first job. Everything was going to turn out right. He was going to make a go of the business. Lumley's Sunshine Gardens Ltd. But not limited. Unlimited. He was going to go places. He could feel it in his bones.

Sunday morning at Reed Court, the sunshine striking through the window of the breakfast room, setting the silver on the table ablaze, warming the cold snow of the damask table cloth, and Miss Rainbird in a bad temper because she had not slept well. For the last two nights she had not slept well, despite her sherry. She had known she had dreamt but on awakening could remember nothing. And awakening early she had lain in bed and found herself thinking more and more of the utter outrageousness and discourtesy of Edward Shoebridge's dismissal of the Rainbird family. Someone, she thought, should teach the man a lesson in manners. Who did he think he was? Illegitimate, a product of Harriet's stupidity, brought up by that loathsome chauffeur who had been Sholto's crony – and calmly sending her a message telling her that she could keep her position, her money, Reed Court, all that the Rainbird family had stood for for over hundreds of years. He wanted none of it. The byblow of an Irish adventurer and that spineless sister of hers. It had been a wound to her pride which she could not take easily. Would not take. She was not a woman to be dismissed in such a cavalier fashion. If anyone was going to be peremptory then it would be her. She would go and see him and put him in his place, tell him that he had got the wrong idea from Madame Blanche, that Madame Blanche had been acting entirely without authority, that she, Miss Rainbird, had had no intention of offering him anything at all, that not in the remotest way had he any claims on the family so far as any pecuniary matters were concerned. She rang the bell for Syton and told him that she wanted the car in half an hour. Mr Shoebridge might deal discourteously through an intermediary, but not her, not Miss Rainbird. If something unpleasant had to be done to restore one's peace of mind, then one should do it oneself. That was something she had learned long ago.

Sunday morning and ten minutes to go before morning chapel, which Martin Shoebridge meant to miss, no matter the trouble he would land himself in. Chapel was a bore and he was going to walk over to the farm where he kept his ferrets. A few days before he had bought a polecat ferret jill from a gamekeeper and he wanted to try her out along the farm hedgerows. There were plenty of young rabbits around now. He would be punished but punishment meant nothing to him. If you could be clever enough to avoid it you did, and he was becoming quite experienced in avoiding it, but if it were inevitable then you just took it. In two days' time he would be home for the holidays. There was no punishment there, only understanding and a way of life which suited him absolutely. He walked, hands in his pockets, fair-haired, well built and wiry like his father, whistling to himself, fifteen years old and missing nothing, seeing the distant movement of sheep on the downs, the quick flirt of wren and blue-tit in the hedges, and the clumsy triangular spoors of a rabbit in the mud by a field gate. While he was with his ferrets the farmer's sixteen-year-old daughter, Mabel, would probably come hanging around. Well, she would be unlucky this morning. He wasn't going to waste any time mucking around in the hay of the big barn with her. A kestrel came down wind then hung hovering at the far end of the field. He stood watching it. It was a male, head lowered, watching the ground below. He suddenly saw the great sweep of the Mendip hills rolling away from Highlands House ... He loved the place, but one day there would be another place, miles, miles better which he knew he would love more. His father had promised it. He walked on whistling gently. Life was full of promise and good things. You just had to know what you wanted, that was all, and then take it.

Sunday morning and the wind was coming in west and warm from the sea. The Shoebridges had slept late and Edward Shoebridge had just awakened. His wife slept still. The bedroom was on the north side of the house and they slept always with their curtains drawn back. Lying in bed he could see through the crystal-clear air the long line of the hills and then their slow drop to the plain and the sea beyond. April was in and spring was taking the land. The big early-run salmon would be coming in from the sea to the rivers. The cliffs of Steep Holm and Flat Holm would be full of nesting seabirds. On the hill slopes the lapwings had long paired off and he could hear a morning lark singing. He lay drained of all feeling except contentment and found himself thinking of the Archbishop's writings, which he had read through before letting the man take them away with him. They had formed an examination of Christian ethics, a criticism and a consideration which had interested him in a way no other theological work ever had. But he guessed that they were a personal statement and would not be published. In different circumstances he would have been interested to talk to the man about them. He quarrelled with nothing in them except their misunderstanding of the nature of man. The world would have had to retrace its steps to find the virtues that the Archbishop argued had to be cherished above all others. Adam and Eve had stepped out of paradise and within half a mile had taken the wrong turning. There was no hope for mankind. It was beginning to destroy itself. Nothing could halt the progress of slow annihilation. Even the small paradise which he was going to create for himself, his wife and his son would eventually be over-run in the time of the sons of the sons of his son ... perhaps sooner, perhaps later, but it would come. There was no inviolable virtue in what he wanted to create. It was as personal and limited as another man's ambition to become chairman of a company, head of a college or a church, but it was the thing that he had to do. If it could not be done then there was nothing he wanted. It was what the diamonds in the washleather bag on the dressing-table would give him. The world would soon become a rubbish dump populated by scavengers. All he wanted was to escape during his time and to take the people he loved with him.

The front door bell rang. He looked at the bedside clock. It was a quarter past eleven. He got up and put on his dressing-gown. The bedroom window gave no view of the driveway. He went to the head of the stairs and looked out of the window over the front porch. He could just see the front of a car. It was an old Ford Capri, mud-splashed. There was no suspicion in him. What he had done had been well done. He went down the stairs and opened the front door.

The two men stepped in quickly and killed his first movement of recognition and reaction. They held him expertly and the bigger of them clapped a hand over his mouth. The other ran a free hand over him quickly to check him for weapons. When they were satisfied that he was unarmed the big man moved his hand quickly from his mouth and squeezed his throat in a choking grip. The other flicked a scarf from his pocket and tied a gag around his mouth. The whole assault was a rapid routine in which they were well practised.

They stepped back from him and he was covered by their two automatics.

The big man, bearded, a monocle dangling loose over his breast, said, 'We've met before, of course, but never been introduced. I'm Grandison and this is Bush. Just turn round and go quite normally to wherever your wife is. When we get to her we'll take the gag off.'

For a moment or two Shoebridge stood unmoving. There was no panic or fear or bitterness in him. Through the open door he could see the back window of the car. It was covered partly with crude holiday stickers of places visited, the flags and shields marking Weymouth, Brighton, Southend and Blackpool. Slowly he turned and led them along the hallway and up the stairs. Somewhere, something had gone wrong. To speculate on when and where and how was idle now because he knew his time was running out and there would be no satisfaction or comfort in knowing. Behind him were his executioners. He knew something of the department and its power by now. There would be no formalities, no law processes. These men worked with and without the law. They had nothing to fear.

He paused by the shut bedroom door. Bush moved him aside and went in. The woman was sitting up in bed. She wore a black silk nightdress, her arms bare, and she was brushing her hair, hair as dark as the nightdress. She was good-looking

229

and firm-bodied. For a moment she stared past him to her husband and Grandison behind, her right arm poised, frozen in the act of brushing her hair. Slowly her arm came down.

Grandison took the scarf from Shoebridge's mouth and said, 'Get into bed with her.'

Shoebridge moved to the bed and slid in beside her.

'Keep your hands where we can see them,' said Bush. His eyes went swiftly round the room, cataloguing, absorbing everything. He saw the washleather bag on the dressing-table. He backed to it, picked it up and handed it to Grandison.

Shoebridge, his right hand holding one of his wife's, said, 'For myself I don't care, but is there nothing you can do for—'

'No.' His wife interrupted him sharply.

Grandison said, 'There is nothing. When you started all this you must have accepted that. Luck, the gods, were against you. They were against you from the moment of your birth. You made no mistake. It was made for you before you were born. All our mistakes spring from the infinity of time past.' He raised the leather bag in his left hand. 'What were you going to do with all these?'

Shoebridge shrugged his shoulders. 'Buy ourselves a place to be and time to be in it.'

Grandison nodded. 'Every man has that dream in some shape or other. Few do more than dream about it. All right – you have ten seconds.'

Shoebridge released his wife's hand and put his arm around her shoulders. His cheek just touched hers but they did not look at one another. Shoebridge's eyes went from Grandison to Bush and then back to Grandison.

'Be quick,' Shoebridge said and he held his wife closer to him.

Grandison nodded and his right hand came up. He and Bush fired together. There was no need for them to fire more. Bush walked to the bed and pulled the loose cover clumsily up over them.

Grandison said, 'I'll look after it up here. You do it from the kitchen.'

Bush went downstairs, leaving Grandison in the bedroom. In the kitchen he found the electric toaster and switched it on. He picked up a Saturday newspaper from the table and laid it across the top of the toaster. When it began to scorch he struck a match and dropped it on the brown, curling paper and it burst into flames. He fed the flame with another paper and trailed it to the kitchen curtain above the sink. The flame fought for a hold on the material, gathered strength, and began to lick upwards. Bush stepped back. There was a plywood breakfast tray with a small wickerwork border by the sink. He edged it into the mass of burning paper and the thin, dry wickerwork flared into instant flame. He worked quickly, efficiently, laying the groundwork for a Sunday morning tragedy; the clumsy husband getting breakfast for his wife, tossing a paper down by the toaster while he went back to his wife to ask her something, the kitchen door left open, causing a draught to turn a page of the paper and lift it on to the toaster.

He backed out of the kitchen, leaving the door open. A slow pall of smoke followed him, obscuring the doorway. From beyond it came the sharp noise of burning wood and the deep sighing sounds of flames gathering power.

He stood at the end of the hall and watched the fire move out of the kitchen, long tongues of flame curling and licking around the door framework and reaching up and racing in a flat, rippling flood across the ceiling.

Grandison came down the stairs. At the landing top a small eddy of smoke, thin and spiralling, whirled around like a ghostly dancer.

Without speaking the two men stood by the front door, watching and listening to the holocaust take possession. When it was no longer safe for them to stay they went out and closed the door.

Bush said, 'There's a dog somewhere and his birds.'

Grandison said, 'Leave them. That's how it would have been.' He got into the car on the far side. Bush took the wheel and they drove to the bottom of the drive, and turned up the narrow lane that led to the side road. It was all over. The bodies would be hardly recognizable as human. The questions if they came officially would be answered officially . . . causing no embarrassment.

On the side road they stopped and looked back. The house was out of sight now behind the elms. There was the faintest trace of smoke above the trees. The house inside by now would be an all-consuming furnace.

Miss Rainbird arrived at the top of the narrow lane at one o'clock. The road was blocked with a police notice and a police car was drawn up on the verge. Two fire engines were at the house, but there had been trouble with the water supply and they had been able to do little. A thick, slow, black spiral of smoke rose lazily above the elms.

The police patrol man was polite. He explained what had happened and said that he could not let Miss Rainbird through. Miss Rainbird, containing her shock, heard herself say, 'I think you must let me through. Edward Shoebridge was my nephew.'

The policeman said, 'If you'll wait for a moment, madam, I'll have a word with the Super.' He went back to the car and began to speak on the radio. A few minutes later Miss Rainbird's car drove down the lane towards the house. Sitting in the back Miss Rainbird was now completely composed. For Edward Shoebridge, and his wife, she could have little feeling. But she knew what she had to do if only for Harriet's sake.

CHAPTER TWELVE

FOR THREE YEARS Miss Rainbird had been happier than she had ever been in her life before. After the Shoebridges' shocking deaths there had been no hesitation in her about where her duty rested. She had taken Martin Shoebridge into her house and made him her own. He was her great-nephew, and all that remained of the male line of the Rainbirds.

At first he had been withdrawn and shy, and even a little difficult at times. But slowly she had won him over and in doing so had become fond of him, even doted on him and – to her joy – he had slowly responded until now there was a smooth, sweet relationship between them which was making the last years of her life full of happiness. She had long ago forgotten that she had taken him in out of duty. He was now part of her life, and his future was all of her concern. The companionship between them was something, she realized, which she had longed for all her life. If he had faults, and what boy hadn't? – though he was boy no longer but a young man of eighteen – then she could forgive and tolerate them. She had had to send one or two maids packing, because she was sure that they were primarily responsible for the small lapses in which he had indulged. Anyway, it was natural for a young man of his age to be interested in young women. He was very popular in the district and always in demand. One day, and she prayed that she would be alive to see it, he would marry some well-connected girl and bring her to Reed Court as his wife. If God were good to her she might live to see his children. After all she was not eighty yet and still in good health, although she had to admit that there were long periods when she did not sleep well at night, teased and disturbed by dreams that fled from her memory on waking. And sometimes she did have bad bouts of migraine.

She stood at her bedroom window now and looked out over the garden. It was a beautiful June evening, the tree shadows lengthening, a movement of wildfowl on the small lake, and the far meadow speckled with the gold of great kingcups. Her own happiness and the beauty of the evening was a slow, deep richness in her. She put out her hand for the sherry decanter and refilled her glass. She kept a decanter always in her bedroom now. Sometimes on a bad night a couple of glasses would help her to oblivious sleep. She drank now from the need to mark the joy in her. They were times when she had to be, or tried to be, strict with herself about the sherry. Martin, it was true, showed no interest in drink, but there was always Sholto's example at the back of her mind. Thank goodness, however, when she had had four or five glasses, she remained exactly the same. No one could possibly tell. And, anyway, at her age, one needed some small stimulant.

From the far side of the lake she saw Martin come out of the trees. The sun glinted on his fair hair. He was carrying one of his hawks on his wrist. She smiled at the sight. Hawks, fishing, shooting ... he was mad about all country things. She had let him turn one of the stables into a mews for his birds. If she had been married and had had a son she would have wished for someone exactly like him. He came up the side of the lake with a dog at his heels and disappeared into the walled garden.

Miss Rainbird turned from the window. It was seven o'clock and she knew that he was coming in to change for dinner. She finished her sherry and then, on a whim, decided to change her dress, and had another glass of sherry while she did so, humming gently to herself and looking forward to dinner with Martin and hearing about his day. Some time soon they would have to have a serious talk about his future. He was eighteen now and had attained his majority a few months previously. She had given a dinner and dance for him. It had been a wonderful evening and at the end of it she had told him that she had changed her will in his favour. Reed Court and everything she owned would become his one day. He had been suitably impressed and grateful.

She went out of the room and down the stairs to the lower landing. The sun struck a great beam of light across it and suddenly she remembered the dream she had had of Madame Blanche standing with her here ... the both of them laughing and talking like old friends. Madame Blanche ... she hadn't thought about her for a long time, or that vulgar man ... Lumley? ... yes, Lumley, that was it. What an age away all that seemed. She turned from the window to the stairs and saw Martin come across the hall. The hawk and dog had gone. He looked up at her, grinned, and waved a hand and then began to come up towards her, moving easily, a compact, healthy, wiry young man.

He put an arm around her and kissed her.

She said, 'Have you had a good day, darling?'

'Splendid. Am I going to be late for dinner?'

'No, there's plenty of time. I'm just going down to have a drink. Hurry up and join me.'

She put up a hand and touched his cheek, brown and warm. He leaned forward and kissed her on the forehead.

Miss Rainbird put out a hand to steady herself on the balustrade and looked down the stairs. Martin Shoebridge stood behind her, looking at the small, frail figure, the smell of the sherry she had drunk sour in his nostrils. Miss Rainbird of Reed Court, he thought, his great-aunt, doting and half-tipsy as usual. His face tightened with disgust and cold hate. He thrust out his right hand and pushed her violently.

He stood at the top of the stairs and watched her fall down the steep flight. Her body hit the balustrade, slewed sideways, crashed against the wall and then somersaulted twice before hitting the floor below, her head smashing against the polished boards. He watched her as she lay there, sprawled out like a broken doll. If there had been any sign of life from her he would have gone down and finished her off. But she lay still with her head and neck twisted unnaturally to one side. He waited a few moments to make sure that she did not move or cry out.

In those few moments Miss Rainbird, before she died, saw him, saw the sun catching his fair hair from the window behind. But he meant nothing to her, even though vaguely she realized with her fading senses that he had pushed her. Yes, he had pushed her. Just as years and years ago she had deliberately, out of cold hate, pushed a drunken Sholto down the same stairs ... pushed him out of her life so that she could live in peace. She died ... hearing Madame Blanche's voice saying, 'Something terrible happened here.'

Martin Shoebridge went up the stairs to his room. Syton and the cook were in the kitchen. Syton might find her. If he didn't then she would be there when he came down. She was dead, and everyone knew she drank too much in her bedroom. There would be no trouble. A tipsy tumble. And now he really had freed himself ... freed himself to do what his father and mother had died trying to do. He knew to a penny what his great-aunt was worth. He knew everything, because with sherry in her she was a great talker ... knew about the Harriet dreams, about Madame Blanche and her suicide ... just as he had known all his father's plans and about the kidnappings of Archer, Pakefield and the Archbishop, because his father had kept nothing from him ... And he knew, too, that there had been no accidental fire at Highlands House. Something had gone wrong because Madame Blanche and the Lumley man had traced his father for Miss Rainbird. Because of them his father and step-mother had died. His dog and his hawks had been trapped and burnt alive ... And now he was free, but before he could move off to find what his father had always sought there were others to be dealt with. It was a debt he owed his father. There was this man Lumley ... a prospering garden contractor. He would go next, and then there would be the two men his mother and father had told him about ... the two who were always there when the diamonds had been collected. Finding them and dealing with them would be harder, more dangerous. But it would be done. He was young, he had time, he had money, and he liked hunting.

He went up the stairs, whistling gently to himself. seeing the pattern of revenge in his mind, knowing he must and would complete it before he was absolutely free to turn his back on the world and live as his father had dreamt of living.

Victor Canning   40p
The Melting Man

'Canning – one of the finest thriller writers in the world'
Reader's Digest

'Splendid entertainment with his excellent private eye, Rex
Carver, haring around Europe at the behest of a beastly
millionaire in search of a stolen Mercedes. He is dogged by the
millionaire's beautiful stepdaughters, a couple of politely
villainous Africans, a coloured man-crazy Amazon (delicious
type), an Interpol man and various others . . . Victor Canning
at the top of his form' *Sun*

Ian Fleming   40p
The Man with the Golden Gun

James Bond 'twisted like a dying animal on the ground and the iron in his hand cracked viciously . . .'

'Pistols' Scaramga: Professional assassin for KGB and other criminal organizations. A paranoiac and sexual fetishist, he used a gold-plated Colt with silver bullets to avenge himself upon humanity.

Mary Goodnight: 'A naked arm smelling of Chanel No 5 snaked round Bond's neck, and warm lips kissed the corner of his mouth.'

'Fleming keeps you riveted' *Sunday Telegraph*

'Some of the best ingredients of the Bond sagas'
Bristol Evening Post

Dick Francis
Rat Race   35p

'Yet another winner' *Sunday Mirror*

'Impossible to stop reading' *Daily Telegraph*

'Top-class novel about a taxi-plane pilot involved in a fraud scheme . . . exciting (there is an in-the-air rescue sequence that would make you really and truly angry if you had to put it down) and a splendid read' *The Times*

'A thriller that really thrills' *Daily Mail*

Slay Ride   45p

'Racing in Norway is the setting for this superstar of thriller-writers' latest adventure . . . a spine-chilling affair' *Financial Times*

'Francis at his brilliant best . . . with plot and character beautifully interwoven, sex and violence, revelation and mystery suberbly blended' *Sporting Life*

'Enthralling, finely written and full of real live people' *Sunday Telegraph*